Promise to Mellita

Promise to Mellita

By

Rollin L. Hurd

*I hope you enjoy the novel —
God Bless
Rollin Hurd*

DocHurd@aol.com

From Blanche —

ISBN: 1-58500-266-6

About the Book

Promise to Mellita is a novel inspired by the true experiences of brothers during World War II.

* * *

Nick Jordan, the youngest brother, joined the army and became a combat medic in the 42nd 'Rainbow Division' In Europe, he saved many lives while going through harrowing enemy fire. Against orders, he cautiously enters a mine field to treat and bring out a wounded GI. A surprise German attack left him cut—off and surrounded for days. He was listed as missing—in—action. Another time, while treating a platoon member, he's captured. Marching to the rear with a group of P.O.W.'s, he seizes an opportunity to make a break for freedom. Later, wounded and hungry, he enters a house where a Fraulein, Mellita, befriends him. They become lasting friends. When Nick has to leave, he makes a promise to help her get to America. The war ends and Nick looks for Mellita, but instead he's picked up in the Russian zone and put in prison.

Meanwhile, Wylie Jordan, the eldest brother, a fighter pilot in the Pacific Theater is flying his P—47 on numerous missions against the Japanese. On one occasion over Japan, he is wounded and his plane riddled with holes. He is barely able to get back to base safely. Another time, he is forced to land in China on a sandbar next to a mountain stream. Wylie's best friend was shot down and killed. The day before his friend had convinced Wylie to write to a girl. It began a pen—pal relationship that after the war ended in marriage.

A couple years after being mustered out of the army, Nick and his high school sweetheart get married. After having four daughters, family responsibilities took over their lives. Twenty—five years later, a phone call from Mellita's relative reveals that she is trapped in East Germany. Nick and Wylie devise a plan to get her out so Nick can fulfill his promise to her. Many surprises follow until the exciting finish of the book.

DEDICATION

This fun effort is dedicated to: My mother Blanche Crandall of Napa, California. A champion golfer and expert bridge player, Blanche is an inspiration to all of us.

Carolyn my high school sweetheart and wife for over 50 years.

My four lovely daughters Nancy, Lisa, Laurie, and Janie each unique in her own way. A daughter is a special part of all that's cherished in the heart. My fabulous grandchildren: Mark, Jon, Mike, Jeff, Julianne, Nick, Mary, Michael, and Adam.

Finally, Brother Ed, his wife Ann and their precious family.

ACKNOWLEDGMENTS

Brother Edgar Hurd's mammoth contributions helped tremendously.

Bernice's writing group was invaluable in improving my writing so it could be readable. The group included: Bernice, Sonny, Laurel, Marypat, Ron, David and Mary.

Carol Lake for her capable guidance.

Peggy Anderson whose teaching skills pointed me in the right direction.

I want to thank everyone at 1st Books for helping me to attain my goal of being a published author.

Chapter 1

New Year's Day, France, 1945

As his breath puffed white in the cold air, Nick Jordan stretched and shifted against the side of the truck. Spending hours inside a big army truck, not knowing where you were going, was a bore. He stared out at the rough winding road and wondered if the convoy would ever stop. When it did, would they be staring into the eyes of Germans? A chill went through him.

As if reading his thoughts, the huge private across from him growled, "When the hell are they going to stop this clunker?" Most of the men in the truck were strangers to Nick, but he'd noticed this man. With deep-set eyes and heavy brows, his face was set in a perpetual scowl. Earlier, someone had called him "Branch". Just being near such a sour-looking person made Nick uncomfortable. Branch started to rise and almost fell on Nick as he bounced with the motion of the vehicle. He regained his balance, unzipped his pants, and took a leak over the tailgate. At that moment the truck lurched forward and he almost tumbled out. As he struggled back to his place, a couple of GI's chuckled. Wycoff, seated by the tailgate and one of the few men Nick knew by name, winked. Nick smiled.

Nick glanced over at Branch, the private was staring at him. He pointed to the red cross on Nick's helmet. "I wouldn't want to be in your shoes -- that cross makes a great target for the Krauts."

Nick leaned back. "I hope not. The Geneva convention says they're not supposed to shoot at medics. For whatever that's worth."

Branch snorted, and the tall skinny man next to him grinned. "Not much, I'd guess. How'd you get to be a medic, anyway?"

"After high school, I took a first-aid course. That did it!"

"No shit? Didn't take much, did it?'

Before Nick could defend himself against the implied criticism, the brakes screeched. He braced himself as the truck rambled to a halt. The men filed out, stretching their muscles while they squinted around in the dark to get their bearings.

As he followed his platoon away from the trucks, Nick thought about his mother's birthday. This would be the first time he'd be unable to at least talk to her on her special day. He'd miss that. His home and family seemed so distant -- another world, another time -- one he'd be able to rejoin soon, he hoped.

The rot of decaying leaves hung in the air, and through a gap in the clouds the first star shone above. He heard distant rumblings and looked in awe at the eerie sky which lit up periodically like a giant flash bulb exploding. So the rumors were true. They were headed into front line action. Nick's fear mounted with each step forward.

His feet numb from the cold, he crunched across the gravel after the others. The air was as chill as well water, and the ground was rough and ridged with frost. He shivered. Soon, the countryside would be blanketed with heavy snow.

As the men ahead of him filed into a large warehouse on the outskirts of the small town, Nick

1

glanced around at the shadows. He wondered where the Germans were. Shouldering his pack and carrying his first aid kit he followed the others into the building for briefing.

Inside was a single square room. Each platoon assembled in groups. As Nick dropped his gear on the floor next to the first platoon, he overheard Branch mutter, "Hurry up and wait for those shit-ass generals to figure out what to do next."

Nick looked around at the serious faces. Most of the soldiers were around his age and not long out of high school. The officers and sergeants were older. Were the others afraid as he was, but just didn't show it on the outside! How many of the men in the room would survive the war? He prayed that he would.

At that moment, a French officer caught the attention of the Americans as he strode smartly into the building. His colorful outfit consisted of a beret, red neckerchief, blue shirt, baggy pants, and boots. "Bonjour!" he called out. "You can get a good night's rest. This has been a quiet area. There has been no enemy activity for weeks. Au revoir." He turned and left quickly.

There was silence, then a buzz of voices. "Who was that?" someone asked.

"He belongs to a group called the Free French,"

Lieutenant Kane, Nick's platoon leader, said, "They fight underground and sabotage the Krauts. Viva La France!"

Having the French underground nearby was a comforting thought to Nick. He watched Kane move off to talk to the officers clustered at the front of the room, and Nick and the others sat down, resting their backs against the wall.

As they waited, Nick thought about the questions the man in the truck had asked. Did he have enough knowledge to treat a wounded man properly? The weeks he'd spent in training suddenly seemed pitifully short. What if he panicked under fire? The unanswered questions stabbed into him like a knife.

Kane's voice broke into his reverie. "First platoon, grab your gear. We're moving to our rendezvous point."

The group lifted their packs and followed Kane. Nick looked at the men around him. Not yet friends, but each would depend on the other for survival. They stepped outside into the cold.

Nick took a deep breath of the night air. He moved his face muscles as they stiffened in the cold. The men hiked together until they reached an isolated schoolhouse. Nick reflected on how similar it looked to country schoolhouses back home. Inside, the chalky smell of school drifted in the air, its ordinariness adding to the unreality around him.

The desks were shoved to one end of the building near the blackboard. The wall clock no longer ticked. How long had it run after the children left the last time? On the other side of the room was a group of three-level bunk beds.

Pictures drawn by school children hung on the walls. They were so similar to what kids did back home. They showed people, houses, trees, flowers, and puppies in bright colors of red, yellow, orange, and green. Where were the French children who'd done these pictures? Were they dead? Imprisoned? Hiding? Free? So many innocent lives altered because of this senseless war made him angry.

When all the platoon had entered, they crowded around the Lieutenant. Just as Kane was getting ready to give the assignments, a soldier walked in and said, "Okay, guys. Windbreaker pants. Pick out your own. It could be a long cold winter."

The men surrounded the box. Nick grabbed a pair and tried them on. They were too large and hung on his thin frame. He looked over at Branch who was fighting a losing battle with a pair of government-issue windbreaker pants that were obviously too small for his bulky frame.

"Trade you," Nick said.

As they exchanged, Lieutenant Kane whistled to get their attention. "Davis, your squad goes to the pillbox to the north. Collins, you take the other one to the south. Thompson, you stay here."

"Medic, ah…" Kane looked down at his roster and found Nick's name. The lieutenant's somber dark eyes searched out Nick. "Jordan, are you able to take care of things if someone gets wounded? I don't want to die because some dumb medic doesn't know his job."

Nick's face reddened and he felt everyone's eyes on him. The question was one he'd wrestled with all day. He hesitated and then said, "I'm not a doctor. All I can say is, I'll do my best."

The men stared at him, but Nick's eyes never flinched. Kane nodded as if satisfied and turned toward the door. "Medic, you go with Davis's squad."

Disappointed to leave the comfort of the school, Nick picked up his gear.

"Anybody got any questions?" the lieutenant asked. Nobody did. "Okay. Thompson, put someone on guard outside. I'll be back soon, so stay on your toes." Someone laughed. Kane's gaze swept over the group. "Don't laugh. I'm serious. The password is 'Chevy coupe.' All right, Davis' and Collins' squad, let's move out. I'll show you where the pillboxes are." At the door he turned. "On second thought, Medic, you stay here."

Nick picked out a bunk and dropped his gear. He felt relieved at not having to go out into the cold night, but a little guilty at being spared. He sat on the bunk and watched the men file out. Somewhere out there the enemy waited. He could tell by their faces that everyone was thinking about it. Each face had a trace more apprehension than it had before.

Nick slid off his bunk and walked across the room to look at one of the children's drawings. It was a happy picture of a girl with her puppy walking up a flower-lined lane to a house. The longer he looked the better he felt. He even grinned at one drawing of a dog that looked more like an elephant. As he turned back toward his bed, his eyes met those of the soldier assigned to the bunk below his.

"Doesn't seem possible we're in France, does it?" Nick asked.

"So true. The sooner we get out of here and back home, the better. I looked at that picture too, and thought of my dog back home. She must think I deserted her." The soldier looked young and lost.

Nick climbed back up onto his bunk. "I wouldn't worry. Animals don't forget. She'll be happy to see you when you get back. What's your name?"

"Al Nelson. What's yours?"

"Nick Jordan. I guess we're in this together. Where are you from?"

"Right in the heart of the country, St. Louis, Missouri; cold in the winter and hot in the summer. How about you?"

"Small town in Washington State."

"I've never been out west."

"You'll have to come visit after the war. See you in the morning,' Nick said.

He rolled into his blankets and soon drifted off to sleep.

Nick felt something far off pulling at his unconscious mind. Another tug. His first thought was that a dream was disturbing him but as confusing sounds became clearer he awoke with a start.

3

For a second he wasn't sure where he was. Then he remembered, and fear hit him like a lightning bolt. He heard gunfire, closer now, and yelling outside. He leapt out of the bunk onto the floor, threw on his clothes, grabbed his medical gear and was out the door.

"Medic! Move it!" Kane shouted. "Follow Thompson into Drusenheim. We're under attack!" He leveled his M-1 at a group of Germans a hundred yards or so away.

Nick saw the eerie figures swarming toward them through the early morning fog. My God! he thought. There's no chance! We're being overrun. Sprinting after Thompson, he spotted Branch stumbling out of the schoolhouse.

"This way!" Nick yelled. Branch swerved their direction on the run, while pulling his M-1 rifle into position to fire.

A burst of gunfire caused Nick to duck instinctively to the ground. Shaken, he took off again, half bent over and weaving from side to side to make a tougher target. As bullets whizzed by him, Nick ran for his life toward the houses on the outskirts of the village of Drusenheim. The others were scattered about running with a single desire; to get into town without being killed.

Suddenly, out of the fog rushed a German soldier almost crashing into Nick. Stunned the two men stared at each other a minute. Then the German began to lift his gun into position to shoot. At that moment, Branch came sprinting up to them. In one swift motion, he swung his rifle like a baseball bat and the bayonet slashed the Germans throat. Blood spurted as the soldier gasped, dropped his gun and grabbed at his throat.

Nick shivered as he watched the young good looking boy with blonde hair and blue eyes struggle but fail in his battle to live. It was a site Nick knew he'd never get out of his mind the rest of his life.

Branch jerked his arm and they ran off together up the road to town. After a short dash onward, Nick heard a whistle followed by a thunderous blast. The ground shook. Another loud whistle. Mortar fire! He jumped to the side and threw himself on the ground against the stone wall separating the road from a field. The next blast was even closer. Nick pressed himself against the ground and the wall, wishing he could crawl into his helmet.

Powder fumes stung his nose and eyes. A feeling of helplessness and anger surged through him. He didn't want to die right here and now like the young German did. He spat out a mouthful of dirt.

Another blast came -- and another -- then the sound of more whistling. Would it never end? His back was cold with sweat, and his mouth was dry, from fear and dirt. He didn't want to be a coward, but he'd never been so scared. He looked around. Branch was nowhere in sight.

He got up and ran. After about ten strides, there came a thunderous blast. Nick sprawled to the ground, not sure if he'd been hit. Covered with dirt and his ears ringing, he struggled to his feet. He looked back and stared at a huge hole near where he'd been on the ground before. How lucky he'd ran when he did. He sprinted off, thinking the Germans weren't playing games. They are serious.

Chapter 2

Nick's wobbly legs didn't take him far. He stopped abruptly. A soldier lay face down before him on the icy ground.

He reached down for the man's shoulder and, with only a slight hesitation, gently turned him over. A pool of blood covered the frozen ground. A young face, ghostlike and unrecognizable, stared up at him, the blank eyes seeing nothing. He glanced at the nasty shrapnel wound in the man's neck.

Nick turned his head away, feeling sick inside. He felt the cold wrist. There was no pulse. As he looked into the man's face, a wave of nausea swept over him. This could have been me, he thought. Nick wanted to run away, but realized he had a duty. He reached into his aid kit and pulled out his record book.

He picked up the blood-stained dog tags and read the name: Alfred R. Nelson. It was the soldier he'd spoken to just last night. The one who'd loved his dog so much. Now he was dead. Nick's hand trembled while he recorded the name, rank, and serial number. Nick wondered what would happen to Nelson's dog, when its master didn't come home.

In spite of the burnt powder floating in the air, Nick took a deep breath. He glanced at his watch and went on recording, filling out the form as he'd been taught.

Drusenheim, 6:45 AM. January 2, 1945.

Cause of injury -- mortar shrapnel

Location of wound -- neck

Cause of death -- loss of blood

He tagged the original document to the body. Somehow, he'd never expected his first tag to be made out for a dead, rather than a wounded, man.

As he started to move away, something made him turn back. He moved Nelson's legs and shifted the torso so the body was in a natural sleeping position. Did it make a difference? It did to him, Nick decided. He felt strange, light-headed, but with a heavy feeling in his chest.

What a shock to come for Nelson's parents. Maybe someday he could look them up. But what would he say?

Nick glanced around. Not a pretty place to die, in the dusty road with the drab grey walls on each side. The town, with its colorless houses, depressed him. There were no grass yards, no beautiful flowers, nothing like the picture in the school house. There were no Germans in sight, thank God. Just Nelson, all alone next to the hole that the mortar had left in the street. Unfortunately, there was nothing more Nick could do for him.

Disheartened, Nick ran toward the center of Drusenheim. Halfway there, he heard the whistling sound begin again, and fear grabbed him as another blast shook the ground. Leaping to the side of the road, Nelson's white face flashed before him. Cold sweat coated his body as the shells impacted around him for what seemed like hours before they stopped. Shaken, he got up and ran on.

Up ahead, he spotted the broad shoulders of Branch, with his rifle draped over his right arm. Del Toro stood next to him. Nick caught up with them just as Lieutenant Kane, wide-eyed and haggard, said, "Spread out up this street. Take a quick rest. I'll get our orders and be right back." He hurried up the street.

Nick threw his aid kit and pack to the ground and slid down against a dirty building. He looked around at the handful of stores and office buildings in the area. The town seemed to be a small one, with a population of only a few thousand people by the looks of things.

Before the lieutenant was out of sight, Branch had lit a cigarette and was leaning against the wall, blowing smoke rings. He grinned at Nick. "We're lucky, Doc. Those mortars scared the hell out of me. I thought I was dead for sure."

"Nelson is. He caught a fragment in the neck." Nick shuddered as he visualized the death scene.

Branch's face paled. "Fuckin' Krauts."

After a moment of silence, Nick said, "I heard from Wycoff that the rest of our platoon were all captured or killed. They were overwhelmed before they knew what was going on."

"Shit," Branch muttered.

Nick shivered, partly from the cold, but more from the thought of how close he'd come to being sent out to the pillbox the night before. Just then, Kane trotted up to them and motioned everyone to assemble around him. "The Germans have us surrounded. There's no place to run. We're making our stand right here in Drusenheim."

He hesitated, then went on, "They don't know we're undermanned. Our platoon is down to eight men, and there's a company from the 36th defending Drusenheim as we speak. They may be content to keep us surrounded. Let's go! We need to dig in around the perimeter of town."

Kane motioned the men to follow and the platoon moved after him. The air was cold. The sky was overcast with the look of snow about it.

He tried to keep his mind off the terror of the moment, but fear gnawed at him.

They soon arrived at the outskirts of town. Kane pointed out where the line of defense would be. "Two of you dig together. When the foxhole is finished, take turns, standing guard. Stay low, and watch out for snipers."

As if to emphasize his words, a shell whistled over their heads. Nick thought of the German soldier and Nelson. Death was so sudden and final.

He and Branch were teamed together. The day before when he first met Branch; Nick would never have predicted that the very next day he'd be happy to have him as his foxhole partner. Branch had learned in basic training what to do when in hand-to-hand combat, and it saved Nick's life.

They pulled their military issue shovels out of their belt pouches. "Let's do it, Doc. Keep your eye out for krauts." Branch shoved his shovel into the frozen dirt.

They dug side by side in silence until Branch said, "I hope this isn't our grave."

Nick's throat tightened. He kept digging. His hands ached with each jab of the shovel into the hard ground. The sky turned gray and the air colder.

A half hour later Kane walked over to check their progress. "Not deep enough," he said, walking on to check the next foxhole.

Branch scowled at the lieutenant's retreating back.

"This ain't Texas. There's no oil down here," he muttered, but they dug deeper. Branch, a strong man, was getting twice as much dirt out as Nick. Something gnawed at the back of his mind, but he couldn't put his finger on it. Something he'd forgotten to do. He glanced up and saw fluffy white snowflakes drifting down.

Branch lit a cigarette and pointed up at the sky. "Don't like the looks of that. Hope we don't get too much. Where are your windbreakers, Doc?"

Nick's eyes widened. Now he knew what he'd forgotten. "I shot out of that schoolhouse so fast, I forgot about them." He glanced at the snow floating down. The windbreaker would have been nice to have tonight. There was nothing he could do about it now. He looked at Branch, whose face was half blanked out by a cloud of cigarette smoke. "A kraut could be wearing 'em now. I wish I'd remembered to grab 'em."

Branch flipped his cigarette butt to one side, where it landed in the snow with a hiss. "Don't worry about it, Doc. You'll be all right."

The snow was rapidly covering the ground. Nick squinted out into the eerie white field. Visibility was becoming poor. The Germans could attack at any time, but from what direction? They could be close right now, and who would know? But then, Nick reminded himself, they couldn't see us either.

"That looks plenty deep enough," Branch said. "I'll take the first shift." He folded up his shovel and slipped it back onto his belt.

Nick did the same, glad to be done with the job. He rubbed his hands and fingers together, then jammed them deep into his pockets. He was so cold already! Would they survive the night? While Branch stared out into the field, Nick dozed fitfully between shivers and thoughts of Germans attacking their positions.

Two hours later, when he took his turn at guard duty, Nick gripped Branch's rifle, after carefully checking the safety. As a medic, he didn't carry a gun. Like a child, he felt the trigger and twisted the weapon into different positions. It was heavy and awkward, but the longer he had it in his hands, the better it felt.

Nick thought back to Camp Gruber, Oklahoma, when he'd won his sharp-shooter medal with the M-1. This was different, though, he reminded himself. Now his life was on the line. The Germans could be creeping up on them in the darkness at this very moment. He had to stay alert. Could he shoot a man? Yes, if there is no choice.

It was so quiet. Nick's glances scanned in every direction across the white landscape. He seemed to have been standing there for hours, though he knew it had only been a few minutes. His ears were numb from the cold. He wished he'd remembered to bring the windbreaker, with its warm hood.

His mind raced through the day's dangerous encounters. The shock of waking to gunshots. Sprinting from the schoolhouse and confronting the German soldier. Then Branch arriving at that moment to save his life. The image of the young German's and Nelson's death would never leave him. The thought of them left Nick with an uneasiness, rage and the nearly incomprehensible feeling of waste and dismay.

In his mind, he visualized another scene, Nelson's mother answering the doorbell. He pictured a man handing her a yellow envelope, saw her sign for it. The man left, never to be forgotten. She read the crushing news, her stricken face contorted in anguish. He prayed that his own mother wouldn't have to go through that torment and that he and his brother Wylie would survive the war.

He admired his mother, She was so strong. If she had an opinion, which she quite often did, no one could change it. He knew she'd be thinking of him, on this, her special day. "Happy Birthday, Ma," he whispered to himself.

His thoughts drifted to Marilyn, her beauty vivid in his mind. He remembered the deep love he always felt when he'd look at her as they walked side by side. Dark eyes, prettier than any he'd ever seen. Silky black hair that hung to her shoulders. The warm and exciting thrill that surged through him each time he held her close.

The snow was falling more heavily now. If there was a German lurking in the white blur, he'd be impossible to see. He hoped the Germans wouldn't attack, content to keep them under siege.

He checked his watch. Time was up. He shifted over to Branch and nudged him. "It's two. Time to take over."

"How did it go?" Branch stretched and reached for a cigarette.

"Quiet. Nothing going on."

"I'll bet you froze your ass off."

Nick shook his head. "I kept my mind on other things."

Branch laughed. "Like laying that French floozy we saw last week."

The girl had been young and innocent, embarrassed by the attention she received from the hordes of soldiers rolling through town. Nick had felt sorry for her, and wished there were some way he could protect her from the whistles and catcalls.

Nick huddled in a corner of the foxhole and put Both hands under his armpits. He knew it wouldn't get him warm, but he forced himself to think of other things. He thought about Fort Lewis where his Army life had begun. He remembered the train ride to Oklahoma, and the conversation with the soldier next to him. The soldier had said, "If you've got a girl friend, don't expect her to wait for you. They never do."

The agonizing possibility that Marilyn might not wait forced him out of his dream world with a shiver. He gtanced at Branch staring out into the night with his rifle in one hand and a Lucky Strike in the other.

Nick curled up and pulled his jacket over him to keep warm. Out of the silence came an explosion that sounded very close. Too close. Was this the beginning of an attack?

As he relaxed again, a shot rang out jarring him alert. Branch's helmet clattered as it bounced across the floor of their foxhole. Branch's left hand went to the top of his head. He still clutched his M-1 in his right hand.

"Son of a bitch!" Branch cried out as he slouched low. "You hit?" Nick asked. With the small amount of moonlight, he could see a shallow gouge across the top of Branch's head.

"You lucky, bugger. It's only a slight scalp wound. You came as close as you could to being killed."

"Some Kraut bastard had me zeroed in. Probably saw my cigarette. That's the last time I smoke on guard duty."

Nick picked up the helmet and cringed when he saw the hole. "How close can you get? Look at that."

"Oh shit! I want to go home, Doc."

Chapter 3

Wednesday, January 3, 1945
Hoquiam, Washington

Wednesday was Blanche Jordan's day to shop. She drove into town and stopped at the gas station. The strong odor of gasoline penetrated the air as she handed Hugh, the attendant, her precious ration coupons.

"Helluva note this rationing, huh, Blanche?" He shoved his grease-stained cap farther back on his head.

"Well, I can't say the rationing has done much for my golf game, but I suppose winning the war is more important."

"Yeah, I guess," Hugh chuckled. Then, giving her a look of concern, "How're the boys?"

"Haven't heard for awhile." She bit her lip slightly. "I'm heading for the Post Office now. Nick's 'Rainbow Division' is in the middle of the action in Europe, and Wylie is in the Pacific flying his P-47." She held up her hand. "Want to see my nails?"

"What nails, for Christ sake? Never thought you were the nail-biting type."

Blanche sighed. "When it comes to my boys, I am."

"Don't worry, Blanche. That bastard Hitler is getting his ass kicked. They'll have to give it up soon. Then we can take care of the Japs." Hugh's greasy hand swept across his mouth leaving another black smudge as he moved away.

She laughed and her eyes sparkled mischievously. She turned on the ignition and called after him. "Hugh, would you get a new cap? That one looks ridiculous. How long have you had it, anyway?"

He turned and grinned. "I just bought it yesterday."

"You jackass! You've had it at least twenty years."

He laughed and waved as she pulled away and swung to the right. A few blocks away, she could see the flag flapping high above the Post Office.

What a difference the sight of the flag meant these days compared to before the surprise Japanese attack on Pearl Harbor. She remembered how the radio had shattered the Sunday-afternoon quiet with the news. The next day President Roosevelt's speech had galvanized the country, turning a calamity into a national calling.

Like most of America, Blanche and her husband Paul and their sons Nick and Wylie had huddled around their radio to hear the message. In a masterful seven-minute speech, Roosevelt had forged their molten emotions of shock, anger and fear into a hard sharp spear of national will. He achieved this by presenting a straightforward account of the damage the Japanese had inflicted and an unflinching assurance that America would prevail.

As she drove, Blanche could still remember her exuberant feeling of relief as the President's positive words rang forth. "Yesterday," he intoned, "December 7th, 1941, a date that will live in infamy, the United States of America was suddenly and deliberately attacked by naval and air forces of the Empire of Japan...."

As he reached the end of his speech, Roosevelt's voice had turned to steel as he pledged vengeance and victory. "No matter how long it may take us to overcome this premeditated invasion," he vowed, "the American people in their righteous might will win through to absolute victory."

Telegrams of support had poured into the White House. Newspaper editorialists and radio commentators had praised Roosevelt's decisiveness and leadership. In Europe, the British and Soviets, desperately trying to hold off Hitler, breathed a sigh of relief that the United States was finally and wholeheartedly joining the fight.

All across the nation, men had lined up at the military recruiting stations. Some, like Nick, were too young and had to wait to enlist. Others, like Wylie, couldn't sign up fast enough. How strange to think that her boys were no longer children, but men, set on a course which would take them so far from their home and family. Their eagerness to serve had made her both proud and fearful.

As she pulled to a stop in front of the Post Office, she sighed. Only three years had passed since Roosevelt's speech, yet it seemed an eternity, so much had everyone's lives changed. Such grand moments were all very well in their place, she supposed, but she couldn't help wondering if even the President had realized how hard the suspense of wartime would be to live with on a day-to-day basis.

She glanced up at the nondescript little brown building that housed the Post Office. Ironic that such an ordinary-looking place had assumed such importance in the life of the town. Running up the concrete steps, she felt her heart beat faster. Every day she and many other parents made the same journey and every day the same strong hope swept through her: Would there be a letter from one of the boys? Please, God, she prayed, let this be the day. It had been so long since she'd heard from either of her sons.

She pushed open the heavy door and went inside. In the lobby, she turned left, passing the long counter.

"Hi, Blanche." Vera, the short cheerful woman who worked behind the counter, waved a plump hand. "You got some good mail today. I tried to call you, but you weren't home.'

Blanche's heart skipped a beat. Good mail! It must mean a letter from one of the boys at last! She smiled and waved, but kept walking, too anxious to stop and chat. Blanche stood at the wall of little bronze square box doors looking for number 536. With the afternoon sunlight streaming in through the window from the west and casting a glare on the wall of boxes, it was hard at first for her to locate her own. Her hand shook as she put the key into the lock and swung the box door open. As she grabbed the pile of mail, she wondered which son the letter was from. She leafed through the stack of envelopes until she spotted Wylie's familiar scrawl.

Moving to the window sill, she dropped the other mail onto the ledge and tore open Wylie's letter. As she skimmed through it, she sighed with relief. Thank God, he was all right. All was well in the Pacific, he wrote. A weight lifted from her shoulders. Now if only she could be sure Nick was all right, too.

She reread Wylie's letter, slowly this time to savor each word. When she had finished, she took a deep breath and picked up the rest of her mail. She walked briskly toward the door. She held up the stack of letters. "You were right, Vera," she called with a smile. "Good mail today. Wylie is doing fine. Now let's hope we hear from Nick soon. Thanks, Vera, and have a good day. Keep that mail coming!'

Vera smiled back. "I sure will. I'll call if we get something."

Adjusting her little black hat, Blanche went out the door and down the steps, thinking how

10

nice it was to live in a small town with friends like Vera and so many others who were interested in the boys.

Driving home, Blanche thought of the day before, her birthday. The whole day she'd had strong premonitions of danger. She'd tried to be cheerful for Paul's sake, but filled with a heavy feeling of dread, she worried that one of her boys was in trouble. Nick especially had been in her thoughts.

She loved both her sons of course, but always marveled at how different they were. Wylie, the oldest, was breezy, exuberant, outgoing, and though she loved him, She really didn't worry that much about him. There was something of the brash survivor about Wylie, and in her heart she'd always felt sure he'd come back.

But Nick -- ah, now, Nick was different. Sometimes, even when he'd still lived at home, she'd worried about him. He was a dreamer, sensitive and introspective, someone who felt things deeply and who always seemed to carry the weight of the world on his shoulders. Sometimes, he was so much like Paul she thought her heart would break.

The boys' attitudes to the war were reflected in their choices. Wylie, in search of adventure and glory, had become a pilot, while Nick had become a medic, seeking a way to help save the lives of others.

She glanced down at the mail on the seat beside her, grateful for Wylie's note. It made her feel younger, more hopeful. She bit her lip. Now, if only they'd hear from Nick, what a wonderful belated birthday present that would be.

She slowed in front of the neat two-story house, painted white with brown trim. She and Paul had built the house, and lived in it since the boys were babies. Switching off the engine, she looked up at the basketball hoop above the garage door.

If she listened carefully, she could still hear the boys whooping and hollering. They'd spent hours practicing, dribbling and shooting, though basketball was really Nick's game more than Wylie's. Like Blanche, her older son preferred golf.

Gathering up the mail and opening the car door, she smiled, remembering the boy's school games. She'd always been their number-one fan. She screamed for them, often drawing attention for her over-zealous reactions, to their embarrassment and Paul's amusement.

She opened the back door and entered the house. How quiet it was. If the boys were home, they'd be roughhousing and arguing. Right now, she'd even welcome that, just to have them back.

In the dining room, she dropped her purse on the table and pulled out the pins to remove her hat. Picking up Wylie's letter, she sat down and read it again. It always gave her a lift to read mail from one of the boys. She visualized them as though they were right there beside her.

Going to the telephone, she gave the operator Paul's number. She hated to get or give bad news over the phone, but good news was different.

After two rings, Paul's voice came on the line. "Hello?"

"Paul! We got a letter from Wylie. He's fine. It's one of his usual short ones, telling how many push-ups and sit-ups he can do. More than anyone else, of course. Wylie is unhappy about being assigned Jim McKay, the arrogant kid he didn't like, as his roommate. Their personalities are opposite from one another's. Hopefully, they'll get along all right. Nothing about the war except that he's out on flight every other day. No word from Nick, though."

"I'm glad Wylie's doing well. Knowing him he's liable to poke that McKay in the nose. He's not the most patient person. And don't worry," he said soothingly. "I'm sure we'll hear from Nick soon. I'll be home on time tonight. See you then. Love you."

11

Blanche replaced the receiver and glanced at the stairway, and was drawn toward it. The carpeting on the steps was old, the familiar pattern almost worn away in places. The hardwood exposed on each side gleamed, though. Just because there was no new carpet to be had on the entire West Coast due to the economy, it didn't mean she had to let her cleaning slide.

It was no wonder the carpet was nearly worn out. As she climbed, she thought of how many times the boys had run up and down these stairs. She couldn't remember them ever walking. Usually they took the whole flight in four or five leaps going up and two or three leaps coming down.

Reaching the landing at the top, she turned left and looked into Wylie's large bedroom. It had been meant for both the boys, but there was no way those two could exist in the same room together. The last straw was the time when Wylie, in the middle of the night, had leaped screaming onto the sound asleep Nick. The next day, with Blanche's approval, the exasperated Nick had moved into a tiny room no larger than a jail cell. Originally intended for storage, the room barely had space for the smallest-sized bed and a dresser and wastebasket but Nick loved it. Later that year, to make his nest complete, he got a little radio for Christmas.

Blanche peered into the room. The radio on the battered dresser reminded her how Nick loved to listen to Leo Lassen broadcast the Seattle Rainier baseball games. Nick knew every player and all their statistics.

Where was Nick now? In her heart she was sure he was still alive, but it was still a giant worry. Please, she prayed, let's get this war over with, so all the boys can come home.

She opened the drawers one by one, looking at the small assortment of Nick's belongings which he'd left behind. In the bottom drawer was the scrapbook they'd worked on together. She lifted it out, sat on the bed, and opened the book.

Each newspaper clipping brought back strong memories of the actual event. She proudly skimmed the headlines:

HOQUIAM WINS STATE BASKETBALL TITLE...
NICK JORDAN BREAKS MILE RECORD...

Suddenly Blanche realized the phone was ringing. She dropped the scrapbook into the drawer, shut it, and hurried downstairs. She was breathless when she reached the wall phone.

"Hi, Mrs. Jordan. This is Marilyn. I don't suppose you've heard from Nick?"

"No, but we got a letter from Wylie today. He's doing fine. Paul says Nick hasn't had a chance to write. We'll hear soon, I'm sure." She was surprised by how calm and assured she sounded, as the pangs of loneliness she'd felt while reading the scrapbook gradually receded.

Marilyn sighed. "I hope so. Every afternoon I stalk the mail box in hopes of a letter from him. Even when I don't get one, I keep on writing anyway. The poor guy will have tons to read when they finally catch up with him."

Blanche laughed, picturing Marilyn busy scribbling away. "He enjoys your letters, Marilyn. He's written that he does better than anyone else at mail call."

"Good! Hope we hear from him soon," Marilyn said.

"We will! Soldiers in combat don't get a chance to write often. We'll just have to be patient, it seems.', Blanche paused, then said, "So, how's school?"

"Fine. I'm looking forward to getting out this year, though. The boys have been giving me a hard time."

"Why's that?"

"They say I should be loyal to my class and go out with them, instead of mooning around, waiting for Nick."

"I wouldn't worry about it. Just ignore the idiots."

"Believe me, Mrs. Jordan, I do!"

Blanche smiled. What a nice girl Marilyn was. Their shared love and concern for Nick formed a bond between them. There was a small pause. Reluctant to have the conversation end, Blanche said, "This rationing is tough, isn't it?"

"The sugar is the worst. I can't bake any cookies, and Dad's upset about the cigarette shortage."

"How's your Victory Garden?'

"Ours is doing fine. We've gotten a lot of production from the little area we planted. I hope the war ends soon. So, we can all get back to normal and everyone gets back home. It's been nice talking to you Mrs. Jordan. I'll call you again soon."

"Thanks for calling, Marilyn." As she hung up, Blanche thought again what a nice girl Marilyn was. Beautiful too, with her brown eyes and long lashes. No wonder Nick had fallen for her.

Later, Paul arrived, and after giving Blanche a hug and a kiss, said, "Dinner smells good, dear. How are you doing?"

"Fine! I'll get Wylie's letter for you," she said, reaching for her purse. "It's another little V-mail letter. You need good eyes to read it."

She handed it to him, and he stared at it for a moment, then chuckled. "Short and sweet, that's Wylie. It'd be nice to know what's going on over there. It's a small world that he'd end up being a roommate with the kid he met and disliked in Nebraska.

"You know their mail is censored, Paul. We'll just have to read the papers and listen to the radio like everybody else, I guess."

"I never knew anyone so stingy with the written word. Although, he does write about that cocky Jim McKay every letter he writes. He doesn't like that boy." Paul paused a moment, then smiled. "There I go again, talking Wylie down. For some reason, I never had patience with him like I did with Nick. It became a habit. I love them both the same, though."

That night, before going to bed, they followed their usual routine of switching on the late-night news, the war progress was always on their minds. The broadcast was droning along as usual, when suddenly the words leaped out at Blanche as though the volume had been turned up.

"The 7th Army in France was shocked today by a strong overwhelming early morning German attack. Hitler's elite SS troops punched through Gambsheim and Weyersheim, two small towns ten miles north of Strasbourg near the Rhine River, capturing both of them. Drusenheim to the north is under siege with remnants of the 42nd Infantry Division courageously holding the town. The 77th and 42nd Divisions have taken heavy losses in the German advances....' The volume on the radio seemed to fade away.

Blanche felt as if someone had punched her in the stomach.

Nick was with the 42nd Division. Where was he tonight? Alive and hunkered down in his foxhole? Injured in some chaotic field hospital? Or perhaps he was already dead, lying in the cold mud with his dog tags glistening in the moonlight?

What would she and Paul do if something had happened to Nick? And what about Marilyn? She had a sudden vision of the girl's lovely young face, contorted with grief.

13

With all her heart and soul, she wished Nick was upstairs in his tiny room, listening to the baseball game on the radio. She swallowed hard and reached out to grasp Paul's hand. He squeezed it with a tender response.

He switched off the radio with a snap. "That's the last time we're listening to the late news."

She patted his hand. "You're right dear. Let's go to bed. Perhaps the news will sound better in the morning.,, Trying to shake off her phantoms of disaster, she got up and briskly set about getting ready for bed.

As they silently undressed, washed, brushed their teeth, she wondered what Paul must be feeling. Was he as fearful as she? She took a deep breath and let it out. It helped, but she still felt hot.

Soon they were in bed. She turned out the light and lay down. "Paul?" she whispered. "Let's go to church on Sunday."

"Yes," he said, his voice trembling.

She closed her eyes and lay rigid and still in the darkness, willing herself to sleep, but all she could do was worry about Nick. Was he alive and well? She knew they wouldn't find out for a long time to come. News traveled slow during war time and it wasn't always good. But her positive attitude, helped to carry her on with the strong belief he'd be all right. He'd come back home again when the war ended. It shouldn't be long. The Germans were showing signs of crumbling under pressure of the Allies coming at them from all directions.

Blanche's mind roamed in all directions but settled on the dynamic words of the boys Commander-in-Chief, "Franklin Delano Roosevelt, "The only thing we have to fear is fear itself." For some reason, the words soothed her emotions. Then another of his statements came to mind, "This generation of Americans has a rendezvous with destiny." A strong positive feeling swept over her leaving her feeling better. She whispered to herself, "The boys will be just fine."

Chapter 4

Nick woke with a start. As he raised up on his elbows, the cold air hit his face. He listened closely for any sound, but there was only silence. It seemed strange to think even war had its moments of quiet and comparative peace.

He glanced around. Branch leaned against the edge of the foxhole, peering out towards the scraggly line of trees and the rocky hummock where the Germans were.

Sometime during the night it had stopped snowing. The sky was overcast, though, a lightening of the grayness around them was the only indication of daybreak. He shivered, cursing himself for forgetting his windbreaker when he'd left the schoolhouse.

Branch shook a Lucky Strike out of the pack from his pocket. "Morning, Doc. Not exactly the Ritz, is it?" He put the cigarette to his lips and lit it in one swift movement.

The comforting aroma of the burning tobacco drifted in the air. They stood for awhile, watching the empty field in front of them.

"You know, Doc, those Germans are dumb bastards."

"Why's that?" Nick yawned. "They can't even speak English."

Nick chuckled for the first time in a long while. "My teacher told me I wasn't too great either."

Branch blew a smoke ring, his eyes watchful. "Funny, isn't it? If they'd kept on with their attack, we'd be dead now."

Before Nick could reply, they heard a whistle. They dropped to the ground. Fifty feet away, as a mortar blast shook them, the cloud of smoke slowly dispersed in the chill morning air.

Branch unconsciously wiped a speck of mud off his cheek. "Shit. I hoped they'd forgotten us."

"No such luck." Nick edged forward on his elbows trying to see where the fire was coming from. There must be hundreds of Germans out there. They'll be hard to hold off. Please God, he prayed, let me get home again in one piece. Keep missing. A thundering blast, a dozen yards away, shook the area. They hugged the ground with the strong smell of the explosion engulfing them. Shells pounded the ground nearby, fear overwhelmed him. He pictured himself and Branch splattered in the mud, pulverized and unrecognizable.

Finally the mortar barrage let up, to be replaced by small arms fire. Nick listened, picking out the different weapons by their sounds. The German burp gun was the most unnerving, as it sporadically spit forth its bullets.

Nick looked up and down the line. Several GI's began to drop back, trying to get to the houses before the Germans overran their positions. As they regrouped into town, it was like closing the drawstring on a gathered purse, trapping the GI's inside. With the Germans advancing, they couldn't stay where they were. They had to retreat.

Branch fixed his bayonet and frantically worked his rifle in defense of their position. "Watch it. They're coming. We'll have to make a run for that white house behind us." He slipped Nick two grenades. "In case you need them, Doc."

Branch pulled the pin on a grenade, waited a second and threw it hard. When it exploded Nick flinched. There was a low moan in the distance. Branch fired his rifle again.

Nick tensed when he recognized the blue uniform and characteristic helmet of a German creeping toward them. His hand shook as he pulled the pin and lobbed the grenade. After the blast, there was a second of eerie silence. The German soldier had disappeared.

"Good shot, Doc." Branch's voice boomed out with enthusiasm. "Now, when I throw this one, go like hell." He took a couple more shots in the general direction of the Germans, then yanked the pin on the grenade and pitched it toward the trees. "Go, Doc," he yelled.

Nick leaped up and sped toward the house, keeping low. Shots rang out, spraying him with flecks of mud and snow. He hit the ground hard, then leaped up and dashed on toward the house. More gunfire. He threw himself headlong on the ground. If the red cross on the helmet did make a target, it didn't seem to be doing much for the German's aim.

Ahead of him, the house looked tantalizingly close. Just one more dash and he'd be there. Come on, Nick, he whispered to himself. You can do it. Just like the hundred-yard dash at school. You know nobody in town could touch you.

He sprinted around the back corner of the house and wrenched open the door, breathing heavily. Branch was next to him, gasping for air. Nick blinked at him in surprise. How had the big guy stayed so close? He'd always felt no one could keep up with him in a race.

The room was bare. Someone had cleaned it out completely, presumably the family that lived here. Del Toro and Pettinato were already at the windows. They fired off a volley of shots from their M-1's.

"Doc, check out the basement and watch yourself," Branch said.

Nick spotted the stairs and cautiously stepped his way down. The sound of gunfire was muffled here, and he immediately felt safer. At the foot of the stairs was a door. He turned the knob and pushed it open. Nick almost jumped out of his shoes when he saw huddled in the candle lit room a group of people. Feeling in danger, he backed up and was about to run. But his eyes adjusted and the fear left him. He realized it was a family taking refuge and praying together. The first person he noticed was an old man holding a large worn Bible with a tattered leather cover. Nick glanced around and saw no weapons, just a jumble of discarded household items, a bin with a few potatoes, and a small pile of coal. The walls were loaded with shelves holding a variety of preserves.

He'd expected the house to be empty and stared with surprise into the circle of startled faces. The family looked back at him, obviously frightened. He shook his head in amazement. He wondered who they were. They must be the owners. Nick was shocked by how much they looked like U.S. civilians. He felt a sadness for these innocent people caught in the middle of the war. Americans had never experienced the nightmare of foreigners occupying their homes. He hoped they never would.

The unreality of the scene he'd stumbled into was unnerving.

Nick embarrassed at intruding on such a private ritual, stepped back and said, "Excuse me." He closed the door.

Nick continued his search and found another small room that reminded him of his own back home. He sat on the floor with his back against a wall. There was no electricity in the house, and it was dark and cold. Exhausted, he leaned his head back and looked upward. He had the sensation that he wasn't alone. The feeling had been with him ever since he'd left Nelson's body by the road, but now it was stronger.

The harrowing experiences which began at the schoolhouse, crowded into his mind. First, there had been the confrontation with his platoon leader about his credibility as a medic. Then the Lieutenant's last moment decision to keep him in the schoolhouse. A decision which had saved his life. He thought about the faces of the men he'd watched leave for the pillboxes. Were any of them alive today? The handsome young German soldiers face and Nelsons, appeared clearly in front of him, and he knew their images were burned into his soul forever.

Nick looked around his basement cubbyhole. A small picture of a country vineyard decorated one wall and a small empty shelf hung on the other. He'd like to stay right there until the war ended. He sighed. No chance!

His mind turned to home and his mother. She was the best 'Ma' in the world. So strong and vivacious, she radiated energy with every movement.

Nick removed his combat boots and massaged his feet and toes. They'd been cold for days, but he'd ignored it. His mind had been on surviving the action.

At that moment, there was a loud noise and the house shook. He scrambled to his feet and hurried to the stairs wondering what had happened. He climbed them rapidly, and gaped at the hole in the ceiling. The jagged edge pointed down where a shell the size of a softball had penetrated the room, but hadn't exploded. It protruded from the wall two feet from the doorway.

Nick grinned, "I'm surprised you guys are alive. Talk about luck."

"Yeah, I'm still shaking. It scared the shit out of me." Pettinato said, as he walked to the window and peered out.

"Hey! Pet, you must be tired of living," Branch yelled. "Get your ass away from the window. Just because that shell didn't go off, doesn't mean the next wouldn't."

Pettinato laughed, but moved away from the window.

Nick sat next to Branch and stared up at the hole in the ceiling. After a short time, he got up and took his turn at guard duty. An hour later, the sound of gunfire picked up. He felt more nervous as time went on and was glad when Branch showed up. After Branch took over and the gunfire slowed, Nick headed back toward the basement.

Branch yelled after him, "We're supposed to get a hot meal today." Seeing Nick's puzzled look, he explained, "Evidently the 36th Division is sneaking it through the lines somehow. Best not to count on it, Doc; it's probably just a rumor anyway."

Nick went on downstairs and reclined in his little room to see if he could push the war from his mind. His thoughts went to home again until he heard Branch yell. "Doc, get up here. The hot food is here."

Nick rushed upstairs in time to hear Branch say, "Leave some for Doc."

Nick appreciated Branch watching out for him, but the two shriveled up pieces of chicken didn't look very appetizing. The hot meal was cold and tasteless. He ate it anyway.

Later, he wondered how the food had gotten to them. Dropped by air, he surmised. Time dragged when he wished it wouldn't. He dozed off only to be awakened by a noise. It came from above. He went upstairs and found the men holding their stomachs and looking green. They'd been throwing up.

"How're you feeling, Doc? That chicken was spoiled," Branch said.

"I'm OK, so far." Nick moved to the window and peered out. Nothing was moving. The men were so miserable they'd forgotten about guard duty.

Nick picked up Del Toro's rifle and took watch. A short while later, a wave of nausea swept him. When Pettinato vomited, Nick did the same. He handed the gun back to Del Toro and carefully took the stairway down. Before he reached the bottom step he threw up again, and one more time when he reached his little room. Nick spent the day so sick he wondered if he was going to survive.

The next afternoon when GI's broke through the German line and ended the siege, the 1st platoon soldiers quickly recovered from their food poisoning. The men shouted and whistled for joy when a Company of doughboys marched past the house. The fresh troops yelled back congratulations for holding the town until they could break through.

"What a sight, seeing those guys!" Nick said.

"Yeah, it is." Branch answered.

Their eyes met and displayed a mutual sigh of relief.

They overheard two men that were at Normandy say, the shelling of Drusenheim was as bad as what they'd gone through before. Later they heard, the Germans took over the town, soon after they left. Most the Americans still holding their positions were killed. How lucky for the little squad of Company G to make it through safely.

Chapter 5

Trucks poured into Drusenheim to pick up the defenders who had heroically kept the Germans from sweeping through the town. Nick climbed into a truck with Branch, Pettinato, Del Toro, and several others. As they drove through the winding streets, Nick thought of the family he'd met in the basement. He wondered if they had survived the artillary bombardment that never let up the whole attack.

The convoy bounced over the rough and rutted winter roads for several hours. Finally he and Branch found themselves at a battalion aid station, soaking their feet in water.

"My feet were numb, but I didn't think of frostbite," Branch said.

"I'm the medic, and I didn't either," Nick said. "I guess we had other things on our minds."

"Yeah, like puking our insides out. God, that chicken was foul." Branch guffawed at his pun, and some of the other men around them joined in the laughter, too.

Nick's commanding medical officer, Major Edwards, appeared in the doorway. Nick jumped to his feet, almost dumping the pan of water, and saluted.

"Well, Corporal Jordan, glad you made it back. We figured you'd been captured or killed. We had a missing-in-action letter ready to go out. Fortunately, we didn't have to mail it after all."

Nick nodded. For a second, his heart seemed to stop beating as he considered the effect such a letter would have had on his parents, especially his mother. "Thank you, sir. Glad to be back. We were lucky."

"Hmm. Maybe not entirely." The major pointed to the tub of water. "Henderson said you both had minor hypothermia and frostbite. He clasped his hands behind his back and rocked back and forth on his heels. A little rest and you'll both be fine. Good luck!" He turned and strode away.

"Wow! How come you're so important?" Branch punching Nick in the shoulder. "No one came to see me."

Nick grinned. "I suppose being the only medic missing compared to all the infantry guys."

"Yeah, well. I told you that red cross on your helmet made you conspicuous."

After two days of rest at the base camp, Medic Sergeant Stoner picked up Nick in a jeep and delivered him back to where Company G was rebuilding. Fresh replacements had arrived from the States to take the place of those who'd been wounded, killed, or captured in the Battle of Drusenheim.

But troops weren't the only thing which had arrived. The incoming trucks also brought the most precious commodity of all, mail from home.

Nick was delighted when his name was called out seven times. He counted five letters from Marilyn and two from his folks. He hurried back to his quarters to be alone when he read them.

He picked out the five thick letters from Marilyn. The feel of them sent a thrill through him. He checked the postmarks and placed them in order. For a moment he looked at the stack of letters, savoring the feeling of anticipation. He put them aside, like a kid saving his dessert for last, and turned to the letters from his mother.

Her positive approach always gave him encouragement and strengthened his love for her. As he began to read, her bold handwriting seemed to make the war disappear. He breathed a sigh of relief. All was well at home, and his brother Wylie was all right. He returned the letters to their envelopes and put them aside to reread later.

He picked up the first of Marilyn's letters. A prolific writer, she always used thin airmail paper to get more in the envelope. He began reading.

Dear Honey,
I miss you so much. I think of you every
day. I can't wait to hear from you, it's been
so long ....

Her writing flowed like a river, and her descriptions included every possible detail. What talent she had! It was as though he were there enduring the shortages of sugar, gasoline and cigarettes. The words raced across the page, and he read on.

A wave of jealousy washed over him when she told of the fun she'd had at a school dance. The feeling grew even stronger when she mentioned taking Pete, a classmate of hers to the cranberry bog with her parents one Sunday. That had always been his special place to spend time alone with her. If she was serious about Pete, though, he didn't 'think she would have written about it. That thought eased his mind, and he continued to read.

In the next letter, Marilyn reminisced about their first dance together. It was strange. The dance seemed so long ago he might only have imagined it, yet he remembered it as if it had happened yesterday. The ecstatic feeling of having her close in his arms when they danced. She'd smile up at him and he could tell she was enjoying it as much as he. The dance was the beginning of a mutual love that grew with each passing day.

Marilyn's letters were a delight but there was a helpless feeling about Pete, whose name cropped up several times. Maybe his train companion was right, and it was unreasonable to expect Marilyn to wait for him. She was young and lovely, it seemed natural that every boy in town would be attracted to her, just as he was.

But the end of the last letter made him feel better. In it, Marilyn stated over and over how much she missed and loved him. Nick's face broadened into a smile. He longed to be with her, and placed the letters deep in his pack for safe keeping.

The next few days Nick wrote letters to Marilyn and his folks and dreamed of home.

As it turned out, the rest and relaxation was over all too soon, and then Nick and Company G were back again on the front lines. They waited for their orders at the edge of a clump of fir trees that reminded him of home. This fighting would be different, Nick knew, they'd be on the attack, rather than defending their dug in positions.

It was strange how time seemed to slow down, almost stop, before a battle. Even Nick, after one battle, sensed the difference. There was a hushed feeling about the group as they waited, like being backstage before the curtain goes up at a play. He realized these hours might be his last; his senses were more alert. He could taste, smell, hear, feel things more clearly than at any other time. The anticipation of the dangers facing him sent a shiver through his body.

As he waited, he glanced up at the grey sky, thinking about Marilyn and his mom and dad. He missed them so much. It would be a long time before he'd get to see them again and that thought wore on his mind. The men around him were subdued and silent, as if they too were lost in thoughts of people and places far away.

At last the command came, and they began to move out in single file, down a trail which led off through the trees. The thick underbrush reminded him of places where he'd hiked at home. Though the thin coating of snow on the ground helped to muffle their footsteps, the dry leaves and twigs crackled underfoot. He hoped the Germans wouldn't hear them coming.

He glanced into the trees and brush, nothing moved, not even a bird or a squirrel. It was as if the forest held its breath, waiting for what was to come. He held his aid kit to keep it from swinging too much, and followed the man ahead of him. His face felt stiff and numb from the cold air, but the walking warmed the rest of his body. Nick felt tense and his left eye had started to twitch, yes, he was scared but he'd keep going wherever his platoon had to go.

He thought of Branch's words about how the sergeant took orders from a unknown officer who got his orders from God only knew. "It all starts with some General in the rear echelon who looks at a nice clean map which is probably outdated, and comes up with a plan. The jerk doesn't know his ass from a hole in the ground, and we get to carry out his orders, no matter how ridiculous."

The sharp scent of pine and fir drifted in the air. Nick took a deep breath. The air was crisp with the promise of snow.

He looked up at clouds just as the silence was shattered by an explosion. The unexpected shrill blast sent a jolt of adrenaline through Nick and his heart pounded. It was similar to waiting for the starting gun before the mile race.

"Medic!" -- the chilling word sounded out from the column far ahead.

Nick shot forward on the run. He guided his feet down the path trying to avoid the roots, rocks and other obstacles. His athletic ability came in good stead as he glided along careful not to slip on the patches of snow. The men moved aside as he spead past concentrating on his mission. He glimpsed Branch beside the trail, "Take your time, Doc. No one is going anywhere."

Nick nodded and trotted past him, glad to have the support of a friend. His hands were clammy, but to his surprise, there were more encouraging remarks as he hurried on toward an unknown situation he hoped he could handle.

He felt a surge of pride. His platoon was counting on him, He needed to come through now and he would.

Nick's foot caught a maverick root and he stumbled almost sprawling to the ground. He fought to keep his balance and managed to barely do it.

Finally, he saw the platoon's first sergeant lying on the ground, scanning the forest, with his bayonet-fixed readied for action. "It's Goodwin -- over to your right. He stepped on a mine." The sergeant said.

Nick spotted Goodwin laying motionless flat on his back. The scene anguished Nick to no end. What a rotten thing to do to another man especially to a nice guy like him. Another perfect example of man's inhumanity to man that was being played out by Hitler.

Nick started toward the wounded man when the sergeant reached out and held him back, "It's not gonna work." The sergeant shook his head. "Don't know how you can get to him."

Nick looked at Goodwin again and hesitated. His legs trembled and his mouth was dry. As the sergeant pointed, he spotted amongst the thin layer of snow, protrusions where the mines had been planted. Goodwin needed his help now, not later. There was no one else but him. Stepping off the Path to get to Goodwin was the hardest thing Nick had ever done, but he had no choice. It was his duty. Cautiously he placed his feet between the small protrusions, praying there were none hidden so well that he couldn't see them.

Even in the cold air, he felt the perspiration on his back as he got near Goodwin. His face was so ashen it was hard to recognize the man. He was trembling probably more from the shock of the wound than the cold. Nick knelt over the patient and observed that most of the right boot and pant leg had been blown away. Raw muscle and bone was exposed and blood coated the leg and ground around it. The foot was mangled and the boot threaded but secure above the ankle.

First, he needed to get all the boot off.

"Having much pain?"

"No," Goodwin whispered. Nick saw the fear in his eyes. The numbness from the injury would soon wear off, and the pain would come. He dug the morphine out of his kit and injected it into the thigh of the injured leg.

"How's it look, Doc?"

"Your foot's messed up, but nothing that won't heal."

Nick hoped to God that was true. How terrible to lose a foot. He felt it would heal and Goodwin would be sent home and that would end the war for him.

Goodwin raised up on his elbows.

"Don't move," Nick said. "Mines on both sides of you." Goodwin stiffened, beginning to panic. His eyes darted from side to side.

Nick rummaged in the aid kit. A pocket knife. He needed a pocket knife. All his military training and now the first thing he needed he didn't have. He looked back at the sergeant who still lay on the trail with his eyes fixed on Nick.

"Sergeant, do you have a knife? I need to cut the boot off."

The sergeant pulled his knife out of his pocket, then hesitated.

"Throw it!" Nick called.

"It could land on a mine."

"It won't.", Nick caught it one-handed. The sergeant had made a good throw, like an easy lob from pitcher to first base. Easy out, he thought. Just like in the city championships.

He flicked open the blade and cut the boot off. The wound looked nasty, jagged and raw. He cleaned it, sprinkled sulfa powder, and bandaged it. It felt strange working in the middle of a mine field, and he couldn't wait to get out of there. He felt good about helping

Goodwin. During the procedure their eyes would meet, and Nick could see the appreciation written in Goodwin's.

"Think you can crawl out of here?"

The wounded soldier nodded and struggled to turn over. "Mines -- there and there." Nick pointed. He stepped in front of Goodwin to guide him toward the trail. After advancing a short distance, Nick said, "Hold it!" He shifted behind Goodwin and lifted his dragging leg to one side, away from a mine. Working together they struggled forward. Nick moved a leg a couple more times before reaching the trail.

To Nick's surprise, litter bearers arrived promptly at the right time. Frank Lawson, a medic Nick had trained with in Oklahoma, was in charge of the litter. While Frank and his Partner lifted the patient onto the stretcher, Nick told them briefly about the treatment he'd given Goodwin.

Frank nodded. "I'll tag him when we get back." He held out his hand. "Great job, Nick." Then, in a moment he knew he'd never forget, Goodwin struggled on his good leg, stood all the way up, and shook Nick's hand. "Thanks, Doc," he said, then their eyes met for a split second and he sank back to the stretcher. Nick blinked, unable to believe what had happened. He'd never conceived a battlefield with people shaking hands.

"Frank will take excellent care of you. Good luck with your foot. It'll be fine."

Frank and his assistants lifted the litter and hurried away toward the rear. As he watched the group depart up the trail, Nick remained baffled on how Goodwin had found the strength to stand.

He turned to the sergeant, who'd scrambled to his feet. "Strange there are no mines on the trail."

"Krauts were in a hurry. Wouldn't be easy to dig up the hard pathway." The sergeant turned to the men up the trail that had been waiting to see what was next to come. "Move out! Stick to the trail, single file. No side trips."

The men of Company G moved past the mine field, deeper into the forest and assembled for a rest and further orders. During the period of relaxation, Nick felt good about what he'd done. But what made him feel even better were the respectful looks he was getting and the snatches of conversation he heard floating from under the trees.

"Did you hear what our medic did?"

"Didn't even hesitate going into that mine field." "Got Goodwin fixed up with no problem." "Nice to know we've got a good medic."

As he leaned against a tree, Nick enjoyed the beauty and freshness of the winter forest. But he knew the images of the German soldier, Nelson, and Goodwin's foot would be with him for a long time and probably forever. He was quickly finding out what this war was all about. It was frightening to think you could be healthy and happy one minute and dead the next.

As he lifted his wallet out of his pocket to look at family pictures, his mind shifted to the moment he reached where Goodwin lay motionless in the middle of the mine field.

"You can't go in there!" The Sergeant said.

Nick looked over at Goodwin, and then inspected the ground. He carefully stepped his way to where Goodwin lay. Later, the Sergeant wouldn't throw his knife because it might fall on a mine. Nick said, "Throw it."

A yellow torn newspaper clipping floated from his billfold. Nick picked it up and read:

Somebody said that it couldn't be done,

But he with a chuckle replied that maybe it couldn't,
but he would be one who wouldn't say so 'til he'd
tried.
So, he buckled right in with a trace of a grin
on his face, and if he worried he hid it.
He started to sing as he tackled the thing that
couldn't be done and he did it.

There are thousands to tell you it cannot be done,
There are thousands to prophesy failure,
There are thousands to point out to you, one by one,
the dangers that wait to assail you.
But just buckle right in with a bit of a grin,
Just start to sing as you tackle the thing that
"cannot be done," and you'll do it. Edgar A Guest

Chapter 6

As Company G moved onward, Nick observed the soldier ahead with his huge pack. The soldiers brown overcoat was rolled and held by the backpack's flap. An M-1 rifle dragged at his shoulder by its strap. He seemed over loaded with equipment but trudged along like it wasn't a problem. Nick had the same gear, except in place of the gun, he had an aid kit. The man's gas mask bounced on the back of his pack. The mask was one thing Nick didn't want to have to use.

Vivid memories of a gas mask drill when he and other GI's were gassed during basic training flooded his mind. He had managed to get his mask untangled at the last second only because the officer in charge had come to his aid.

He'd never forget the heavy coughing and uncomfortable nausea that had swept through him as he left the chamber. But what he remembered the most was when the gruff obnoxious officer came over to him afterwards, put his arm on his shoulder and smiled, "Are you all right, son?"

"Yes, sir, I'm OK." Nick had responded. He realized the officer had been putting on a tough front, but underneath, he was a caring person. He wondered, how many other tough acting sergeants and officers might also be nice guys.

His thoughts came back to the present, and he shivered in the cold air. This was the real thing, no game like back in Camp Gruber. This was a long way from warm Oklahoma, and he felt like a worried chunk of ice.

G Company hiked for hours until darkness overtook them. The column slowed, and the man in front of him said, "We're stopping for a rest." The message had passed back, man to man, until it reached Nick, the last man in the chain. It was a natural feeling for him to follow up the rear being the medic. A few minutes later, the men dropped their packs and huddled together on the ground as they tried to catnap.

"Doc, get closer," the soldier next to him said. Nick noticed the patches of snow on the ground wasn't melting and the breeze made the chill factor well below freezing. Nick not having anyone on one side of him shivered from the breeze He didn't sleep until just before it was time to move on. They'd been resting an hour and a half when Nick was nudged awake. As they hiked along, the starlight sifted through the passing clouds, creating mysterious shadows that stretched out from the bushes and trees and kept him alert for any Germans who might be lurking there ready to ambush them.

They were surrounded by silence, but when Nick thought about it, he realized that silence was rarely quiet. Silence merely consisted of the small sounds you heard when larger noises disappeared. In the background, Nick could hear the soft rustling of leaves in the calm breeze. Two hours later, still in darkness, they stopped.

"We're near enemy lines, so no talking or smoking," Lieutenant Kane whispered. In the night, the glow of cigarettes could make for a good target for the Krauts. Nick's platoon waited behind a hill.

Later Kane came by and said, "They'd be taking a narrow road through the forest and around a sharp curve and then straight ahead a quarter of a mile. They'll cross a bridge over a small river and hold it 'til the next day."

Nick breathed in and exhaled slowly while watching the cloud of air from his lungs puff into the cold air. Just as Branch had said, this is another situation where you had no control of your destiny. Nick prayed he'd survive whatever danger lay ahead.

The GI's near him began to whisper amongst themselves as they moved nervously about. As daybreak arrived, the word came to move out. They marched forward and when they reached the curve in the road, Nick heard a strange noise. He glanced to his left and saw Dan, a GI who he knew slightly, sobbing. Another soldier had his arm around Dan and led him toward the rear.

"Dan's nerves got to him." Del Toro said.

Nick felt sorry and embarrassed for Dan. Shell shock could strike anyone because of the constant stress and fear. Nick hoped it didn't happen to him.

The platoon snaked down the hill and through the trees. When they reached the bridge, Lieutenant Kane led them across. The group dispersed along the far side of the river. Kane told Nick and Harris to remain near the bridge under a clump of pine trees. "Our mission is to hold the bridge until morning. A tank corps is to cross for a surprise attack." Kane said as he squinted across the small river. "This is a good spot for our headquarters."

The GI's found old trenches and tunnels and took up their positions. Since it was calm, they figured the Krauts had no idea of there presence. However, Nick wondered what would happen when they were found out. This thought popped into his mind often and it was a giant worry.

"Harris, you stay with, Doc, here." Kane stopped at the edge of the screen of pines and called back, "Keep an eye on the bridge and watch for the tanks. They're due at dawn and sure as hell better show up. Be alert!" He ambled off into the fog to check on the rest of his men.

Nick peeked at his watch, it was 5:15 A.M.. Harris moved his M1 in his hands appearing nervous. To pass the time Nick tried to picture the platoon's position out in the fog. Where was Branch? He missed his familiar gruff ways. Harris, he hardly knew but seemed nice enough. Lieutenant Kane was the only link between him and the others in the platoon. He looked over at Harris and he was looking more agitated.

"How're you doing?" Nick whispered as he rubbed the back of his hand against his sandpaper like chin whiskers.

"Freaked out! What if those damned tanks don't show?" Harris's voice sounded strained.

"What time do you have Harris? I think my watch has stopped."

"I've got 5:40. What a drag," Harris said as Kane reappeared. The Lieutenant leaned his carbine, a smaller rifle, against a tree and sat down next to Nick.

"How's Branch doing out there?" Nick said."

"Funny you should ask. He asked about you. He's not happy. I pity the Kraut that gets in his way."

A flurry of shots echoed through the trees. "Shit!"

Kane muttered. He grabbed his gun and took off.

"Damn it! We've been found out," Harris said as he held his rifle ready. The gun shook, so Nick touched Harris on the shoulder.

"Those tanks will get here and we'll be all right." The gun steadied.

Would they show up? Cold sweat trickled down Nick's back.

When Kane returned, he said, "A Kraut came face to face with Davis. We're in trouble now. The fog is lifting, and still no sign of the tanks."

The persistent gunfire continued nearby. Kane mumbled something, Nick didn't catch, and left. A red-faced sergeant named Crawford dashed into camp. "Where's Kane?" he panted.

"Checking the men. He'll be back soon," Harris said.

Crawford crouched beside Nick. "I'm not wandering around this shooting gallery. I'll wait."

Five minutes later, a distraught Kane arrived. "Damn Germans are picking us off one at a time. We can't hold on much longer."

Crawford nodded. "That's why I came over. What now?"

Kane looked at him, but before he could speak, Crawford said, "I'm surprised your medic is with you. I couldn't get ours to come. I threatened him, but it did no good. What a coward! He said, he wasn't required to go with us. I'm going to get his ass."

The lieutenant looked at Nick. "Really?" he said. "Our medic sticks with us no matter where we go."

Nick's mouth curled into a slight grin. The remark made him feel good, but had he done the right thing by coming along. Maybe by this time tomorrow, Crawford's medic would still be alive and he wouldn't be. He'd never thought there was a choice. He always stuck with his platoon.

"Well," Kane said, "We've got orders to hold this bridge, but if things get too hot, we'll make a run for it--one at a time--or if we're forced to, I guess we'll have to surrender."

The word surrender shook Nick to the core. He wanted to run across the bridge and up and over the hill onto the other side and keep running, from the horror and the constant fear of death. He glanced around the desolate place and wished he was anywhere else.

"We'll keep in touch," Kane continued. "I'll send Harris over to your headquarters in half an hour. Where are you?"

Crawford pointed down the hill. "See that clump of trees about a hundred yards down river? That's it."

"OK. Good luck." He waved at Crawford, who bent over and raced away. He turned to Nick. "Come on, Doc. Follow me. There's wounded."

As Nick followed the lieutenant, a sense of futility swept through him. He felt the sweat flow over his body. Together they entered the maze of trenches, Nick reluctant but close on Kane's heels.

Kane whispered, "The Krauts have concussion grenades, so keep your mouth open. It'll keep your eardrums from rupturing if one goes off."

Nick nodded and followed Kane around a curve in the trench. A soldier named Worthy sat against the dirt wall. "I'm OK, Doc. Just get me out of here."

Nick didn't think he looked OK. Worthy's blood-soaked jacket had a huge gaping hole right where his heart should have been. Nick reached into his aid kit, praying he'd do the right thing. If only he was a doctor! He couldn't believe Worthy was still alive. Somehow the bullet had missed the man's vital organs and large blood vessels. The bleeding had stopped on its own, and though the wound looked fatal, it wasn't. Thankful the man hadn't gone into shock, he powdered the wound with sulfa and bandaged it.

"You got lucky, Worthy! Try to make your way back to headquarters. We'll catch up with you later," Nick said.

He followed Kane farther down the trench, and they found Lindell. He'd been shot in the leg, and his pants had been torn away. The hole exposed the beefy red muscle, ripped apart, with white bone uncovered. Nick inspected the shattered thigh and gave Lindell a quick injection of morphine. He felt his efforts would be inadequate, but treated the wound with the usual sulfa and bandages.

They moved on to Private Olson. A jab of nausea swept Nick when he saw the bloody wound. Olson had been hit in the stomach, and the bullet had exited his back. He gave Olsen a shot of morphine. Nick felt helpless and compassion for the young man. More than anything Nick wanted to be able to help, but he couldn't. O1son, needed to be in a hospital with doctors to take care of him.

"Let's get back, Doc," Kane shouted over the sounds of the battle.

Nick turned, anxious to get out. Shots broke out near them. Kane and Nick hit the dirt. Nick's face was pressed tightly against the brutally cold frozen ground littered with dry leaves and scratchy brambles. He felt vulnerable with the eye-catching red cross on his helmet. He kept his head low and moved crab-like toward their headquarters. As they passed the pasty white Lindell, Kane said, "Try to crawl out of here; otherwise we'll get back to you."

Nick knew they wouldn't get back, and Lindell couldn't move far. Lindell was going to be captured or die, and there was nothing he could do about it. Nelson's face flashed in his thoughts, and an empty feeling gnawed at his stomach, but he kept moving.

On their way back, they caught up with Worthy, crawling along in the dirt. As he and Kane squeezed past him, Nick said, "Keep going, you're doing great." Worthy gave him a frustrated glance but struggled on. Nick hoped none of the men held their agony of battle against him. The brass wouldn't send doctors to the front lines. They were too valuable. Instead, they sent expendable medics to do a doctor's job. Their basic first aid training made the assignment impossible.

Nick and Kane got to headquarters and found Harris shaking with fear. Nick could hear the German firepower building up as the Krauts closed in for the kill.

Lieutenant Kane looked down river towards Crawford's location. Nick saw soldiers putting up white flags. The shooting didn't slow up anywhere as far as Nick could tell.

As he squinted into the lifting fog, Germans were overpowering the Americans all up and down the line.

Kane pulled his shirt and undershirt off. "I'm going to raise a white flag to test them." He tied the undershirt to the bayonet on his rifle and held it as high as he could. An instant later, Nick felt the ground shake as machine gun fire swept past his feet, spattering him with mud and snow.

Chapter 7

Kane dropped his white flag and slipped away to pass on instructions to the men in the trenches.

Nick crouched behind a tree. He glanced around, wondering where the shots were coming from. He couldn't tell. The Germans were hidden on three sides, and bullets blasted around them more often, coming closer each minute. His hand trembled as it rested against the tree. Would they have any chance of getting out alive, he wondered.

Worthy very weak but still moving made it to headquarters, and other GI's began to arrive.

Kane rushed back into the clearing and said, "Harris, take off across the bridge. We'll cover you."

Without hesitation, Harris crouched and dashed off at full speed.

One by one, the men ran across the bridge through a hail of bullets that came from all directions. Nick saw two get hit and stumble to the wet snow patched ground. He wanted to take off, but he held back, waiting Kane's word. As usual, being the medic, he'd be one of the last to leave. Still huddled near the tree, he glanced down the hill toward Crawford's platoon. They had white flags up, and the men had their hands up as they walked toward the Germans.

Kane Yelled, "Go, Doc!" Nick, engrossed in watching Crawford's men surrendering, nearly missed the signal. He'd been called to go sooner than he'd expected. There were several others set to take off. Adrenaline surged through him like a lightening strike. He scrambled to his feet and raced to the bridge. Without stopping or turning around, he crossed and started up the hill, anticipating the worst as gunfire boomed around him. Nick, hunched over and moving side to side in hopes of not being hit by the enemy fire continued on through the gauntlet of bullets. He knew the Krauts were behind him, and at any second, a bullet could strike him down.

Nick bounced and sprawled to the ground. He was hit! He lay there, gasping for breath. He expected pain, but there was none. He twisted to look down at his ankle. He'd only stumbled after all. Terrified, he could feel his heart beating in his temples.

He jumped up, ready to dash onward, out of the range of the German guns. Unfortunately, there were no trees on this hillside to hide behind. Nick felt exposed to easy enemy fire.

Then Nick saw him--a GI lying about twelve feet to his right. The soldier's helmet lay beside him, and Nick saw an ugly wound on the back of his head.

He crept through the mud and snow to the unconscious GI. A slow seepage of blood came from the wound, so Nick took a compress from his kit and pressed it against the injury. Then taped it tightly. The soldier didn't respond and at last, Nick had to leave him and go on.

When he darted forward again, he noticed Del Toro standing next to a concrete block shed watching him approach. Nick had no idea what this structure was doing sitting half way up the hill. There was no other building as far as the eye could see. It had three sides and a roof with the open side facing up the hill. A perfect spot to be protected from gunshots. It was a relief to be able to relax. Nick gave a sigh and grinned at Del Toro.

"You hit?" Del Toro asked.

Nick shook his head. "I stumbled. It happened so quick, I wasn't sure at first."

"Hey! Let's get the hell out of here. We need to get over the hill." Del Toro headed upward.

Nick was in no hurry to leave the safety of the building.

"I'll catch my breath and follow you in a minute." He held his side, taking a few deep breaths before sprinting over the top of the hill. Del Toro was waiting for him.

"Look at that, Doc," he said as he pointed to his boot. There was a hole through the toe.

"Did it get your foot?"

"Not even a scratch, damn it. If it'd caught my toe, I'd be heading for the rear and a long rest. Lousy luck."

They both collapsed to the ground. They felt safe now as though the Germans had left the country. Nick noticed the sun was low in the sky. How the time had sped by since the Germans had spotted them and began their attack. Also, the small shrubs and grass where they rested made him wonder if the area had been logged in the past. He glanced into the valley where the trees were plentiful. All of a sudden, he sat up, scanning the men one at a time. A sinking feeling engulfed him.

"Have you guys seen Branch?" Nick asked.

"He didn't make it," Hunter yelled back.

Nick jumped up and walked down to where Lieutenant Kane was resting. "Sir, did you see Branch?"

Kane shook his head and rubbed the back of his hand across his haggard face. "No, not after he made it to headquarters."

"Sir, can I have permission to look for him?"

"Forget it, Doc. We can't afford to lose our medic."

Nick felt a surge of anger and knew his face was flushed. "He's a friend. I can help him."

"The Krauts have taken over the area. You couldn't get near him. You'd get killed."

"He's one tough guy," Nick insisted. "He could be just wounded."

"I'm in charge here, and I say no. That's the end, Doc." He pointed to a hollow in the hill. "Go rest up. You did a great job."

"I owe it to him, Lieutenant."

"You haven't been listening. I said no, and I meant it. Sit down and forget it."

Nick walked to the hollow and sat down. He knew he'd be crazy to endanger himself for what might be a lost cause. He listened to the gunshots in the distance and glanced back and saw the Lieutenant watching him. He pictured his friend back at Drusenheim peering out of their foxhole with his gun in one hand and the old faithful Lucky Strike in the other.

All Nick had to do was walk away. Nobody would know the difference or care, especially the alcoholic parents Branch had told him about the week before. The hell of it was he wanted to do this for a man he hardly knew. But he knew Branch would do the same for him.

He felt he was being driven by his own conscience into a situation where he might die an unpleasant death. He would rather be almost anywhere else, doing anything other than this. Still, he knew he had to try.

Nick walked over to Del Toro. "I'm going after Branch. Will you come along?"

Del Toro looked at Nick as if Nick had lost his mind. "Sorry! I'll give you whatever you need, but I wouldn't go back there for a million bucks."

"OK! I need your helmet, pistol and three grenades. I appreciate it."

Del Toro took off his helmet and handed it to Nick, then gave him his pistol and three grenades.

"Thanks." Nick removed his helmet with its conspicuous red cross. He put on Del Toro's and

30

grabbed a flashlight from his pack and stuffed it in his medical kit.

Del Toro watched as Nick attached the pistol and the grenades to his belt. "You're somethin' else, Doc. Good luck, you'll need it!"

While Kane was occupied talking to another survivor, Nick slipped over the hump of the hill into the foggy twilight and crept down the other side. He moved toward the concrete shed where he'd stopped before. Taking cover behind it, he scouted the landscape below. In the failing light, he could make out the remains of the damaged bridge the Germans had blown up after the platoon crossed it. Nick could still see the German soldier creeping from the brush and slinging the explosive under the bridge then turning and sprinting back to his cover before the blast went off. From where Nick stood, he could see three bodies and knew there were probably more concealed by the slope of the river bank.

Debating whether or not to forget it and head back, Nick forced himself down the hill toward the river being careful not to slip on the patches of snow and mud. He approached the first GI laying motionless and it took him a minute before he recognized that it was corporal Joe Bentz. Nick saw no signs of life. He paused next to a football sized rock and two small brown shrubs, and listened to the bursts of gunfire in the distance. Keeping as low as he could, he slid his way down the hill to the next victim, this man he didn't recognize. He squinted over the edge of the slope but saw nothing in the gathering darkness.

A shot broke the silence. Nick jumped and froze. Were they shooting at him, he wondered. As another shot hit close by, he took off zigzagging toward the ruined bridge. He dove forward and rolled down the embankment, ending up near the bridge abutment where he crawled behind a beam.

Nick remained still for a short time and then pulled his pistol out and held it ready to fire. In the darkness, he couldn't tell where the enemy was hiding. He waited a few minutes, then noticed a movement fifteen yards farther up the the river bank.

In the fading twilight, Nick pulled the flashlight from his kit. He was about to switch it on when he thought better of it and shoved it back into his kit. There was no use giving his position away. There was not a sound. He prayed the German sniper had given up on him. Stealthily, he crawled toward where he'd seen the movement. When he got there, Branch raised his head, and they stared at each other for a moment.

"I knew you'd come back for me, Doc."

"How're you doing?',

"Shitty! I'm hit in the back and in my right leg."

Nick inspected the wounds. Branch's back had a small hole there with blood slowly dripping from it. The leg was shattered badly. No wonder he couldn't move, Nick thought. It didn't look good for Branch. Nick prayed he would survive. There was a bullet lodged in his body that should be removed as soon as possible.

"I'm going to carry you out of here."

"You're not that strong. Where are those other assholes?"

"I'm alone. I can do it. So believe it." Nick said with what he hoped sounded like conviction. Several shots erupted near them, and Nick heard footsteps on a remaining timber of the battered bridge.

He lifted the grenade from his belt and pulled the pin, holding the release tight. His hand was slippery with mud and sweat, and he hoped he wouldn't drop the grenade and blow them both to bits. Waiting until he saw a flicker of movement, he lobbed the grenade at the bridge. He ducked just before the blast.

Their ears rang, but Nick knew the grenade had done its job. "C'mon, Branch, we've got to get the hell out of here. Can you get up on your knees?"

"Doc, I can't."

"Yes, you can. Get your ass up now!"

Branch moaned and turned onto his knees. Nick grabbed him by the waist and hauled him up, then slid under him, lifting with all his strength until at last, he managed to get Branch across his shoulders.

"How much do you weigh, for Christ sake?" Nick wheezed. "You're no branch. I feel like I'm dragging the whole damn tree." Branch started to laugh but groaned as it turned into a cough.

Nick could barely move as they started up the steep incline of the river bank. They'd only gone a few laborious steps when scary German words he didn't understand echoed in his ears. "Halten Sie! Hebst dein Hande auf! Jetzt!"

Nick froze, almost stumbling to the ground as he looked up into the faces of two armed Germans who stood above him on a bridge timber. He wanted to reach for his pistol, but with Branch on his back, there was no way.

Nick was sure they were finished--dead--no chance. He looked into the barrels of the guns aimed at them. Branch's weight suddenly seemed heavier. Nick slipped to his knees, slowly slumping to the ground.

Then came a burst of gunfire. Nick was flat in the mud with Branch on top of him. He gasped for breath and waited for the pain to begin. Was this it? His time to die? He twisted to look at his attackers, hoping for mercy. He prayed they'd take them prisoners instead of shooting.

A booming voice came out of the darkness, "Hunter, Smith! Grab Branch and move out!"

Americans! Nick lay there, stunned. Was that Kane?

Hunter and Smith pulled Branch off Nick's back and started up the hill. Kane stood and looked toward the bridge, his rifle in his hands, ready to fire. "You OK, Doc?"

"Never better,', Nick said, as he began to regain his lost composure. "I thought we'd had it."

"We were lucky." Kane turned and motioned up the hill. "Let's go."

As Nick hurried along, he wondered about Branch. Would his friend survive? Nick believed that he would. His rescue mission had turned out as good as he could have expected. They continued up the hill. Nick was exhausted when they reached a safe rest area. Hunter and Smith looked beat and collapsed to the ground.

Kane grinned at Nick, a cigarette dangling from his lips. "Well, Doc, I can still see you with Branch on your back and those two Krauts looking down at you. What in the hell were you going to do then?"

"I don't know. I thought I'd had it until I heard your voice."

Kane laughed. "Gotta hand it to you, Doc. You may not follow orders very well, but you've got nerve. After all that, Branch had better make it."

He will. He's tough," Nick said solemnly praying it was true. Then, looking Kane in the eye, he said, "Thanks for showing up when I needed you."

Kane shrugged. He shook Nick's hand. "A good medic is hard to find. We can't afford to lose you." He clapped Nick on the shoulder. "One thing, though Doc. Don't do it again."

Nick grinned convinced Branch would make a full recovery. Kane had no need to worry he'd ever try it again.

It was probably the dumbest thing he'd ever done. It was pure luck he and Branch hadn't been shot dead in their tracks. No wonder Kane had told him not to do it. That's why he was the platoon leader and Nick the medic. His blunder could have been fatal. Thanks to Kane it all turned out all right. They'd go on to fight another day and eventually win -- so they could head back to good old home.

Chapter 8

Nick and the men of Company G plodded forward, chasing the stubborn Germans through forests, fields, and towns. After a week of slogging through the mud of the desolate countryside without running into a single German, they were sent back to the rear lines for rest and relaxation at Weyersheim.

When they marched into the quaint little Alsation town, the men were assigned to sleep in vacant houses. Nick enjoyed the beauty of the colorful buildings, each had its own unique patterns of red, yellow and blue. Weyersheim had been by-passed by the destruction of war.

After the long spell outside in the chilling weather, Nick was grateful to be indoors. He didn't care about a lot of creature comforts such as beds with mattress's and soft pillows. The house he entered had no furniture just bare floors. There was only a small window in his room and he didn't care.

The next morning, after eating his K-rations and wishing he had more, his next thought was of mail from home and Marilyn. Nick realized disappointedly that it wouldn't have caught up with them yet. It took weeks and sometimes a month to get overseas from Washington state. He'd heard the battalion aid station was in town, so while he passed the time until they headed back into combat, he decided to check it out. He looked forward to seeing some of the friends he'd gone through medic training with in Oklahoma. He'd been at the front for the past month, and this would be the first time he'd had a chance to talk to any of the medics stationed in the rear.

He glanced around the large bright room that had booths along the outside walls. His medic buddies sat at several of the tables playing cards. Nick looked around eagerly at the familiar faces, thrilled to see them again. As he walked near the booths, he expected a rousing "Hello!" or some kind of acknowledgment of his presence, but to his disappointment, no one even noticed him.

He spotted Wozniak in the corner by himself, "Good seeing you, Sergeant. How're you doing?"

"Hungry and bored stiff waiting around for chow-time and today's mail call."

"You're not a card player, huh?" Nick said.

"No! Never got into it. I spend my time writing letters home." Wozniak looked down to his lap at his writing pad.

Wozniak looked at Nick and said, "Nice seeing you. I still think about the fun we had on that three day pass to Tulsa last year." He turned to his writing.

Nick walked away realizing these guys had no idea what he'd been through. They didn't know what the real war--his war--was like. His war was fighting, dying, wading through the mud, being so bone-weary he had wondered if it was possible to die of exhaustion. Each day he narrowly escaped being killed. He wanted to shake them, to yell, "Hey! Wake up! I'm alive! It's great to see you!"

But he couldn't make himself do it, instead he walked to the back of the room where two other sergeants were asleep in bunks. He recognized one he'd trained with. The man opened his eyes, glanced at Nick, then closed them again and went back to sleep.

Nick felt invisible as he turned and walked back to the front of the building. When he reached the door, he swung around and glanced at the men he'd trained with. He still wanted them to notice him, to call out to him by name, ask how he was. They didn't.

In bitter disappointment, Nick turned and left the place. How could he have thought these bastards were his friends? He didn't care if he ever saw them again. As he walked away, Major Edwards came around the corner of the building and they nearly collided. Nick managed a quick salute.

"How are you, Corporal Jordan?"

"Fine. Thank you, sir." After the cold reception he'd received inside, Nick appreciated the Major knowing him by name all the more, especially since he'd only met him once, after the Drusenheim siege.

"Are you stationed in the aid station now, Corporal?"

"No, I'm back for a rest and came by to say, 'Hello' to the guys I trained with, but they acted to busy playing cards to notice me. So, I left feeling disappointed they didn't seem to care about me."

"Corporal Jordan, I'll never forget what you went through at Drusenheim. I'd given you up for dead. When you got back to us it was a great releaf for me. They gave you the brush off, huh?"

"Yes! I guess, just being an aid man for a rifle company isn't good enough for the battalion aid station group. Most of them out rank me as you know." Nick said sadly.

"We'll see about that, follow me Coporal." Major Edwards marched to the front door with Nick close behind. The Major entered and stomped his feet on the filthy throw rug.

Wozniak was the first to see him and he shouted, "Attention!"

The men dropped their cards and stood at attention. Those sleeping leaped from their bunks.

The Major's deep set hazel eyes underneath his heavy dark eyebrows scanned each one of the medics with a penetrating glare. The men instantly knew there was something upsetting their commanding officer.

"Men! Since we arrived at the front and launched into combat, Corporal Jordan here has been out in the trenches busting his ass under enemy fire. He's known to have saved many lives while exposing himself to constant danger.

When he drops by to see how you're doing, I expect him to get the respect he deserves. Understand?"

Mild 'yes' responses came forth from the soldiers.

"I can't hear you!" the Major retorted brusquely.

In unison came a loud 'Yeh!', response that left Nick holding back a laugh but he couldn't help smiling. "Thank you, sir." Nick said.

Major Edwards with the corners of his mouth showing a slight grin, winked at Nick and turned back to the others and said, "Now, let's clean this pig sty. I'll be back later to check it out. At ease!" He and Nick turned and left the building.

Outside, they chuckled together and Nick again thanked the Major before they separated.

As Nick walked back to the house where he was staying and thought about the humorous episode at battalion aid station, his thoughts were interrupted by a sergeant standing in front of him.

"Are you on duty?" the sergeant asked.

"I'm attached to Company G. We're on R and R."

"We have an emergency assignment and we need a medic now."

"I can't leave my company," Nick answered.

"You're a medic, and you're the first one I've seen. We're going to relieve a machine gun position not far away for a few hours, and then you'll be free. I have to order you to come with me." The sergeant pointed down the street.

Trapped, Nick had no choice but to go. The sergeant made it sound like a routine mission, but Nick had an uneasy feeling. He knew if Lieutenant Kane had been around, this wouldn't have happened.

He climbed into the back of a open bed green Army truck with a group of other men he'd never met. The men were equipped with bazookas, machine guns, rifles, and ammunition. He sat in silence glancing around the area as they bounced along in the truck. His fellow soldiers appeared relaxed as they spread their legs in contorted positions and rested their arms along the top of the trucks bed frame. Nick didn't care for the flat bare terrain that left them exposed to any enemy that might be lurking unseen. The weather was clear with a few white fluffy clouds drifting here and there. Nick could see almost a quarter of a mile ahead as he peeked around the side of the truck cab.

Before long, Nick became annoyed. The sergeant had hinted the ride would be a short one, but it was going on and on.

Suddenly, Nick was jolted from his thoughts by a burst of machine-gun fire accompanied by rifle shots.

"Out of the truck!" screamed the sergeant. With ditches on each side of the road, there was no way to turn around and they were sitting ducks in the truck. The only thing was to leap out and make a run for cover.

The men scattered. Nick leaped to the ground and scrambled after them as the shooting continued around him. There was no cover for hiding and the ground was flat with rocks scattered here and there. They'd been ambushed by Germans who were hidden from view somewhere down the road.

"Head back to town!" the sergeant yelled. Turning to Nick, he said, "Follow up the rear in case anyone gets hit."

Nick felt a surge of anger. Here he was again, stuck in the same old agonizing situation. He wanted to run for cover with the others, but he had to hold back because he was the medic.

He sprinted after the men, who kept low, zigzagging, then lying flat before they rushed away again. Several times, he nearly overran the man in front of him and had to wait to keep his position at the rear of the group. The shots were still too close for comfort. What if one of the men did get hit? It would be impossible to transport an injured man to safety.

As the shooting continued, they kept running. Nick wondered why he'd let himself get talked into joining this squad. How dumb! He should have forced the issue and contacted Lieutenant Kane. The men hurried back the way they had come. Nick's mouth tasted bitter and metallic as he ran with his head down. He prayed a bullet wouldn't rip into him. He didn't dare take the time to look behind to see where the shots were coming from. His only thought was to get away in one piece.

A sinking feeling swept over him when he heard a scream of pain. Someone had been hit. Nick hesitated while wondering how bad the man had been hurt. He hoped he could take care of him, and still get away from the Krauts. He moved to where he'd heard the cry until he found the source, a wounded soldier, lying in a gully. His buddies had all run ahead.

"Don't leave me," the man begged, his eyes wide with fright. "My knee is out. I can't move! You've got to help me!" Fear stretched the man's voice to a keening wail.

Nick pulled the pants leg out of the combat boot and felt the already swollen knee. He'd never unlocked a knee before and wasn't sure which way to twist it, but he grabbed the man's foot, knowing he had to try. He extended the leg and gave it a twist to the right. To his relief, it worked.

The soldier gave a yelp of joy. "You did it! You saved my life!" He tested his weight on the leg and winced. Damn, I can't put any weight on it. You gotta help me, Doc."

A wave of frustration washed over Nick. He thought he'd taken care of the problem, but now he still had to help the soldier move along, and that would slow them up.

Defeated, Nick put his right arm around the man's waist. The GI put his left arm on Nick's shoulder, and they headed off after the others.

"Thanks again, Doc. I owe you," the soldier said gratefully.

Their progress was painfully slow. Nick couldn't see any of the other GI's. They were far ahead, out of sight. Ever so often, they'd come to a shallow gully and Nick had to practically carry the man down and up the other side. Somehow, he did it.

Abruptly, shots sprayed near them, and a German voice boomed out. "Halten Siel Schnell!"

Nick looked over his shoulder and saw the blue SS uniforms and familiar german helmets on three enemy soldiers aiming rifles at them. Nick and his companion stopped and put up their hands as the Germans surrounded them.

Lieutenant Kane wasn't around to save him this time. Nick's heart was pounding and his mouth felt loaded with cotton. Would these ferocious-looking Germans kill them right in their tracks?

The Germans were talking rapidly together, and Nick strained to understand. Two of them seemed to be ready to shoot him, but one cooler head finally prevailed. Using is rifle barrel, the man pointed the way, and Nick and the GI were marched off toward the German lines.

As Nick helped his frightened companion, he'd never felt so helpless. How would he survive now? Would he ever see his Mom and Dad or Marilyn again? Had his luck run out? Was this the end?

His heart sank in despair as they walked toward the unknown.

Chapter 9

The SS guard shoved Nick in the back. "Schnell, schnell," he spat; his lip curled into a snarl. Nick stumbled, but managed to keep going without falling. He bit back a retort and kept his eyes downcast so the German wouldn't see his anger. His toes ached with cold, and his nose was numb. His ears felt as though they'd fall off if touched.

He and the GI with the bad knee had been forced to hike for miles to join up with this group of prisoners. During the march, Nick's thoughts had been in turmoil. He wondered what Kane had thought when he didn't return. He worried about Branch. He thought about his mom and dad and Wylie. And Marilyn, especially Marilyn. Would he ever see any of them again? He dreamed of returning home. Somehow, he had to survive, He watched the three German guards as they herded their prisoners down the narrow gravel road. One guard looked like a career officer, disciplined and intelligent, but the other two were little better than animals, kicking and spitting at the prisoners.

He wanted to keep his spirits up, determined to take whatever happened. He tried not to think about the stories he'd heard of men dying in prisoner of war camps. From what he'd read and heard, the Third Reich didn't teach mercy, and most of the Germans would as soon kill you as not. Had Kane saved Nick's life so he could die in a Nazi stalag?

He was glad he'd taken two years of German in high school and studied it later, for it enabled him to pick up most of what the guards said.

The stout, hard-looking German with the small beady eyes kicked at a stumbling prisoner. "Gerhardt!" he shouted to the career officer. "Halten Sie eine minute." Then, by Nick's approximation, something like, "It's crazy to take these prisoners back. Why don't we walk them into the woods and shoot 'em?"

Fear shot through Nick as he interpreted the words. His knees felt weak and his chest tightened. Sweat seeped over his body.

"Nein, Mueller," the trim and straight Gerhardt replied. "We have our orders. Verstehst du nicht? General von Beck is expecting prisoners for interrogation."

Nick sighed with relief, relaxing a bit. So they were safe, for the moment anyway. 'Prisoners for interrogation.' What a laugh. Not one of these GI's had any idea what was going on. They were all just following orders. The general would be furious when he found out how little they all knew. Nick wasn't looking forward to his reaction.

"Ich verstehe nicht," Mueller growled. "I'll take care of a couple of these swine. The others will sprint the rest of the way."

Nick glanced at the ornery Mueller. "He's the swine!" he said to himself

Gerhardt frowned. "Nein. Let's keep going. Macht schnell!" He looked back to the rear of the line and shouted, "Keep them moving, Schmidt. We need to get back to town before dark."

Nick had a good feeling about Gerhardt, as he watched Mueller move up and down the ranks, prodding the men onward with the butt of his rifle. Nick saw his gaze settle on the limping soldier he'd helped. The GI dragged behind, too tired to keep up with the others. Mueller took a viscious swing, his foot slipped on a loose rock. The GI ducked, and Mueller fell hard onto the road.

Nick froze as he watched the German guard squirm in agony. Mueller spouted out fierce sounding German words, but Nick only understood fragments.

Gerhardt halted the column of prisoners. "Are you all right, Mueller?"

Mueller, ashen faced, held up his bleeding hand. "Nein. I gashed my hand on a rock."

Gerhardt looked around until he saw Nick, and said, "There's a medic prisoner. He'll bandage it."

"Ja, Ja. Schnell!" Mueller shouted angrily.

Nick's nerves tensed, and his heart pounded, but he didn't move. He had a hunch it was better the Germans didn't realize he understood what they said. He waited while Gerhardt pulled a first aid kit from his gear and walked toward him. The German handed him the kit and pointed to Mueller. In English, he commanded, "Fix it up."

Nick took the kit. Leaning over Mueller, he examined the hand. The cut was about an inch long but didn't look deep. He hated to work on this bully but knew there was no choice. He took a sterile gauze and pressed it against the wound and in a couple of minutes the bleeding stopped. He sprinkled antiseptic powder on the cut and wrapped the hand and wrist leaving the thumb free.

As Nick worked on the hand, Mueller swore under his breath. Nick was glad to be finished with it and anxious to move away from the mean German.

Gerhardt checked the neatly bandaged hand. His eyes met Nick's. For a moment, they studied one another. Nick felt what he hoped was a mutual respect.

Gerhardt took the aid kit and motioned for Nick to get back in line. He went quickly, happy to be away from Mueller.

The weary prisoners had watched the tense encounter in silence. Their faces showed the worry and anticipation of their helpless situation. Being a prisoner of war could mean starvation, torture, or even death facing them down the road. Even though he knew only the man with the bad knee, Nick felt a deep common bond with the others.

The guards commanded them onward again. Nick looked at the desperate and frightened faces around him and wondered what lay ahead. It was as though he was living out his worst nightmare. Although cold out, the men perspired freely as they stumbled on becoming weaker and more thirsty with each step. As the miles passed, Nick had come to a decision. If the opportunity arose, he'd try to escape. The thought of remaining a prisoner of war repulsed him.

For now, though, he'd keep a low profile and wait. He glanced to the right where tree-covered hills followed along the northerly direction of the road. The fallen leaves on the forest floor and the stark, barren trees led his mind to drift back to a similar day two years ago, when he and Marilyn had scuffed through the decaying leaves at the Hoquiam City Park. A sudden ache for home and family brought a lump to his throat. Were they worried about him now? Probably not-- they would have no way of knowing, about his predicament. A weakness gripped him as though energy was seeping from his pores. The thought of never seeing Marilyn again was more than he could stand. The emotion that swelled in him whenever they were together was always on his mind. Their dreams for spending a life together had to be fulfilled. Somehow, he had to find a way out of this nightmare.

He glanced up at the spotty dark clouds against the blue background. To his left, brown grass patched with green spread across the valley. Snow remained in shady areas. As he trudged along, he spotted the pine trees about seventy five yards to the right. He loved woods; as a child, he'd played and hidden in tree-covered hills exactly like these.

He felt a glimmer of hope. If he could make it to the trees, there wasn't a German in this world who could catch him. Nick thought about when he and Wylie were children and with their friends had spent hours playing in the woods. No one could keep up with him or find him during their endless games of hide-and-seek. He'd savored those fun moments of contentment alone in the trees, and how he loved the powerful feeling of being invisible. These woods were no different than those back home. So, Nick felt confident that he could discover places where no one could find him.

Suddenly, Gerhardt shouted, "Halt!" The column of prisoners came to a stop. Nick peered around. Why were they stopping? Their captors sat down and pulled out their canteens. Nick heard the Germans gulp the water, and his thirst grew. He tried not to think about his deep craving. He shifted his position on the hard rocky gravel road; to keep his mind off his thirst.

The GI next to him whispered, "Those sons-of-bitches." Nick nodded but didn't reply.

When the Germans were rested, and their thirst quenched, they ordered the prisoners to move out. The prisoner next to him muttered, "Bastards!"

The line of prisoners straggled forward again, moving north, away from the front lines. Nick eyed the deep but narrow ravines and creek beds running up and down the hillside from the tree line at top of the hill to the ditches beside the road. Some of the gullies zigzagged down, making a variety of patterns. These were caused by the rush of water, when the melting snow and rain filled them.

If Nick could get into one unseen, he might get away.

With his sore hand, Mueller though subdued, still looked mean. He watched the men with a sadistic gleam in his eyes, and the prisoners looked downward. They didn't want to attract his attention and possibly his ire.

Nick studied Mueller's huge frame and wondered how much fat was under that uniform. The big man reminded him of an oversized playground bully.

"Schnell!" Gerhardt shouted. Nick froze. Another shout, this time from the short chubby guard. What was going on? The three guards were pointing to the sky, and at the same time scrambling off the road. Nick spotted a speck off in the northern blue sky.

The SS guards motioned to move off the road. Since the Nazi Airforce wasn't active any longer, the guards must have been sure it wasn't their plane.

Nick hurried off the road and dropped to his knees. He watched as the shorter guard sprawled into the ditch, and up front, Gerhardt directed the prisoners. Mueller's eyes darted back and forth from the men to the plane, and he crouched as low as his large body would allow.

Nick's mind raced. He wiped his sweaty hands on his pants, and his face flushed.

"This may be the moment I've been waiting for." He glanced at the guards, "Would Mueller kill me if I got caught?" Should I run for the ditch now?" He noticed the guards distracted by the plane. "I may never have another chance."

Nick said a quick prayer and made a dash for the ravine. He didn't look back for fear of seeing a gun pointed at him. He tried to run carefully so as not to stumble. If he did, his escape might end right there. He was already breathing heavy. His puffing reminded him of a steam engine chugging down a track. Wet with sweat, he hunched over and sprinted toward cover. He shifted side to side to make a harder target. The plane overhead was the only sound. Each step took him closer to safety and freedom.

Chapter 10

Nick sprinted forward and rolled into the ditch, his heart pounding so hard he could barely breathe. He glanced over his shoulder. The Germans hadn't noticed he was gone. Crouching low, he ran up the creek bed. If he could make it to where the gully turned right, thirty yards ahead, he'd be safely out of view.

As he scrambled over the rocks, his movements seemed thunderous, even with the roar of the airplane overhead. In his haste, he stumbled on a rock and sprawled to the ground. Soaked with sweat, he lay there panting for a second, trying to catch his breath.

Nick looked back at the road. No one had noticed his disappearance. Squinting up at the trees, they seemed farther away than they had when he had considered them from the road. The plane had passed now, and he had to get moving. He dashed toward the curve in the gully.

Moments later, a rifle blast rang in his ears. Fear shot through him. As he struggled forward up the hill, another shot tore into his right thigh knocking him flat.

He clutched his leg, and grimaced. Another shot rang out as he crawled around the bend, out of range. He ripped his pants leg apart, and gaped at the exposed raw muscle. Blood streamed from the bullet hole but there was no spurting. Relieved that an artery hadn't been severed, he pulled a clean handkerchief from his pocket and pressed it against the wound, then tied it around his leg. The whole leg throbbed with sharp jabs of pain. He felt sick.

When another shot whizzed over his head, he forgot the nausea and flattened to the ground. He tasted the dirt but kept crawling toward the trees.

Mueller's voice boomed out, "Kommen Sie bier! Schnell!" "Come back here! Immediately!" Nick would have known what that meant even if he hadn't known any German.

Over the sound of Mueller's shouting, Nick heard one of the prisoners yell, "Go man! You can make it--don't give up!" More shots rang out. Had the GI been shot?

He kept sliding his body along the cold earth, heading for the cover of some bushes up ahead. He wasn't going to let himself be caught now, not after getting this far. He couldn't. Mueller's cruel face flashed before him. Nick knew, if they caught him now, they'd kill him.

He peered through the bushes over a knoll. The three Germans had their rifles aimed in his direction, but only Mueller with his bandaged hand had walked up the hill toward him. Nick scanned the terrain. The gully came straight down from the woods, but to the right was a closer group of trees. Either way, he'd be exposed to more gunfire.

Mueller moved upward. With every second, he was getting closer. Nick took a deep breath and raced for the nearest tree. He pushed on through the pain that had begun to feel like a knife in his thigh. He moved as fast as he could, but it felt like slow motion. Nearly to the protection of the trees, the first shot rang out. Nick tumbled to the ground.

Mueller gleefully screamed, "Gut, gut! Kaput!" Lowering his gun, he scrambled forward.

Nick forced himself onward to the nearest tree. By the time Mueller raised his gun and fired, Nick had made it behind a bushy pine. The German kept firing into the woods.

Nick heard him shouting, "After I finish him off, I'll be right back."

Nick, knew he was in trouble. As Mueller came closer, knowing he was leaving a trail of blood, Nick limped deeper into the woods. He was glad there were no dogs involved. Nick knew he couldn't outrun Mueller; he had to outsmart him. The pain had decreased; the will to survive had taken over. He looked around for a quick place to hide. Not the thick brush, that's the first place Mueller would look.

Nick heard Mueller crashing through the undergrowth. Time was running out. He spotted a tree he thought he could climb, he strained every muscle to pull himself up. Then got into a position where he'd be hidden.

Nick's ragged breathing sounded like a freight train in his ears, and his arms trembled as he waited. He tried to be calm. Silence could be the difference between life or death. He prayed for the strength to survive. He had to win this battle, himself. Before he could beat Mueller, he had to overcome his own fear. No one, not even Kane, could help him now. Beads of perspiration covered his body.

Nick remembered how he and Wylie and their friends had played cowboys and Indians in the woods back home. Nobody could find him, not even Wylie. This too was a game, with deadly stakes. He tensed and held his breath. Come on, Mueller. Where are you? Nick scanned the rugged beauty of the natural and peaceful forest. He'd never forget this quiet serene scene surrounding him while he waited for the SS Kraut that was out to kill him.

A moment later, the silence was shattered by the sound of Mueller's boots scuffling through the dead leaves and branches. Nick held his breath and waited. Mueller stopped under the tree. Nick shivered at the thought of being seen. He knew it was time. His only chance to catch the German off guard. Hanging onto the tree branch, he dropped down and swung into Mueller from behind. As the German fell forward, his gun slipped from his grip.

Nick clenched his teeth, grabbed Mueller's helmet and jerked it back. Mueller reached back, trying to pull the helmet forward to relieve the pressure of the neck strap on his windpipe.

As Mueller rolled over, Nick lost his grip. The German broke loose and stood up. He brought his leg back, and kicked Nick in the head. Nick rolled away. He grabbed Mueller's foot in midair, and lifted it high and jerked. Mueller flew backward and Nick seized the chance to leap on top and pummel him with both fists.

Mueller's hand slipped to his belt. As he raised his hand, Nick saw the flash of a knife blade. He leaped sideways. The knife flicked at him like a snake striking.

As Nick brought his good knee down on Mueller's forearm, the knife flew from his hand and out of reach. Desperate, Nick bounced on the big man's stomach.

Mueller bellowed and doubled over on his side. His face livid with anger, he raised up and threw Nick off like a feather.

"Dumkopf Schwein! Du bist alles kaput!" Mueller growled.

"Stupid pig," Nick understood. "It's all over for you." The German darted over and swept up the knife, and before Nick could duck, he felt the blade slash across his face.

As pain seared through his cheek, Nick's wild swing caught Mueller on the nose. His head snapped back and Nick heard a crunch of breaking bone. Blood streamed from the faces of both men.

Mueller seemed stunned by the blow, and raised both hands to his face. Nick, leaped at the German and threw him down. They struggled, Mueller reached for the gun, his bloody face contorted into a viscous grin. But the smirk changed to a grimace when the knife blade plunged into his chest. Nick shuddered simultaneous with Mueller when his hands grasped his chest. The gun dropped to the ground.

Mueller gasped for breath. He crawled to a nearby tree. Leaning against its trunk, Mueller grasped the knife and pulled it from his chest with a retching groan. His head lay back in an awkward position, one hand pressed to the ground. Nick stared at the pool of blood forming near Mueller's elbow.

Blood trickled from the corner of Mueller's mouth and a bubbling croak came from his chest. His blank eyes fixed on Nick. "Schwein," he whispered.

A deep howl seemed to rise from him, guttural and pain filled. There is no sound so terrible as a man's sorrow for his own death. His eyes opened wide and lost their focus. As Mueller's blood-covered hand fell limply to the ground, his head rolled to the side, and he was still.

Nick stumbled backward, staring at the German. He couldn't believe he'd killed a man. He was a medic, for God's sake! He was supposed to save lives, not take them. But to survive, he'd had no choice.

He slumped to the ground, exhausted. It was over--he'd won, but it didn't seem real. Hope flickered in his heart; he still had a chance to make it home alive.

Chapter 11

Overwhelmed with fatigue, Nick realized he had to regroup and move on. More Germans could come after him any minute. With Mueller dead, they'd shoot him on sight.

Nick grimaced as he dragged himself upright. First, he went through the Germans pack and discarded what he didn't want. He kept the food, blanket, ammunition and Mueller's coat. He snapped the canteen of water on his belt. There was no time to take a drink.

He used Mueller's shirt for a rag, and wiped off the bloody knife and slipped it into his belt. He picked up the gun, and checked the mechanics. It was similar in size and weight to U.S. guns, but stubbier. He hoped, if he had to, he'd be able to work it.

He cradled the gun in one arm, and limped toward the tree line. He was amazed no one had come to check on Mueller. He peered around a tree and spotted the short SS guard coming slowly up the hill about fifty yards away. He leveled Mueller's gun and pulled the trigger. The recoil spun him around. He regained his balance and moved behind a tree. Nick squinted and saw the Guard crouched low with his rifle pointed in his direction. Nick fired off another round. He heard a yelp and the German darted down the hill. Nick started to shoot again but instead turned and headed back to where Mueller's body lay. The pain was unbearable whenever he moved but he forced himself onward. His life depended on finding a place to hide, and the farther from here the better. He'd have to ignore the pain.

Nick glanced at Mueller's body as he went past, still unable to believe he'd killed the man. An image of the fight flashed before him; Mueller's grin changing into shocked surprise as Nick plunged the knife into him with all his strength. The memory made him sick. Yet, Nick knew if he hadn't done it, he'd be the dead one, and Mueller would have swaggered back to the road.

For an hour, he trudged around thick laurel shrubs and unfamiliar gnarled trees of different sizes. Some had leaves and some didn't. He headed south away from where the P.O.W.'s were going. Finally, he couldn't go another step. He collapsed on a fallen log for rest. The thought of Krauts hunting him with dogs sent a chill up his spine.

As the sun dipped low on the horizon, Nick moved deeper into the woods. Time to find a place for the night.

He pushed through the dense underbrush, and found a well concealed hollow between two fallen trees. Nick crawled into the spot. He took a deep breath of fresh air, and inhaled the pleasant odors of the forest, but was too tired to appreciate them. He checked his wound and didn't like the inflammation there. Unable to do anything about it, he tried to relax, but the cramped quarters made it difficult. The ache deep in his thigh kept him awake until fatigue swept him into sleep, and the nightmares took over.

Nick woke before dawn, shivered, and his leg throbbed with a peculiar numbness. He lay in the darkness and listened to the slight whisper of the pines. He wondered if the Germans were close.

He pulled himself to his feet and tried his weight on his sore leg. A jolt of pain exploded through his thigh. Nick gasped, unable to move. He wanted to lie down but knew he didn't dare.

He moved his leg, and the intial burst of pain began to subside. The memory of the instant when the bullet smashed into his leg was vivid in his mind. Nick limped out of the brush to the edge of the forest. As the sky paled with the approach of sunrise, the improved visibility gave him confidence that he'd get back to the American lines. He continued on in a slow limping gait.

He came upon a viewpoint which overlooked a narrow valley and was relieved to see the empty road about a hundred feet below. He skirted the edge of the woods, and followed the road. Perhaps there was a town ahead.

Nick struggled on for another hour until fatigue forced him to rest. He stopped for a few minutes, and held onto a tree branch for support. Then, he started again, dragging his wounded leg behind. Even though he was tired, cold, and hungry, he limped on.

A half hour later, he'd covered only a few hundred yards when the pain became unbearable. His knees gave out, and he collapsed. When he tried to get up, he felt dizzy. Nick didn't remember where he was or what he was doing. Then as the fog in his head cleared, he remembered -- and stumbled on.

He strained his eyes, as he searched the horizon. The town had to be close. Pain sent shock waves through his leg. The idea of spending another night alone in the cold terrified him.

Nick remembered how brave Branch had been in spite of his serious wounds, and how Kane had saved his life. He couldn't give up now. He had to get home again. Marilyn's pretty face gave him the strength to take one laborious step after another.

No longer able to judge how much time had passed or the distance he'd covered, Nick plowed on doggedly.

It was no use. Near collapse he crawled into deeper underbrush. He chose what he hoped was a good spot. Then, he collected fallen branches and leaves for a bed. After arranging his makeshift shelter, he settled in for another frigid night.

His leg throbbed, keeping him awake, until eventually he drifted off as the night wind stirred the leaves. At last, the interminable night ended. He raised his head and looked around. No sunrise this morning, just dirty grey clouds and a hint of snow in the sky. When he tried to sit up, his injured leg felt heavy and numb. The brutal pain hadn't dulled during the night. If anything, it was worse.

This must be how it feels to die. A wild wave of panic fell over him, and he dug his fingers into the foreign soil. He must live! He must! He could not, would not let himself die.

Chapter 12

Nick studied the slowly drifting, light and dark, grey clouds ringed in what appeared to be white fluffy cotton, and knew it was time to get up and move. He willed himself to sit up. He struggled to his knees. Nick stretched to reach the branch above, but his cold hands were too weak to grip. He thrust his arm over it for leverage, and pulled himself part way. With all the stength he could muster, he lunged to his full height and leaned on the branch. It bent under his weight but held.

He began to work his stiff fingers. His blood began to circulate, the last warmth in his body began to stir. His toes felt frozen, and when he touched his face it felt like a mask. He fought to think clearly, but everything was fuzzy. He needed warmth, and food. He must. What was it he needed to do? He shook his head to clear it, he didn't want to die here, alone, so far from home.

He forced himself to move each part of his body. His strength gradually returned. His throat felt dry. In front of him was a small patch of snow hiding under a forest bush, he scooped some up and slid it into his mouth. Even though he'd expected the cold, the icy granules were a shock. He waited while the snow crystals melted and trickled down his throat. No cup of coffee, no wine, had ever tasted so good.

He walked, one painful step at a time. The movement helped make him feel stronger. In a near trance, he skirted the edge of the trees.

It was slow going. He was about to give up in despair when, about midday, he spotted the town. He felt a surge of relief. This is what he'd prayed for. A town with food, drink, and warmth. His spirits lifted.

The afternoon had turned cloudy, and the diffused light flattened the shadows, blending everything into uniform drabness.

Nick worked his way up the hill and studied the houses. Smoke came from a few chimneys. Each house seemed to have been designed by a different architect, one small with a little yard another large with ornate facade across the front. In the center of town, a bell tower stood high above the other buildings. Most of the houses had two floors, but a few three and four stories.

He needed to be cautious. If he was captured again, they might execute him. His appearance clearly pinpointed him as an American, the enemy. He shrunk farther into the cover of the bushes.

Unsure of his next move, he watched children playing, people walking, bicycle riders on the streets. He saw few cars. Nick watched one going through town, and wondered who was inside. Not someone hunting him, he hoped. With a whole army pounding on their door, he wouldn't think they cared about him.

He noticed two women walking down the street. They turned toward a dark empty house near the end of a block. They climbed the steps to the front porch, and unlocked the door.

His heart pounded. The house was ideal for breaking into. Isolated at the end of the block, surrounded by trees and bushes, perfect, he thought. When the women left in the morning, he'd have the place to himself.

He was tired, and could hardly move. He'd have to rest until dark. He lay on the cold dirt trying to get comfortable, but his aching body made it impossible.

He felt confident, he could find a way to get inside and out of the cold. His mom always told him, "If you dream about something and want to do it bad enough. You can!" He remembered when she told him before the county track meet and he broke the record.

He started to touch his face, where there was a constant burning, but pulled his hand back. He didn't want to infect the wound. He and Marilyn would both have scars. They could be called, "The Scarface Twins"

Every time he looked at his scar in the mirror, it would be a reminder of the battle with Mueller to survive.

When darkness set in, he listened as the sounds of the town became quieter. Night seemed softer, like a liquid that surrounded everything. At night all the foliage was blended by shadow, fused and simplified, where daylight divided, setting objects in sharp contrast, at war with one another.

The calm that settled in told him the people retired early. With the war, a night life wasn't a consideration.

Nick, decided he couldn't wait 'til morning. Racked with pain, he limped toward the house. So cold! He had to get inside--but how? Food--he needed food. Something hot to drink. His leg throbbed, but he moved closer to the house taking care not to be seen.

Nick hobbled on, stumbled, and fell. He couldn't move another step. When he was able to get up, he dragged himself over the old wooden fence and into the yard.

On this side of the property, natural foliage grew wild, blended into the nearby woods. Creating a spacious and private area for the owners. On the opposite side of the house, a tall laurel hedge separated them from their neighbors and the street. He stepped inside a woodshed, and burrowed between piles of fresh cut kindling, dry and light enough to be easily moved. Protected from the cold wind, Nick felt warmer than he'd been in days. Tired, the bed of wood didn't bother him, and he soon fell asleep.

In the morning, Nick waited for the women to leave. Through a crack in the siding, he could see anyone leaving by the front door. As he waited, he checked his leg. The wound seemed worse. White pus oozed from the swollen red area, and a nauseating odor drifted in the air. He had to get into the house, to scrub his wound and put antiseptic on it.

He'd developed a fever that made him delirious and he fell in and out of sleep. He was jarred awake by the sound of a door closing. Through the crack, Nick saw the two women walk away from the house. The sight was like a shot of adrenalin.

Stiff and sore he could barely stand. He stumbled out of the woodshed toward the house. He headed for the backdoor. Had the women locked it? He pulled himself up the railing hand over hand, and worked his way up the steps to the porch, and tried the doorknob. It was locked. Nick peered through the kitchen window, longing to be inside. The food he needed was so close, but he didn't dare break a window. He wanted his presence to be a secret.

Somehow, he had to get in the house and take what he needed without anyone knowing. Then later, he'd return for more necessities, until he was strong enough to make his way out of Germany. Nick made his way back down the stairs and around the corner of the house looking for a way in. His patience was rewarded. A shrub partially blocked a basement window that had been left cracked open at the top. He found the answer to his problem -- he hoped!

He tried to pull open the window, but it was jammed. The struggle with the window sapped the last of his energy, and Nick sagged against the wall. There had to be a way. He limped back to the woodshed, picked up a piece of kindling, and pried open the window.

Cringing in agony his breath coming in ragged gasps, he dragged his leg over the sill, crawled through the window and into the basement. It was an unfinished storage room, piled with magazines and boxes.

When Nick reached the stairs his legs gave out. Everything went blurry, and he slid to the floor. When he came to, he checked his watch, and he'd only been out a couple of minutes.

He listened. There was only silence. His strength failing, he moved slow and quietly one step at a time. The thought of food and water drove him onward until at last he reached the main floor.

He stopped. Silence. He was alone. His stomach grumbled with hunger and he started for the kitchen, praying he wouldn't pass out before he got something to eat. In the kitchen, he made his way to the ice box. His prayers were being answered. He'd live and make it back home.

Nick could hardly pull the ice box door open. The smell of different foods drifted in the air. It took all his strength to lift the bottle of milk to his mouth. He couldn't stop drinking, and the milk dribbled down the sides of his face and onto the floor as he stood in front of the open ice box. He'd forgotten how good milk tasted!

Suddenly, a noise behind startled him, he twisted around just as a girl entered and shrieked.

Caught! Nick felt dizzy. Before he could reply, he slumped to the floor, and everything went dark.

Chapter 13

The Fraulein bolted, then stopped and glanced back. Nick lay motionless on the floor. She tiptoed toward him and looked down at his dirt smudged face. His uniform was torn and wrinkled like he'd slept in it for weeks. His pants leg was smeared with blood. Her foot poked his shoulder.

Nick, barely conscious, remained still as his slitted eyes watched her. She knelt above him, and touched the rainbow insignia on his jacket. He saw the concern on her face. He tried to rouse himself, to tell her she needn't be afraid. He felt her shiver, then check his chest for movement.

She stared at his face with an expression of approval. Then glanced at his leg and her look changed to a worried one. She moved toward the door and came back again. Her face displayed concern, but confusion on what to do next.

Suddenly, the girl hurried to the bathroom. A moment later returned with a wet cloth, and began to clean his face. Her eyes widened in surprise when she uncovered the slash wound.

She turned and inspected his leg and paled at the sight of the pus.

She went back to the bathroom, and grabbed the bottle of antiseptic and another cloth. She gently washed the wound, and dried it. Each time she dabbed the antiseptic on the raw wound, she'd flinch. She'd grit her teeth and put more on it.

Nick gasped! Someone was cutting his face again! His eyes flew open. He reached out to protect himself, and caught a wrist and held on.

The girl yelped and jerked away, breaking his grip. She jumped to her feet, and ran toward the door and turned, her eyes wide with fright.

Nick started to speak, but the words didn't come. All he did was release a pitiful moan.

He tried to find the right phrase in german. "I've been shot." He hoped she understood. He looked at her. Please, God, he wasn't going to faint again, was he?

"Aus! Aus! Schnell!" She pointed at the front door.

"Fraulein, bitte," he whispered. "I can't. Too sick. Help me."

"Nein! Aus! Schnell."

"Please!" Nick pleaded, to weak to convert to German, his lips dry and papery. He swallowed, racking his brain for words which would convince her to help him. He managed with broken German to say, "I can't hurt you. I must hide, or they'll kill me."

"Who are you?" she said in English. "You are doing here vat?"

"American," he said, relieved that she spoke some English. He wanted to make her understand, but he was so tired. "Shot. Hungry. Help me. Bitte," lapsing into simple German. "Please."

The girl stared at him. "I find doctor."

"No! No doctor. He'll turn me in." Nick stretched his had toward her. "Hide me, please. I'll swear you didn't know about me if I'm caught. Do you have someplace where I can hide? As soon as I get my strength, I'll go. I'll never bother you again. I promise."

She shook her head, her eyes filling with pity and regret. "Ist verboten. Die shoot people to death for helping da enemy."

"Please," he begged.

She shook her head. "Ist hopeless. My mutter und aunt vill turn you in ven die come home."

"I'll give you no trouble. Besides, the war will be over soon. Then no one will know or care about me. Think about it."

"It might be possible," she said. The indecision showed on her face and made his heart beat faster. What could he say to convince her?

"Vat if someone finds out?"

"No one will."

She bit her lip, obviously tempted. She shook her head. "But mutter vorks for da local SS Field Marshal. She vould never allow it."

"Don't tell her. We'll keep it a secret between us. No one will ever know you helped me."

She stared at his leg, then his slashed face. When he saw her eyes soften, Nick knew he'd won her over. "If you can spare a little food, I'll sleep in the hiding place, then leave in the morning."

She frowned and said, "You vill leave when my mutter und aunt leave in der morgan?'

"Yes, yes, I promise. Thank you. I'll never forget what you are doing for me."

"You can go up the stairs?"

"Yes. With your help, I can." Nick struggled to his feet, almost falling back down. Clutching her arm for support, he hobbled toward the stairway. The Fraulein placed her other arm around his waist. Together they moved up the stairs, finally reaching the second floor.

Nick glanced down at her, and for the first time, he looked directly into her eyes. She met his gaze and didn't look away. Her deep blue eyes reminded him of the ocean on a summer day, and her hair was silvery blonde. Her nearness gave him strength and hope for survival. With a start, he realized he didn't even know her name.

Nick and the nameless girl struggled up the narrow stairway to a small room with very little furniture. She led him across the hardwood floor to another doorway

"My room," she said.

He longed to crawl into the comfortable looking bed. Tucked under the eaves, her room had a peaked ceiling like a tent, the highest point in the center and the sides tapering down. A worn green rug with intermittent diamond shaped black designs clustered across it.

She gripped a knob on the wall, and pulled open a door, Nick hadn't noticed. She reached in and pulled on a light cord.

Nick peered in at the storage area. It was the same length as the girl's bedroom, but the ceiling slanted down until it touched the floor on one side. There were two large trunks, a stack of suitcases, some boxes, and a few framed pictures leaning against the wall. There were no windows, and the far corner was dark even with the light on.

"Perfect! A good hiding place." Nick said

"Wir hah' blankets in der basement."

"Good." He gave her a little smile. He needed a friend now.

The fear she'd shown on her face had faded. She hesitated, and then turned and left the room.

Nick sank into a wicker chair beside the bed. He leaned over and touched his leg and cringed. It was still sore. He looked around the cozy room, and a pleasant smell, that reminded him of his granmothers house drifted in the air. A dresser with a large mirror sat between the bed and the windows. The walls were paneled in natural pine, and a variety of colorful pictures hung on the walls, giving it a homey look.

Exhausted, he wanted to crawl into his hiding place and sleep. Nick took another glance at his leg, hoping it would be better. It wasn't. A chill went through him, but he felt hot. He had a fever, for sure. He remembered back when he treated a wounded man with gangrene in his leg. It was life threatening, and a possible amputation was necessary. He wondered how it came out.

Time dragged, but at last he heard footsteps. Was it her? He froze as the door swung open. What a beautiful sight as she entered with the blankets. He struggled to his feet.

She carried the blankets to the far side of the trunks and spread them on the floor.

"Thanks," Nick said weakly, and worked himself back to the nest of blankets and collapsed.

"Ich bring food later. Meine Tante and Mutter vill be home soon."

"I'll be quiet," Nick promised. "You won't tell anyone, will you?"

"Nein," she whispered.

"I'll leave your house as soon as I can." Exhausted, he leaned back.

The young girl gave him a slight smile and turned and left, closing the door softly.

Nick's body ached as he tried to make himself comfortable on the hard floor. In spite of the pain, he could still picture the blue-eyed, blonde Fraulein. His future was in her hands now. He hoped she wouldn't let him down.

Chapter 14

Sometime later, the Fraulein tapped on the door and opened it, "Food." Then switched on the light. Nick jumped. He blinked, momentarily blinded.

"It's me," she whispered.

As his eyes adjusted, he said, "Hi. I'm glad to see you."

"Ich bringe --" She broke off, embarrassed. "Sorry, I forget to speak English. I bring you food, milk, How are you doing?"

My leg is throbbing, and I feel weak and hot. The food will help." He took a deep breath taking in the pleasant aromas and slowly exhaled.

"Smells good." He forced himself upright as she placed a watery soup with bread chunks and a slice of some kind of sausage in front of him.

"Ist dere anything else du vant?"

"No, thanks. Did your mother and aunt come home?"

"Ja, they're in bed. Dey not suspect." As she sat on top of a large brass-cornered trunk, and watched him chew.

After each bite, he'd glance at her, enjoying her good looks as much as the food. She was young, yet seemed very grown up.

"How old arc you?" he asked.

"Funfzehn Jahre. Sorry, again I forget. Fifteen."

Nick nodded. "I'm glad you speak English. My German isn't good. Was ist deine name?"
"Mellita. Mellita Schwartz. Und your?"

"Nick Jordan. Thanks for your help Mellita."

"Vas nothing." She shrugged, looking at his leg with concern. "You need a doctor, I think."

"No!" he whispered, and smiled to reassure her. I just need food and rest." He hoped it was true. "But I appreciate your concern. Without you, I'd be in trouble."

"I hope soon dere are well. Then you can leave." She glanced down at her hands, her long lashes shadowing her cheek. Her skin looked velvety in the dim light, and Nick longed to touch it.

Instead he smiled. She was right, of course. He knew he had to leave soon, but it made him sad to think that he would never have a chance to repay her.

"I vill get the antiseptic and bandage," she slipped off the trunk and out of the room.

A few minutes later with her hands full, she tiptoed back into the room.

Neither spoke as she swabbed the wound with antiseptic.

She was gentle, but he still tensed at the cold sting of the liquid. He watched as she wrapped his leg neatly. He couldn't have done it better himself, and wondered if she'd studied first aid.

"Ve will treat it again in der Morgen."

"Thanks again."

"Gute Nacht." Mellita pulled the light cord and closed the door. Nick listened to her go down the stairs. Then later he heard her return to her bedroom. He tried to picture what she was doing from the noises in her room. He glanced toward the door. A bright beam of light came through the space between the top of the door and the door jam. Then he looked toward the front of the attic, where he saw pale stars shining through a screen to the outside.

As he stared out at the night sky, he felt encouraged. His thoughts drifted to his family, and he wondered if they'd heard he was missing-in-action. He worried about his brother, a fighter pilot in the pacific. Had Marilyn heard he was missing?

Would she wait for him? He longed to get home again. How great it would be.

When he woke in the morning, he was covered with sweat. He threw the blanket off, and then got a chill. So, he pulled it back over him. The leg still throbbed. He knew the infection was still acute, and was causing his fever.

There was a knock on the door. It swung open and Mellita came in. Her long blonde hair was tied back with a blue ribbon. She looked so lovely it was hard to believe she was only fifteen. He struggled to sit up.

"Guten Morgan. Breakfast." She smiled and handed him a plate with two eggs. "How are you?"

"I've felt better. Have your relatives left?"

"Ja, they left half- hour ago. They not suspect. One time I think Mutter coming up here, but she go back into sitting room."

"Good. Where did you get the eggs?"

"We have five chickens. I look at your leg now."

Together they unwrapped his thigh and inspected the wound. Mellita's eyes bulged. "It not look better."

"Let's put a hot pack on." Nick said.

"I get one." She scooted out the door.

His hand trembled as he spooned the egg into his mouth, he couldn't finish it and slumped against the pillow, nauseated.

Mellita returned and put the hot towel on his leg. "If your mother found out I was here, she'd turn me in, huh?"

Mellita hesitated, as if choosing her words carefully.

"Ja, I think so. She not understand ven so many Germans in United States, why Americans entered the var. But I would try to explain it to her."

"I'm in your debt, Mellita. Danke."

She nodded shyly, putting down the wash cloth. "Now, I must leave. I have vork to do. Later I return mit more hot water. You rest now."

He lay there, and felt the beginning of delirium, at times he thought he was still at home. Each time Mellita came to replace the hot pack, her image grew fuzzier, until he wasn't sure whether she came or just imagined it. One time she started to leave and Nick said, "Marilyn, Marilyn don't go."

That afternoon Mellita slipped into the attic to check Nick one more time before her mother and aunt came home. She touched his cheek. His face felt hot. She rushed for water and tried to get some down his throat. She got him to swallow half a glass before he choked. She put down the glass and wiped his lips.

She stared down at him, smoothing a lock of hair off his forehead. He looked so helpless. She kissed Nick's cheek and held him in her arms. She pulled back and admired his face. Now, she must go downstairs and start dinner, for if it wasn't ready when her mother arrived she might wonder why. Concerned she stared at Nick as she left closing the door softly behind her.

Downstairs, while working in the kitchen, Mellita wondered whether she should tell her mother about Nick. Then, call a doctor for him. She'd wait a little longer and see if he got better.

Later, as the three women sat in the dining room eating their meager meal of potatoes and cabbage, a loud moan came from above. Mellita froze, her hand suspended over the bowl of potatoes.

"Was ist das?" her mother asked, staring up at the ceiling. Mellita's aunt, preoccupied with her food, didn't respond to the noise.

"Oh, that's the neighbor children, Mellita said. "They've been yelling all day. They have been driving me crazy!' Holding her breath as she dished some more cabbage onto her plate, she glanced at her mother, willing her to believe her story.

Her mother pushed her chair back from the table, "Nonsense. It sounded as if it were right upstairs."

Mellita watched in shock as her mother walked to the foot of the stairs, and leaned forward, listening. There was only silence. Mellita stood and began to stack the dishes on a tray, creating as much noise as she could.

Mellita's aunt peered at her sister over the top of her glasses. "Ach, Ilse! It is nothing. Sit down and finish your supper."

Mellita's mother shrugged and closed the door to the stairs. "Ja, I suppose you're right." She went back to the table and sat down.

Mellita, relieved, picked up the tray and went into the kitchen. She turned on the water and began to bang pots and pans.

It was about seven, nearly dark, when she finished in the kitchen and joined her mother and aunt in the front sitting room. She tried to concentrate on her schoolwork, but the evening seemed endless. Would her mother never put aside her mending? Would her aunt never put her book down?

Finally, at around 8:30, they prepared for bed.

She waited until she was sure they were asleep before creeping into see Nick. Through the long night, she nursed him quietly, wiping his forehead with cool damp cloths and tried to get him to swallow a few sips of water. Most of the time, she sat watching him in the dim light. Finally, she realized she could do no more and went to bed.

It seemed as if she had just fallen asleep when she opened her eyes to find her mother standing over her.

"Sorry, I woke you. I was looking for the flashlight."

Mellita, wide awake, realized how close her mother was to the attic door. "It's down stairs in the front closet, I'm sure."

"I looked there but probably missed it. I'll see you later." She turned to go but put her hand on the attic door knob.

"It wouldn't be in there."

"It could use a good cleaning, but I don't have time." She walked out of the room. Mellita gave a sigh and leaned back on her pillow.

Chapter 15

Nick opened his eyes. Gradually his mind cleared. He found himself looking into Mellita's blue eyes, and saw her pretty face smiling down at him.

"Your fever breaks," she said. "You feel better soon."

"How long have I been here?"

"Two days. You vere out most of time. I keep trying to get you to drink water, but I can not. I almost choke you to death."

Only two days, but he felt as if he'd spent weeks in the Schwartz's attic. "Does anyone else know I'm here?"

She shook her head. "Nein, but you cried out und meine Mutter heard you. Do not worry, I tell her it was der neighbor children." She went on, "The other morning she came up to my bedroom while I still slept looking for the flashlight."

"That's scary. I'm glad I didn't make a noise then."

She looked at him, her eyes clear and bright. "I had doubts. About helping you, I mean. I vas sure it was wrong. But you vere so helpless, I was afraid you vere going to die! Thank Gott you did not." She scrambled to her feet. "I bring you some food." She smiled and left him.

While waiting he thought of her young smooth face with the vibrant big eyes that seemed to look at him with such compassion. Her mature figure left it hard to believe she was only fifteen. He'd never heard of the name, Mellita, before but he liked it. In fact, he liked more than the name. She impressed him so much that he couldn't get her out of his mind. He looked forward to her returning. His stomach rumbled. Finally, he heard her foot steps.

She came through the door holding a plate with an egg, some toast, and Milk. As she sat the plate in front of Nick, their eyes met for an instant. He gave her a slight grin and proceeded to devour the breakfast. She seemed pleased that he ate it all. "Gut!" Mellita picked up the dish and left. Shortly she returned with a large pan of hot water, a washrag, and a towel. "You can wash yourself and when I comeback I'll take your clothes to wash. You can stay under the blanket."

"OK! Thanks. My clothes are filthy. I haven't been able to clean up."

After she left, Nick washed his face and proceeded to peel his dirt encrusted clothes off. He scrubbed to get to the white skin. It felt good to be clean again. He threw the clothes toward the door and dried off with the towel. He crawled under the blanket.

It wasn't long until Mellita returned. She gathered up the laundry and said, "Ja, you are right. They are filthy." She held the clothes with the end of her fingers while wrinkling her nose. She ducked out the doorway, and clattered down the stairs.

In spite of being naked beneath the blanket, Nick still felt hot, but he began to improve as the day went on. His fever was down and he felt stronger. He stretched and moved about to get his muscles loosened, but every effort exhausted him. As he began to doze off, Mellitta knocked. He checked the blanket and said, "Come in."

She'd brought him a sandwich and more milk. "How you are feeling?"

Nick shrugged. "Not so bad."

"I'm glad. Your clothes are not dry yet, but it vill not be long. They're in front of the stove and should be dry before Mutter gets home."

"I appreciate it." He took a bite of the sandwich. "The food here is better than what I got in the Army."

"Gut. I am glad you like it."

"I'm going to be spoiled. Especially having a pretty girl to wait on me."

Mellita blushed and glanced away but a smile played at the corners of her mouth.

"You look better," she said. "I vill get my chores done, und bring you clothes." She slipped away.

By the time Mellita came back, he felt even better. A surge of delight went through him when he saw her.

"Your clothes are ready," she placed his things on the trunk, and went back to her room.

His clothes were stiff and a little scratchy, but he welcomed them. At home, fresh laundry had appeared in his closet as if by magic, and he'd never given it much thought. Now, though, he knew he'd never again take clean, warm clothes for granted. They were a luxury he'd never appreciated.

Soon Mellita tapped on the door, and Nick said, "Come in."

She stood shyly in front of him. "My mother and aunt will arrive soon, so I go."

He felt disappointed at the thought of hours of enforced silence ahead when he'd be unable to see her.

"I will bring food tonight. If you are sleeping, I leave food on trunk." She gave him a little wave and smile and disappeared out the door.

Later, he felt nervous when he heard German conversation downstairs. He hoped Mellita's relatives wouldn't need anything from the storage area. What would he do if he was discovered by one of them? He wasn't sure. He prayed it wouldn't happen.

After listening for several minutes, everything remained quiet and he dozed off.

He didn't wake until he heard the squeak of the door. Was it Mellita? He opened his eyes and strained to see a face in the darkness, but he dared not move or make a sound. He waited, fearful he may have been discovered.

"It is I," Mellita whispered.

"I'm awake." The light flashed on. It took and instant for their eyes to adjust.

"Here is a little dinner for you, leavings from ours."

"Leavings? ... Oh, you mean left overs. Thank you Mellita."

"Ja, left-overs. I get dishes in der Morgen. Gute Nacht," She smiled and closed the door with a soft click, at the same time she'd turned the light off.

Nick felt disappointed again that she had to leave so soon. He waited for his eyes to re-adjust to the gloom, then ate the dinner and placed the dishes on top of the trunk. For the first time after eating, he was still hungry. A good sign, he thought.

Weary and ready for sleep, he lay down again on his makeshift bed. He glanced toward the door where a beam of light shone through at the top. He heard Mellita moving about and imagined her getting ready for bed. Nick raised up and stared at the door. He had a strong urge to go over and peak, but he pushed the thought out of his mind. His conscience would haunt him, because Mellita had been so loyal, besides saving his life. Each time he saw her, Nick found himself thinking of her more. He dreaded the day when he'd have to leave, but he knew it would have to be soon. He couldn't place her in this danger much longer. He would be stronger in another day or two, and he'd go.

The next morning, he stretched his stiff body and moved his arms and legs to get the

57

circulation going again, he listened. It was quiet. His leg still ached but it was better. He got to his knees, and without making any noise, inched toward the window. He moved an old wooden box into position, and sat on it. He could peer out the small screened window. He looked at the walk leading from the house, and a block down the street toward town. He felt a certain security in being able to watch without being seen. After looking out awhile, he heard a door below bang shut and he watched as Mellita's mother and aunt walked from the house. When they disappeared, he moved back to his bed. He waited knowing Mellita would soon be there. He looked forward to seeing her.

When she came, she brought a big bowl of mush and hot steaming coffee. He was amazed that she could get him this food without being detected and during wartime.

Mellita set the tray down, using the trunk for a table, for Nick. He glanced at her with a smile. His expression gave away, the admiration he had for her. She turned away, flushing, but looked back showing a pleasure from his glance.

"I'm feeling better and will soon be able to move on. I don't want to get you into trouble."

"But vere you rill go?"

"I'll have to get back to the American lines someway." He hoped he sounded more confident than he felt.

"Vould be too dangerous. Maybe you wait here longer."

"I thought it would be better for you if I left."

"Not now. I worry if you go." She blushed, changing the subject. "Now, I go do list of chores my Mutter leaves me. Later I come back." She left and went downstairs.

Nick finished his breakfast, and moved around the attic.

He even went to the door and looked through the crack. He was surprised at how much of Mellita's room he could see.

After a little while, he felt tired, and his leg ached, so he went back to his bed. His thoughts drifted toward his family and Marilyn and he wondered if he would ever see them again. They surely had received the missing-in-action telegram by now. Were they in shock, or had they grimly accepted the news, fearing the worst? Nick saw an image of Marilyn and his family, mourning for him. If only there were some way to get word to them to relieve their minds.

Chapter 16

Blanche Jordan returned home from the post office where she'd picked up a letter from her eldest son, Wylie. This was the third letter from him since the last time they'd heard from their youngest son, Nick. This was a strong concern of hers. She felt sick. Why hadn't they heard from Nick?

She opened the letter and read:

Feb 15, '45

Dear Ma & Pa,

We found out today that we're being shipped to the Pacific in a couple of weeks. They don't give us details, except to start packing.

My room-mate, Jim Mc Kay will be leaving with me. He and I are getting along better now. After our first confrontation in ping pong, I didn't think we could ever be friends. He couldn't believe I could beat him, With people waiting to play the winner, he kept wanting to play me again after I had won. We played several games and I kept beating him. This guy was rude and arrogant. I had no desire to have him for a friend.

Jim weighs thirty pounds more than I do, and he's three inches taller. He has a round, bullet head set on a powerful neck and mighty shoulders. He lifts weights and thinks he's superman. One day he was acting cocky. It made me mad; you know my temper. I grabbed him, threw him down, got an arm hold and made him say, "Uncle!" Ever since he's been nice as pie. He thought he could lick me easily, but found out otherwise. Nick and I were always stronger than we looked.

Hope you're doing fine and Nick too.

Love

Wylie

Ps ---I got a letter from a friend of Jim's
girlfriend. I'm going to write her today.
Her name is Sally.

Blanche chuckled, typical of Wylie not to put up with much. But a surprise that he would write to a girl. He never seemed interested. She felt nervous about Wylie going overseas. it would be a big worry for her and Paul.

Blanche decided to keep from worrying, she'd stay busy. She went upstairs to clean her bedroom. She was just getting started when she heard the doorbell, she put down her duster and hurried to the front door. She expected to see her neighbor, Cora, but was surprised to see a young man on the steps.

"Telegram for Mr. and Mrs. Paul Jordan," he said, handing her a thin yellow envelope.

Blanche paled. "Oh God! No!" she whispered. Her hand shook as she scrabbled around in her purse to find a quarter for him. Taking the coin, the tall, gangly boy touched the brim of his cap and loped away down the sidewalk to the curb and his bicycle.

She closed the door and stared at the telegram, tears already streaming down her cheeks. Something had happened to one of her sons. But which one? Unfair, unfair! Just because she had two sons didn't mean she could spare one! How could fate be so cruel?

She was afraid to open it, yet she had to know. She took a deep breath, and sank onto the chair in the hallway and tore open the envelope. She brushed away her tears, and raced through the words. She picked out "missing-in-action" and then found the name "Nicholas P. Jordan." Nick.. her baby.

A sudden image of his face -- thoughtful, intelligent, young, so terribly young -- flashed before her. She moaned and her shoulders shook as the tears flooded down her face. She couldn't stop sobbing as she looked at the dreadful yellow message.

Then she felt a flicker of hope. Maybe Nick was hiding from the Germans somewhere? She prayed he was a prisoner of war and would come back after the war ends. But what if he wasn't? Frightening scenarios swirled through her mind.

Her hand clenched, crumpling the envelope. Nick had to be all right; he just had to be. She Couldn't imagine him any other way but alive and safe. She tried to stand, but her knees felt weak, and she sank back down on the chair.

She reread the telegram carefully, but it didn't tell her anything more. It offered no new hope. More tears came; the heavy weight of emotion lay on her chest, and she strained to catch her breath. Paul. I should phone him and tell him what's happened. But she was unable to move.

Perhaps it would be better not to call Paul. Yes, she would wait until he came home from work. No sense upsetting him now so that he couldn't finish out the day.

She wished he were here now, though; she didn't want to be alone. Cora, across the street, was her good friend. Going to the phone, she gave the operator the number. She held her breath, praying she was home. The phone only rang twice, but to Blanche it seemed like an eternity.

"Cora! Please come over!" she sobbed into the receiver.

"Blanche? Is that you? What on earth is the matter?" Without waiting for a reply, she said, "Never mind, I'll be right there," and slammed down the phone.

Blanche held the door open as Cora came rushing across the street. She was still arranging her green blouse as she hurried inside.

"What's wrong?" Cora panted, her face contorted in fear.

Blanche threw her arms around her and sobbed. "A telegram. Nick is missing-in-action."

"Oh, you poor thing!" Cora's arms cinched tighter around her.

"I haven't called Paul yet." Blanche said. "There's the telegram." She pointed at it as if it were a rattlesnake.

Cora picked it up, "Well, they don't say he's been killed. He could be a prisoner. Let's not give up."

Blanche nodded, gravely, "I can't help thinking about the West family. They got a missing-in-action telegram, then a month later the killed-in-action one."

Cora looked her friend in the eye and gently shook her by the shoulders. "That has nothing to do with Nick. It's hard, Blanche, but you know Nick better than anyone. He's a survivor. He'll make it. You know he will!"

Blanche's eyes twinkled, desperate to believe her. "Can't help thinking of all the boys from our small town who have already been killed."

"Now, Blanche, you can't think that way. It won't do any good. You have to believe he's coming back."

"Yes... Yes, you're right." Blanche sighed and wiped her eyes. She straightened and squared her shoulders.

"There, that's better. Do you want me to call anyone?"

Blanche shook her head. "No, I'll wait until Paul comes home. He'll be destroyed when he hears. I'll call Marilyn later. I hate having to do it."

"I'll stay with you until Paul gets home. No arguments, I'll make us some tea."

Blanche sat back down. She could hear Cora in the kitchen, running water, getting out the china. Soon Cora brought the tray with the tea, and they went into the living room. Neither of them seemed to be able to think of anything to say, so they sat silently, sipping tea.

When Paul's car turned into the drive, Cora left by the front door, closing it quietly behind her. Blanche heard the car door slam in the garage, then the creak of the back door as Paul entered the house. She listened as his footsteps echoed down the hallway. How could she ease the pain for him? She couldn't think of a way, and the flood of tears began again. She looked up as he entered the room.

"Christ, you gave me a start," he said. "I didn't think you were home. What's the matter? Then he saw the telegram lying on the table. Without picking it up, he turned to her, "Which one?"

Blanche leaned back, took a deep breath, "Nick. Missing." She began to cry as children cry, deep, shuddering sobs.

He put his arms around her, resting his head against her shoulder, stroking her hair. "Thank God for that, at least," he whispered. "I thought for sure one had been killed." He turned toward the table and picked up the telegram.

As he read, his face reddened. He wadded up the telegram and threw it across the room. "Those bastards, those God damned bastards!" he shouted. His eyes reflected the helplessness he must have felt as they began to fill with tears of frustration and bitterness. He started to take a deep breath but the thought of his sons risking their lives strangled him. He felt it should have been him, not his children, fighting for his country. Paul stood as though in a trance. He looked at Blanche and knelt by her chair. He took her hand, small and cold, and pressed it against his cheek. "Oh, Blanche, I'm sorry. I'm sorry," he said.

Paul picked up the telegram, smoothed it out, and reread it. When he spoke again after a long while, it was in a calm voice, and Blanche marveled at his self-control and the conviction in his voice. "Nick's in good shape. He'll make it all right. It was as if he believed that if he said it firmly enough, it would simply be true. With her mother's heart, Blanche wanted to believe him.

Usually Blanche enjoyed cooking but that evening, supper was uninspired. Neither of them was hungry and the left-overs ended up in the trash.

Blanche prodded herself to call Marilyn. The reaction was even worse than Blanche had imagined it would be. She completely lost control, crying into the phone with long, loud sobs that Blanche thought would never end. When the tears finally subsided, Marilyn could hardly speak. She let out little sobs and gasps for air.

Blanche tried to remain strong; so, she fought off the urge to join Marilyn in a duet of tears.

"Just because we got a telegram saying Nick is missing, doesn't mean he's dead. Paul and I think he's all right. We're not giving up."

"Yes, you're right. I think he'll be Ok!" Marilyn replied with a sniffle. "He's in good shape and can out run anyone."

"I'm going to be praying for him every day, and anxiously waiting to hear something more," Marilyn's voice cracked. "I'll come over this weekend and we can talk."

"That would be nice, I'll look forward to seeing you."

"It was good of you to call, Mrs Jordan. Let's hope to hear good news soon." There was a click as Marilyn hung up.

That night, Blanche was unable to fall asleep. Paul, to, tossed and turned. After a while, they gave up trying and lay side by side in the dark, staring up at the ceiling.

"Do you remember the wagon?" Blanche asked.

"Wagon?"

"You know, when Nick first started really talking, and how he told us about the, wed wagon Wylie buwied in the back yawd. How Nick took us out and pointed, and when you dug, there was the wagon."

"That's right. I remember thinking someone in the neighborhood had stolen the thing." Paul chuckled. It was a reassuring sound in the darkness. "I never could figure out why Wylie buried it. Nick must have known all along. I wonder why he decided to tell us that day."

"Also, I'll never forget the time when Wylie came running into Cora's house, while we were having tea, screaming that Nick was dead. Cora and I ran a half mile down the street and found Nick laying under the ice delivery truck. I was scared to death, especially with Wylie continuing to scream that Nick was dead. Turned out he was fine, not even a scratch. I nearly had a stroke though." Blanche laughed, "There was always something happening with those two kids."

Blanche smiled and squeezed Paul's hand. She listened as his breathing deepened, but it was a long time before she went to sleep.

The next morning, Blanche was in the kitchen having coffee when Paul came downstairs. The lack of sleep showed on his face, and he looked tired and old. "Somehow, I thought things like this only happen to other people." He said.

"Yes, I did too, but not true, I guess." Blanche replied. "Marilyn is coming over this morning, Paul."

"OK!"

When Marilyn arrived, the hysterical outburst with which she had greeted the news about Nick seemed to have passed, and she appeared pale but composed. Marilyn spent the day helping in the kitchen, reassuring them that Nick would come home safely after the war. They talked of memories of Nick. When it was time to leave, she gave them both a hug and kiss.

Through the glass in the front door, Blanche watched her walk away. She was sorry to see her go.

After she left the Jordans' house, Marilyn walked slowly down the street. The sky was clear and the stars were beginning to come out. The crisp beauty of the night made her realize that it must have been a beautiful day. She hadn't noticed before.

Staying calm and cheerful while she spent the day with Nick's family was the hardest thing she had ever done in all of her seventeen years. She shook her head, amazed that she'd managed to do it. When she'd first heard the news about Nick, she had felt as if the floor had fallen away beneath her feet. She bit her lip; the feelings were still close to the surface. She had felt ashamed, sobbing to Nick's mother on the phone, but she hadn't been able to stop herself.

As she reached her house, she crossed her fingers for luck. She tried to make herself believe that Nick would come back to her.

But as she walked up the first stairs her courage dwindled. Bursting into tears, she sprinted up the rest of the steps. She ran to her room and flung herself on the bed, glad her parents were out.

She lay on her bed until she heard her parents' car in the driveway. She looked over at the desk in front of her window. Of all the places in the house, the desk was where she felt closest to Nick. She had spent countless hours there writing to him.

It was where she sat to read his letters, too, rereading them over and over. Closing her eyes, she imagined the slope of his handwriting, as if he was always in a hurry when he wrote. Slowly she got up and walked to the desk. Sliding open the drawer, she stared down at the stack of letters inside. She was going to write to him, as she had every day since he'd left. It would be a way for her to show fate that she wasn't afraid, that she was keeping faith, that she knew Nick would be all right.

She pulled out her chair and sat down. Picking up her pen and a pad of paper, she began to write.

February 20th, 1945

Dear Nick,

Yesterday, your folks received a telegram from the government saying you were missing-in-action. We're all worried for you. But I know in my heart that you're all right, and that we'll be together again. Nothing can keep us apart -- not even the German Army.

Honey, hurry and get home. I love you so much! You're never out of my thoughts.

I went over to Emerson track the other night and walked around it like we used to. I pretended we were together looking up at the stars. I could feel your arms around me just like you were there with me.

Come back to me soon so we can be together for the rest of our lives.

I'm going to pray for you every day until you get back home. So hurry, hurry!

I have to go now. Mother is calling me for dinner. 'Bye for today. Remember, I love you.

Always,
Marilyn

The next morning, Marilyn dropped the letter in the mail. As she stared at the box, she pictured Nick getting the letter and smiling as he read it. Her shoulders sagged, and an ice cold shiver of fear spread through her. Was she fooling herself? Would he ever read another one of her letters?

In spite of her determination to be brave and hopeful, her eyes filled with tears again. Slowly, she turned and walked on to school.

Chapter 17

Nick saw her standing close, with her back to him. Her dark hair cascading in waves down her back. He stepped toward her. He couldn't stop his urge to kiss her.

"Marilyn it's you. Thank God!" Nick grabbed her and spun her around. His mouth dropped, when he saw the blue eyes and blonde hair of Mellita.

Nick woke from his dream, and there he was alone in his attic hideaway. For a moment he thought he was back home. It was a disappointment, when he discovered he was still living out the nightmare in Germany.

He reached for his thigh, and pulled back. It still hurt and the throb persisted. He brushed the back of his hand across his face, and cringed from the raw tenderness.

Nick heard the front door close, and figured Mellita's mother and aunt had gone out.

He rubbed the sleep from his eyes, and hobbled to the vent. He watched the women walk down the street. When they were out of sight, he moved about to loosen his muscles. But all he could think about was that Mellita would soon be there. He sat on the trunk and waited.

At last, he heard her footsteps. She pushed open the door. "Guten Morgen! I have breakfast. How are you today?"

"Better." Nick replied. She wore a pastel flowered dress, and her hair was tied back with a light blue silk ribbon. She set the food on the trunk, and said, "While you're eating, I'll do my chores. Later, I will bring our map so you can show me where you live." She smoothed the skirt of her dress, then turned and hurried from the room.

"Thanks!" Nick called. "See you soon." He finished his breakfast and stacked the dishes on the trunk.

An hour later, Mellita returned with a map of the United States. Nick, sitting next to her on the trunk, pointed out his home town in Washington State on the West Coast.

Mellita frowned. "But I thought only Indians lived out West. Are you a cowboy?"

He laughed. "Not at all. In fact, I've never been on a horse in my life. There are no cowboys and Indians fighting out West any more. That was a long time ago, back in the old days."

She looked puzzled. "It is strange. Not at all like the movies."

"That's for sure. It's modern now, like back East."

They stared at the map and Nick said, "Where do your relatives live?"

She leaned close to Nick and pointed to the State of Florida. "They love the weather and the beaches. They encouraged us to follow them over there, but the war started until it was too late."

Nick noticed the sadness in her eyes and said, "After the war you can do it. Maybe I can help you. Turnabout is fair play, you know." He stared at her marveling at her beauty. Her closeness made him feel warm. She glanced up from the map, meeting his gaze.

"Right now it's hard to believe that could happen, but I hope so." Mellita replied.

Soon, She had to leave to finish her jobs. The moment she'd gone, Nick missed her. He enjoyed her company more all the time. He thought about how if she hadn't helped him, he would have been taken prisoner or executed. It was more her youthful beauty that he thought about though.

Nick limped to the door and looked through the space above it. He was amazed at how much of Mellita's room he could see. Her table and mirror and half of her bed were in clear view. He hobbled over to the vent. As he peered out to the front of the house, he studied the area. Below Mellita's window was the roof of a first floor room. On the side of the porch nearest him, a trellis extended to the ground. When he left the house, all he had to do was go out the window onto the roof and down the trellis.

He saw the two women come down the street, and tried to guess which one was Mellita's mother. Since neither looked like her, he wasn,t sure. Nick slid over to his bed and crawled in. He felt tired and soon dosed off.

When he awoke, it was night. He looked toward the screen. No stars or moon were visible, and Mellita's room was dark. He made out the faint murmur of conversation downstairs, but couldn't hear what was being said.

He thanked God for Mellita, she had a way of keeping his spirits up. He looked forward to her return. As though she knew his thoughts, she appeared. She moved to the trunk and handed him a dish of stew and a glass of milk. The light from the room behind her had turned her blonde hair into a golden halo.

"Sorry, I'm so late," she whispered. "I thought I vould never get up here. Mutter brought a war bulletin home. I've got it for you to read. It's in simple German."

"Good." Nick set his plate on the floor, and took the bulletin, and squinted in the dim light. His high school German served him in good stead, and he began to read:

> Soldiers of the Western Front!
> Your hour has come!
>
> Large Third Reich Armies will strike the
> enemy. We gamble everything, and you
> carry with you a holy obligation to give
> all to achieve our objectives for the
> Fatherland.
>
> -- Field Marshall von Rundstedt

"Wow! This is something. If I knew where the spearhead of the attack was going to be, I could try to warn my unit, and the attack could be stopped and thousands of lives saved." Nick smiled at Mellita. He appreciated what she'd done and realized the danger she'd put herself in by handing the message to an enemy. "Thanks for trusting me with this. Do you know if there's a radio transmitter in town?"

"No, I do not think so. Oh, wait. Yes, there is.

Every month Mutter goes to a friends house to listen to 'The Voice of America'. She hears more of the true picture of what's going on."

Nick, chewing on his dinner, said, "Maybe you can find out about it for me?"

Mellita nodded. "I vill try. If you are better tomorrow, perhaps you can move about the house."

"Sounds good."

She closed the door and soon the light in her room went out. As he lay there, Nick thought about the possibility of getting a message out telling Hitler's plans. There had to be a way.

Chapter 18

Nick woke early, cold and stiff, but eager to get out of his hiding place. Because of the low ceiling, he stood hunched over to keep from bumping his head. he stretched and then settled onto the trunk to wait for Mellita's mother and aunt to leave. When they did, it wasn't long before Mellita arrived.

"You can come out." She smiled when he appeared at the doorway.

Nick stepped into the bright cheerful room. He smelled the cooked eggs before he spotted the steaming omelet on the dressing table. "It's nice getting out of that hole-in-the wall." He rotated his hips to the right and left.

"I found out about the radio, but I'm not sure if it's still there." Mellita said.

"Great! Let's hope it is." He smiled as he sat eager to start on the breakfast.

Mellita's face turned serious as she spoke. "I asked Mutter und she rambled on about it for a half hour. Herr Schneider lives down the street and every month he'd invite some of his trusted friends to his house. They listened to the news from, The Voice of America. It was not censored and truthful, better than what we heard otherwise."

"I'll bet that was against the law." Nick said as he savored another bite of omelet.

"Ja! They could have been executed. Mutter told me long ago not to tell anyone."

"Do you know where this house is?"

"Ja!" She nodded, moving toward the window. "I'll show you." He followed her, enjoying the closeness. She pointed, "See the highest roof, down a block."

"The brown peaked one?"

"Ja, that's it." "No problem."

"What are you talking about? You can't leave yet."

"I'm fine. Do you know where the radio is in the house?" "Ja, it is hidden in a secret room on the top floor. It may not even be there now though. Mutter said the man left town a month ago. She thinks the house is vacant now."

"I'll check and see what I can find."

It was nearly a week before Nick felt well enough to take his first venture out of the house. Mellita knew his plan, but when he went through her room and out the window, she slept through it.

He eased himself onto the roof and climbed down the rose trellis to the porch. It was a dark, moonless night. The chill night wind was a gritty slap in the face. Nick's eyes adjusted as he crept slowly to the sidewalk, and toward Herr Schneider's house. It was quiet except for a distant dog barking at some unknown disturbance in the night.

He circled the tall house looking for a way to enter. Mellita had given him a flashlight, a screwdriver, and a wrench.

Unable to find a point of entry, Nick climbed a woodpile and onto the garage. From there, he pulled himself to the roof of the house. He moved carefully to the edge where he could reach a second story window. He lay flat, placed the screwdriver against the lower edge of the window sill and struck it with his wrench. The screwdriver slid under the sill and he pried. The window moved. Nick got both hands under the frame and pulled, it slid open. He hung onto the edge of the roof, and swung his feet to the window ledge and climbed in. When his foot hit the floor, it jarred his wounded leg, and he almost cried out from the jab of pain that radiated through it. He crouched in the dark room, sweat beaded his brow and a tightness clutched his throat. He pulled the flashlight and wrench from his pockets. The musty odor of stale dust touched his nostrils. The old house even smelled empty.

He moved to the door, and turned the knob and eased it open. The squeak of the hinges echoed through the still house. He froze, but there was only silence.

Nick crept along the hallway until he found the stairway, and went up to the third floor. He tip-toe to the first door and gently opened it. He switched on the flashlight, hoping not to find anyone in bed. He sighed in relief when he saw an empty room. This one didn't fit the description he was looking for. He switched the light off and moved out and towards the next room. It, also, was empty. The third one fit Mellita's description. This was it. The radio was hidden here. Now, if only he could find it.

He explored the place for the mechanism that would spring the door open. Herr Schneider fearing detection by the Nazi's, had been extremely careful, yet courageous enough to disobey their laws. Nick admired the man without knowing him.

Mellita had said there would be a button or switch near the mirror. He scanned the wall with the flashlight. There was no sign of a door or switch. He felt along the surface of the wall. On the lower right corner, flush with the wall, he found a protrusion. He pressed inward, no results. He tried again. Nothing. He found another button on the opposite side and pushed it. No luck. He pushed them both together. He jumped as it slid open. He peered in, and a grin spread over his face.

Nick entered the small space and flipped his light around. Where was the damned radio? He remembered Mellita saying it was on the left wall as he entered. A bookcase covered the wall, he pulled on the outside edges. It didn't budge. He raised on his tiptoes to feel the upper shelve. There's got to be a way to get behind it. Like a cop frisking a criminal, he felt around the bookcase. He bent low to check the bottom, and then raised up and caught his head on the corner of the lower shelve. His hand shot to the pain. He held back a scream. "Christ O'Mighty, what next?" Nick felt like heading back to Mellita's, but instead pulled a few books off a shelf. His head stung, but he ignored it and kept looking.

He took out another book and behind it was a good sized hook. He played around with it a second and then found the secret. He pulled it out and down. He let go and the whole bookcase shifted to the floor. There in front of him was the radio. Herr Schneider had done a great job of hiding it.

Encouraged, Nick studied the workings of the radio, and tried to identify the functions of its switches and dials. He strained to remember what he'd learned from Company G's radio man, he finally figured it out.

"Attention! Emergency call to Allied Forces from behind German lines. Emergency call to Allied Forces. I'm an American. Nick Jordan, Medic, Company G, Rainbow Division. I have important information for you. Can you hear me? Can you hear me? Come in! Come in!"

He repeated the message, then switched from transmit to receive, and slowly moved the frequency band. No reply. Nick wondered if he was working the equipment right. He glanced at his watch, it was still dark but wouldn't be for long. He tried the call again. Still no reply. Time was running out. It was the hour when people would soon be getting up to go to work. This was it for now, he decided. He turned everything off and left it as he found it.

Nick went out the front door and glancing in all directions, hurried back. Next time he had to get to the radio earlier and maybe that would work better. He wasn't about to give up. He would try to make contact tomorrow night.

Nick discovered it was tougher climbing up the flimsy trellis than climbing down. After a struggle, he made it up, sliding through the window into Mellita's room. Every movement sounded like a drum roll as he crossed her room.

Out of the darkness came Mellita's whisper. "How did it go?"

Startled, Nick said, "You scared me! I thought you were asleep. Everything went good, except I didn't contact anyone." His eyes began to adjust to the dark.

"You found the radio und tried it? Mein Gott, I can't believe it!" Mellita said as she sat up, revealing her faded blue nightshirt.

"It wasn't easy. Quite frustrating, in fact." Nick sighed.

"Tell me about it,"

Nick sat on the edge of the bed. She was so close, he wanted to reach out and touch her, but he didn't.

"Fortunately, I didn't run into anyone. I had to climb onto the roof to get in a window. It took me awhile to find the radio and figure out how to work it. So, by the time I sent a message it was late. Next time I'll get over there earlier and have a better chance of getting someone."

"Ja, you must keep trying." Mellita whispered.

"Can you find out more information from your mother? The date and place of the attack would be a help."

"I'm not sure she knows, but I vill try,"

Nick raised his hand gently touching her shoulder. "That would be great. Thanks." With a sudden impulse, he raised his other hand to her left shoulder and leaned forward and gave her a kiss on the cheek. He was relieved when her face broke out in a smile.

"Danka." Mellita responded, forgetting to whisper.

Nick surprised at that reply was speechless. He put his hands down and smiled back. Nick a little embarrassed but pleased with her reaction, stood up and headed back to his room. As he went through the doorway, he gave her a wave and a happy grin.

The next morning while eating breakfast in her room, he asked Mellita, "Any chance I could get a bath? I feel crummy."

"Ja, I vill run the water and set out a towel for you."

Nick hurried through his meal, then went to the window. Everything looked all right outside, so he picked up his dishes and headed downstairs.

Mellita was still running the water when he got there. She handed him a towel and stepped out.

He felt so relaxed in the warm water, Nick was close to falling asleep when he heard loud footsteps. The door cracked open.

"Get upstairs! Soldiers are coming."

He detected the thin edge of fear in her voice.

Chapter 19

Nick struggled out of the tub, yanked the plug and hit the floor. He grabbed his towel and shoes, and headed toward the attic. He saw Mellita, down the hall, wide eyed. He took the stairs two at a time. Loud knocks on the front door roared in his ears.

Nick ducked into the attic and scrambled to the vent. He peered down at the front yard. Two SS Officers stood below him at the door. If they entered the house, he'd try to get out the window. He wouldn't get far wearing only a towel. He crept back and ducked behind the trunk. He dried off and wrapped up in a blanket.

He listened to voices below, then heard boots on the stairs. Sweat washed down his face. The steps came closer. Now, they were in Mellita's room.

The door creaked open and a flashlight beamed over his head. Nick froze as it swept above him. Were they going to shoot?

His face buried against the floor, he waited. Time stopped. The SS men entered the attic. With his boots making a loud echoing explosion on the bare floor, he moved toward the vent. Nick peeked over the trunk and saw him look out at the front yard.

Nick fought to hold down his breathing and remain still. As the SS trooper stood a few feet away, his time could be running out. He heard the boots move on and then stop. There was a dreadful moment of silence. The light went past him again. Nick's fear was similar to the time he wanted to crawl into his helmet at Drusenheim when the 88 mortars exploded around him. God, please save me again, he prayed.

Then, the boots moved out and the door closed. How lucky could he get. Maybe, it was the power of prayer! Nick was thankful for which ever the reason. At one moment when the German had stood still, Nick was sure if he stood up he could have shook hands with him. However, the inclination wasn't there. Nick's body relaxed. His breathing dropped back to normal. He rose and listened. The front door opened and closed. He moved to the vent and saw the two Germans walk away.

He was so glad the soldier hadn't searched very well. It was a close call.

The house seemed too quiet, where was Mellita? He tightened the towel around his waist and went to the stairs and listened for sound below. He heard nothing until he reached the main floor. He went toward the front, and heard the girl's sobs. Mellita was collapsed on the living room sofa, pale and trembling.

"Did they hurt you?"

"No. I was so scared."

Nick sat beside her, and put his arm around her shoulder. "They've gone, you're all right now. What did they say?"

"The young SS soldier told me people are living on turnip soup and the elderly are dieing of starvation. There's been horrible bombings in the cities, killing innocent women and children.

The Americans are moving close and we'll have to evacuate towards Berlin soon. Also, he mentioned that an American war prisoner had escaped in the area, but he was more worried about himself. He was afraid the enemy was closing in and he'd get killed.

It scared me when he kept looking at me. Then, when they were leaving, they whispered together. The younger one stared at me with his cold eyes. The older man grabbed him and shoved him out the door. I was frightened the whole time."

"Mellita, I'm well enough to leave here any time." "If you leave, I will never see you again." "After all you've done for me, I'll be back."

He leaned over and gave her a soft kiss on the cheek. She rested her head on his chest and started to put her hand on his chest and raised her hand to his shoulder, but pulled away: "Your clothes are in the wash tub. I must finish them quick before Mutter gets home."

"Can I help you?"

Mellita giggled and gave him a curious glance. Nick grinned and fought an urge to grab her in his arms. He reminded himself that she was only fifteen. He followed her to the back room and stood close as she ran the clothes through the wringers. Afterwards, Nick carried them upstairs.

They hung the damp clothes on an old drying rack in the attic.

"Oh! I didn't get a chance to tell you. The German attack is scheduled for Alsace near Drusenheim on March 25th. I was surprised that Mutter knew this."

"Wonderful! Thank you."

"I'd better straighten the kitchen, now. I'll see you tonight."

When she'd gone, Nick marveled that even though they didn't always understand the words, they had been able to talk to each other from the start. They were friends. He felt good that she trusted him enough to share the information of the attack.

It struck Nick again how beautiful she was. Her eyes were large and lovely. Her lips weren't too full, or too thin.

He glanced at the mirror in her room. The person he saw didn't look like him. The long wavy hair and scruffy beard made him seem older and tougher. He leaned forward and examined the scar. It looked better. What would Marilyn and his folks think of it? A character mark that made him unique, and would remind him how lucky to be alive. A memory of the war.

Even though he didn't want to, it was time to move on. The whole family, including himself, would be executed if he was discovered.

As much as he appreciated Mellita, his strongest desire was to get back home. He needed to return to the American sector and reach his Company.

Chapter 20

The March rains reflected the gloom hanging over the Jordan family. Ever since Nick was reported missing-in-action, they prayed for his safe return.

Paul and Blanche were staring out the living room window watching the rain drops bounce off the sidewalk and run down the street. They glimpsed a boy in a yellow slicker ride up on his bike, and swing off his bike and head for their front door. Paul moved to meet him hoping for good news about Nick. He accepted the telegram and ripped it open as the boy sped off.

The unbelievable words leaped from the page.

We regret to inform you...
Nicholas P. Jordan, Killed-in-Action...

Corporal Jordan fought honorably for his country.
He will be awarded a medal for bravery--posthumously.

He crumbled the telegram and slammed it to the floor, and slumped to his chair.

"What is it?" Blanche shrieked.

Paul looked up at her, tears in his eyes, unable to speak. He opened his mouth, but nothing came out. His eyes fixed on the floor. He couldn't tell her. He just couldn't.

"Is it Nick?" Her voice barely audible. He could only nod. There were no words in him.

"God in Heaven'! No!" She picked up the telegram and read it. When she finished, she tossed it in the air.

"What have we done to deserve this torture? Nick! It can't be possible. Not Nick! My beautiful Nick. I want to die." Confused and not knowing what to do she spun madly around the room.

"I can't believe this," Paul wailed. "He was such a good boy. I never opened my God Damned mouth. He never knew how I felt. I loved him! He died without me telling him. It serves me right for being such a rotten father," Paul sobbed. "I sat on my ass, playing bridge at the Elks Club when he broke the county mile record. What kind of a father is that?" His fists clenched tight.

They clung together and shared the rage and grief. Then they paced the house. Their emotions out of control, like they were in a dream world. Actually, a living nightmare. Since they received the telegram, Paul's face had aged dramatically.

They took sleeping pills to get through the night but the next morning, the horror and disbelief were still there waiting.

"We have to write Wylie and call Marilyn today." Blanche reminded Paul.

There was a long silence. Finally, Paul said, "That's an ugly task. I'm not sure I can handle it."

"You write Wylie and I'll call Marilyn," she said as the tears began again.

Later that morning, Blanche suggested it would be better to go meet Marilyn to tell her rather than call her.

Paul couldn't find it in himself to start his letter. He decided it wasn't the time to tell Wylie. No use disrupting his life sooner than needed. The bad news could wait.

They left the house in silence and climbed into the car. As they drove toward Marilyn's house, neither looked forward to seeing her under these circumstances. The rain had stopped, but now it began to come down again. The windshield wipers flapped back and forth like metronomes, doing little more than smearing with a thin film of grime.

Blanche let out a yell, "Paul, you went through a stop sign."

A chill went through him. They could have been killed. He shook his head and forced himself out of his daze.

They pulled into the narrow driveway barely wide enough for their car. The telephone post was so close, Blanche could barely squeeze out her door. They hurried up the steps to the porch overhang to keep dry. Blanche hoped she could put the right words together in a gentle way. Paul rang the doorbell.

When Marilyn opened the door, the two of them stood there staring at her unable to speak.

"It's Nick, isn't it?" Marilyn asked softly.

"Yes. I hate to have to tell you, but we have terrible news. We received a telegram ..." Blanche spoke in a weak, cracking voice. She hesitated, swallowed hard, then continued on. "It said, Nick was killed in action."

Silence prevailed as Marilyn's mind consumed the shocking news.

"They don't know everything. He's been missing for a while, so now they're assuming he's dead." Marilyn said, then proceeded, "Come in and sit down."

"Just for a minute." Blanche said. Paul hadn't said a word, yet. He handed Marilyn the telegram and sat in the over-stuffed chair looking drawn and pale. While Blanche sat on the couch, Marilyn stood and read the telegram. Her face paled and she sat down to finish it. She started to cry and Blanche moved closer and put an arm around her.

"It sounds so final." Blanche said.

"I'll tell you, even though it's a great shock, I still don't believe it. You know, every time Nick wrote about his close brushes with death, I've thought back and remembered I'd had an apprehensive feeling he was in danger at about the same time. I haven't had any sort of reaction like that, and I believe I would have."

"God, I hope you're right!" Paul shouted.

"The war will be over soon and then we'll know for sure. He could be a prisoner or even hiding out somewhere," Blanche said with hope in her voice.

"You're right. I'd given up, but thanks to Marilyn, I can see there's hope." Paul said.

"Yes, we can't give up. As long as there is any chance he could be alive, let's believe it," Marilyn said before they left.

The rain had slowed as Paul and Blanche drove home. They talked about how nice Marilyn had been. She had shown such a strong interest in Nick ever since he went into the Army. She wrote him long letters every day and called them often to see if they had heard anything from him.

"Marilyn has been a darling. It's unusual for a girl to be so dedicated. She seems content to wait for Nick. She's popular and cute. I know she could date any boy, but she's not interested in anyone but Nick." Blanche said.

As they drove into their driveway, the sun broke out. "Let's not go in there now, why don't we go down town. We can check the mail while we're driving around." Blanche suggested.

"Good thought." Paul said.

At the Post Office there was a letter from Wylie. They sped home anxious to read it together. They sat side by side at the kitchen table and opened the letter.

Dear Mom and Dad:

I'm still in shock about Nick. I wish I
was home with you to help you carry on with
your burden.

I hope he will turn up and be all right. I
think of him all the time. I wish I had been a
better "Big Brother."
Jim and I are stationed on a small island.
I already had a scary experience. Our first
combat mission took us over the Japanese mainland.
After we hit our target, we pulled up and headed
for home base. I was glad to get out of there
without getting hit. Anti-aircraft shells were
exploding everywhere. I thought about luck and
fate, but I prayed to survive as hard as I could.

We were flying toward our island for about
ten minutes when I discovered my fuel wasn't
transferring from the auxiliary to the main tank.
I knew I was in trouble and wasn't sure what to do.
So, I moved the control stick to the right and
the ailerons caused the plane to bank. I
hoped this maneuver would get the fuel to
move. It didn't. I was scared and felt like
I was going to panic. I began to hyperventilate.
This is dangerous in an airplane you can go
into a coma quickly and not come out. I slowed
my breathing and called my LEAD Colonel on my
radio and told him my problem. He was no help
except saying they would stay close and mark
where I went into the water. So, a PBY could
try to pick me up. The odds of that happening
are not good, believe me. If you ditch in the
ocean, it's almost impossible to be found.

Out of the blue came a voice on my radio,
"Switch off these five circuit breakers and
then pull them back on." The person named the
breakers. I picked the right ones and did it.
There was nothing to lose. I waited what
seemed like forever and then the fuel started
to transfer. What a relief! I started to breath

normally again.

Back at base I tried to find out who the
pilot was that called me about the breakers,
but I never found out who did it. I'd never
heard of that procedure before, nor had any of
my fellow pilots. I searched through our P-47
flight manual, and there was nothing about it.

I'd like to find out who saved my life, but no luck.
Maybe, it was my Guardian Angel. What do think?
I hope you are both OK.
I'll be praying for Nick.
Thanks for the letters.

Love,

Wylie

"After what Marilyn said, and now reading Wylie's letter. I feel Nick is all right. Remember
all those times Nick came close to being killed and wasn't. There had to be a reason. He wouldn't
survive all that, only to be killed. I think our family has someone looking after us, like Wylie said
a Guardian Angel." Paul said with a slight grin of hope on his face.

After watching Blanche for a reaction, he began again. "Your brother Tony survived his freak
accident. The time he was deer hunting alone, and his horse fell on top of him in a deep ditch.
Your other brother, Bill, happened to see him go down with his binoculars. He rushed for miles
to get to Tony. There the horse lay on Tony and wasn't moving. Bill gave a mighty heave and the
horse got up. Besides some broken ribs, his rifle was the only thing ruined. It had a forty degree
bend in it. The horses weight had bent it. Tony could have easily been killed.

Also, Tony's son fell from that one hundred foot high scaffolding that collapsed. He grabbed
a cable out of nowhere and he hung upside down until he was rescued. It was a miracle. People
watching thought he was going to be killed for sure.

There were other occasions of miracle's that saved members of our family but especially
Nick. In Drusenheim, he was one of a few G.I.'s to survive the German surprise attack. Also, he
made it through when his squad was pinned down for hours by German 88's zeroed in on them.

He tip-toed through the mine field to save a buddy.

His own tanks shot 50 caliber shells at him.

A German soldier ran out of a house in the middle of the night, and went right up to Nick and
looked him in the eye. Then turned and sped back to the house. If he'd remembered his gun, Nick
might be dead.

Nick told us about the night in a staging area where the four G.I.'s befriended him. He slept in
their tent one night. The next day he went back to the front. That night an artillery shell killed all
four of the men Nick had been with.

On and on it went with him. He's got to be alive. I believe it, Blanche. Am I right or am I
grasping in thin air! He's got to come home to us. Let's pray for him.

74

When Marilyn's Mother arrived home, and saw her red cheeks said, "What's the matter, honey?"

"The Jordans got a telegram saying, Nick was killed in action." Marilyn's tone was oddly detached.

"Oh! How horrible!" Her mother rushed to her side. "Yes. They are taking it hard. I feel sorry for them."

"I'm so sorry, darling. I know how much you cared for him." She wrapped her arms around Marilyn.

"Mom, I want to be alone now. I'll be in my room." "Pete Nelson called. He said he'd call back."

"Tell him I'm sick. I don't want to talk to him."

"He's such a nice boy. Why don't you? It'll make you feel better."

"I'm sorry, but I just don't want to talk to anyone." She turned and hurried up the stairs to her bedroom. Then closed the door, and walked to her desk. She sat down, pulled out a piece of paper, and began writing:

> Dear Honey,
> We haven't heard from you for what seems
> like a thousand years! Where are you?
> We are worried. We all want you to be all
> right and back home with us.
> I can't stand not being with you. Please,
> please, be alive.
>
> Your folks are in shock because they received
> a telegram saying you had been killed. They are
> distraught because they love you so much.
>
> I'm sure you're still alive, so write as soon
> as you can. It will make everyone happy.
>
> I'm exhausted from the worry and frustration
> the telegram caused. We're having a hard time
> believing it.
>
> I'll dream of you tonight and pray that you
> are alive and well.
>
> I love you with all my heart.
>
> Always yours,
>
> Marilyn OXOXOX

She folded the letter and placed it in an envelope, then sat staring at it for a long moment before she lowered her head on the desk. Her shoulders shook from the sobbing that she could no longer hold back.

She could not picture Nick dead. He had to be alive. Finally, Marilyn collapsed on the bed, tossing fitfully before fading into a troubled sleep.

Two days later, Marilyn opens the morning paper and was shocked by the headline:

"LOCAL ATHLETE KILLED IN ACTION"

Underneath the headline ran a long story about Nick's various athletic achievements and awards, and a brief war history in the European Theater of Operations. The final line said that: "Hoquiam was in a state of mourning for a man that was more than one of its greatest athletes."

When Marilyn read the article, a sadness swept over her. No. He's not dead.

The fun times together flooded her memory. At first they barely spoke to each other, shyly glancing in each others direction. Then the tolo dance opened up their friendship that rapidly turned into a romance. Instantly, they were struck by a strong love for one another that seemed to be implanted forever. She would always love Nick and want to be with him. He would come back to her.

Chapter 21

Nick retraced his previous tracks, and had no trouble getting back to the radio. He was determined to get his transmission out that night.

He flipped the power switch, and made adjustments to the antennae, crystals, and frequency.

"American calling from behind German lines, trying to contact Allied Forces. Come in! Come in!"

Nick pushed the receiver switch and waited. There was only silence for five minutes. He changed frequency, then transmitted:

"American calling with important information."

He repeated the message, then hit the switch.

After a long silence, a crackling sound blared forth, and he jerked to attention. A garble of French words that Nick didn't understand came through the speaker.

When the voice finished, he turned the transmitter "I'm an American. Do you speak English? Urgent message. Come in."

He clicked the receiver on. After a moment, the same voice spoke again. He could make out some of it this time:

"Parlez vous Francals? Pierre in Nancy, France. Frequency 30-70. OK. Come in."

Nick flushed with delight. He adjusted the frequency and transmitted:

"This is Corporal Nick P. Jordan, Medic for Company G, 232nd Infantry Regiment of the 42nd Rainbow Division, with an urgent message from inside Germany. Repeat back to me."

He flipped the switch and waited.

Nick almost jumped from his chair when the words came back, partly in French but with enough English for him to decipher the words.

Nick started again. "Hitler is going to make a final all out surprise attack on the West. He thinks by splitting the western troops in half, they will be confused and defeated. Then, he can concentrate on the Eastern Front and win the war. He's going to throw all his might at the U.S. Forces. If we're ready, we can stop him. Repeat back, please."

It came back correctly, so Nick completed his message:

"Attack to occur March 25, at dawn, in the Alsace area near Drusenheim. On March 24th, camouflaged in white to blend with snow, they will begin moving into position."

Nick continued, "That's it, but also I'd like to ask a favor. Could you notify my parents that I'm alive and well? Thank you. Roger and out."

Pierre's voice repeated what he had sent. Nick was especially excited about notifying his family that he was OK.

His job completed, Nick switched off the radio, pulled the antenna in, heaved a big sigh and smiled. He jumped from his chair barely able to suppress a yelp of joy.

He left everything as it had been, and headed back. He ran most of the way to the Schwartz's house. As he climbed through Mellita's window, he slipped on the ice and sprawled on the floor with a soft thud.

"Nick?" Mellita whispered.

"Yes, I tripped. Do you think your mother heard me?"

"Nein. Ve should stay quiet, though."

After a few minutes of silence, Nick rose and came to sit next to her on the bed. "It's snowing, and there was ice on the roof that made me slip when I came in the window. But listen to this, Mellita: the message is out."

She sat up, her face close to his. "This is marvelous! I'm happy for you,"

He slid his arm around her and kissed her cheek. Mellita wrapped her arms around Nick. His heart pounded as he moved his face to hers. He found her lips and they came together.

Her feminine softness felt food. Nick pressed closer. He didn't ever want to separate. Mellita pushed against him and her hands moved gently on his back.

Was that a noise? They pulled apart and listened. Afraid Frau Schwartz might come in the door, Nick froze, one arm and hand in the air, the other sunk into the mattress supporting him.

It was quiet. She could be sneaking up on them. They waited longer. Mellita hadn't moved. They were both hardly breathing. There was still nothing. They started to relax. They listened once again. Then, they both giggled slightly, and slid together. Mellita's hand found Nick's and she massaged it softly. Her touch sent shivers through his body. His free arm wrapped around her and she cuddled against him. They clung together. Nick felt her soft breasts tight against him.

Since he'd come to Mellita's house, this was the first night Nick didn't sleep in the attic. He enjoyed the comfort, and being with her that night.

He knew though, that the time had come for him to move on. Mellita must know it, too. So, it was comforting to show each other how much they cared. If they waited any longer, it would be too late. The timing was right that night for Nick. Theirs was a love that he would never forget.

Chapter 22

With Mellita's help, Nick prepared to leave the Schwartzs' house. He hoped to get back to his unit.

"I'll miss you Mellita. Without your help, I'd never have survived."

"I'm happy I could help you. My life was pretty dull until you showed up. I'll never forget the days you spent here."

"If I get into trouble, I'll come back. Otherwise I'll look for you after the war."

"Danka. Yes, do come back any time. You'll always be part of my life. I'll pray you are safe."

He felt empty at the thought of leaving her.

Tonight Nick would take one of the Schwartz's bicycles, and go toward Hofen. Then, he'd head to the south and hope to find the U.S. lines.

After scrounging around the house, they had gathered blankets, flashlight, small hatchet, matches, thermos, gloves, clothes, mess kit, paper, and other items. He filled his backpack, and wore his small shovel and hatchet on his belt. He tied the kerosene lantern to the handlebars. Food would be the last and most important to be packed.

Nick slipped out to the garage and checked the bike. It needed the old balloon tires pumped up. He found a pump hanging on the wall, and set to work. When he went back into the house, Mellita had gathered some of her dads' cloths. Nick tried them on and laughed at the brimmed hat. With the clothes, no one could tell he wasn't German.

"When will you be going?" She seemed reluctant to look him in the eye. He saw the tears begin to trickle down her face.

"As soon as it gets dark. I'll pack what I can on the bike and move it into the woods, that way I wont make any noise when I leave." He looked at her sad face, then held her close. They embraced for a long moment. It wouldn't be easy leaving her. He started to speak, but the words wouldn't come. He swallowed, cleared his throat and tried again.

"I'll be back," He took the supplies and tied them to the bike, and wheeled it into the brush.

When he got back to the house, Mellita was hunched in the overstuffed chair in the living room; with her head in her hands.

He knelt in front of her and lifted her chin. Nick looked into her, tear-filled eyes and said, "I promise you, we'll be together again someday." He swung his arms around her, and squeezed her to him. He kissed her gently on the lips, and felt her lips respond strongly to his.

A car pulled into the driveway. They both jumped and rushed up the stairs to Mellita's room. She looked out the window and froze. "Quick, it's the Gestapo," she said pushing him toward the attic.

Nick hurried to the far end of the cluttered room. He heard the footsteps and voices below.

He was so close to escaping, and now he might be trapped. Nick remained silent, and prayed. Time seemed to crawl as he waited. He sporadically heard the voices wondering if Mellita was all right. The noises came from the back of the house, the dining room and kitchen. He was afraid to move, or even breathe.

It seemed like hours had passed. Then the voices came closer. Were they coming toward him? Nick held his breath and listened. Relieved, he could tell they had moved right below him in the living room. Then the front door opened, and he heard them leave. Then, came the sound of the car's ignition, and it drove off.

It was night when Mellita opened the door.

"What happened? Are you all right?" Nick asked.

"Yes, it was Mutter's employer, Field Marshal von Schott. He brought her home. He wanted to be sure they made it safely. His wife died about two years ago, and lately he has been. interested in Mutter."

"Thank God! I was afraid for you. I'm glad everything is OK. I'll leave before something else happens."

Nick pulled her close to him, looked deep into her eyes. He never wanted to let her go. "As soon as the others are asleep, I'll go."

Later, when all was quiet, Mellita returned. Her eyes widened and filled with tears. "You will come back, won't you?" Her voice trembled. "The name of this town is Dambach."

"Yes, you better believe it. My heart is and always will be yours." In a flash, Marilyn came to mind. He hadn't seen her in a long time. She was in a different world, it seemed. Nick took her into his arms. He held her as they moved to the window. He kissed her again, and held her hand until the last. Nick climbed out onto the roof. He took one last look back. He gave her a farewell wave, and moved across the roof and climbed down to the ground.

Cpl. Rollin Hurd Awarded Bronze Star For Heroism

The Bronze Star medal, for his heroic action in service with the army, in Germany, was presented Nov. 6 in Austria to Cpl. Rollin Hurd, son of Dr. and Mrs. Rollin Hurd, Hoquiam, it was learned yesterday.

According to the accompanying citation, Corporal Hurd, 1943 Hoquiam high school graduate and letterman in track, basketball and golf, earned his medal March 19, 1945, near Ludwigstwinkel, Germany.

The citation was as follows:

"To R. L. Hurd, 39212522, T-5, medical department, medical detachment, Company O, 232nd infantry regiment:

For heroic actions on March 19, 1945, near Ludwigstwinkel, Germany. During the deployment of the platoon to which Corporal Hurd was attached as aid man, intense enemy artillery, mortar and small arms fire inflicted many casualties. Remaining behind with the covering force, he unhesitatingly exposed himself to the direct fire in order to treat the wounded and help evacuate them. Corporal Hurd's courageous action and devotion to duty were responsible for saving the lives of many of the wounded men."

Corporal Hurd, holder of the Grays Harbor county mile record, entered the army on his 18th birthday, soon after graduation from high school, and has been overseas for more than a year. At one time during the intense fighting in Germany, Hurd, with his unit, was missing for almost a week, only to return safely to American lines.

Hurds Learn How Missing Son Landed Plane In China Stream

Receiving word yesterday morning in a terse war department telegram which contained no details, that their son, First Lieut. Edgar Hurd, reported missing over Okinawa, was safe, Dr. and Mrs. Rollin Hurd of Hoquiam learned yesterday afternoon the details of their son's rescue and the ironical fact that they could have known about his rescue several days earlier.

Yesterday's war department telegram was the first word of their son's safety that Dr. and Mrs. Hurd had received since a previous telegram Feb. 19 informed them he had been missing since Feb. 4 after a P-47 flight over Okinawa. In the meantime Ensign Herb Rhodes, Hoquiam navyman, had revealed Lieut. Hurd's safety several days earlier in a letter to Rhodes' uncle, James Rhodes, Centralia. The latter, supposing that the parents were aware of the rescue of their son, did not contact them until yesterday afternoon. Learning yesterday that news

without details of Lieut Hurd's safety had been received by the parents, Rhodes contacted Dr. and Mrs. Hurd.

Ensign Rhodes' letter from Shanghia, China, to his uncle unveiled a saga comparable to that of Robinson Crusoe.

"When we were waiting to leave, I ran into Edgar, an old high school classmate of mine and son of dentist Dr. Hurd." wrote Ensign Rhodes, who is on a ship attached to the Marianas amphibious pool and at the time was in Shanghai, China. "He had been flying a P-47 over Okinawa and when the weather closed in he was lost. He headed for the China coast and set the plane down on a sandbar in a mountain stream just as his gas ran out. It took him ten days to get out of the interior although he only penetrated about 27 miles. He flew from Shanghai to Okinawa with me.".

Ensign Rhodes is the son of Mr. and Mrs. Charles H. Rhodes, 614 Lincoln street.

Upper right, Ed Hurd in his p-47 fighter plane.

Upper left, Rollin Hurd

Above, Rollin in the middle with his helmet off. Part of a squad, at the front in Germany.

Above, Rollin Hurd in a German town that just surrendered. White flags hanging out on the houses.

Left, Rollin.

Dachau Concentration Camp Liberated by 42nd Rainbow Division

Chapter 23

Nick concentrated on not skidding on the snow-packed road. He pumped the pedals at a slow, steady pace, as he got farther from Dambach. The bright moon reflected off the white ground, illuminating his path. He needed to be on guard; prepared to make a quick exit from the road through the drainage ditch and into the brush. The thought led him to glance over his shoulder, to be sure he wasn't followed.

As he pedaled on, his mind drifted to Mellita. Not to smart to leave her, he thought, but he had put her in danger. He looked back again, and was startled to see the headlights of a car approaching in the distance that he nearly lost control.

He slowed and dragged the bike off the road, stashing it behind a clump of bushes, and crouched beside it in the undergrowth as the car sped by. When it seemed clear, Nick pulled the bike up, but ducked again as a second car went by him.

He waited a few minutes before moving on. His thigh muscles ached especially the injured leg. There was still no town in sight. He struggled for another few miles before he spotted another light behind him. He moved off the road, and watched a high powered motorcycle approach, and speed past. Nick stared in disbelief, as the cycle hit a patch of ice and began to fishtail. Seconds later, the motorcycle out of control, went flying into the air and off the road. He heard a loud crunch as the bike hit the ground and bounced along. The motor roared, the wheels still spinning.

There was no movement from the wreck. Fearing the worst, Nick let go of his own bike and rushed toward the crash site. He heard a groan. The driver was pinned under the vehicle. Nick found the ignition switch, and turned it off. The wheels slowed and then stopped.

He leaned over the young man. A German soldier, about his own age. As he checked out the seriously injured man, Nick worried that if someone came along now, he would be captured or killed. Aware of his own risks, he reasoned that the man was beyond his help. After all, he was no doctor. Someone would come along soon enough and take the man to a hospital.

Nick pulled his bike up to the road. He started to move when he heard an agonizing moan. He Pedaled a few yards, then stopped.

"Hilfen mir, bitte?" The young man called out.

"Damn." There was no way he could leave now, enemy or not. He moved his bike off the road and hurried toward the injured German. He was conscious, and when he saw Nick, his expression changed to one of hope.

"Bitte, bitte,'danke schoen."

Nick leaned closer, and examined the boy's condition. His skin had the same paleness that he'd seen on Goodwin's face in the mine field. The German's face was contorted in pain; his eyes pleaded for help.

Nick wrestled, the heavy machine moved. He took a deep breath. He saw the grotesque position of the leg. It was broken in several places. However, it was the blood-soaked earth under the leg that concerned him the most. With his pocket knife, he tore away the pants leg, and uncovered a deep gash on the inner thigh. A main artery had been cut, and he was bleeding to death. Nick cut a long strip of material off the torn pants leg and wrapped it above the wound. After the tournequet was tightly in place, the bleeding subsided.

Nick felt good that he'd come back, because the youth would have bled to death. Still, he couldn't shake the thought that this soldier still may not survive. He looked like any boy back home that could live down the street. Nick was concerned for him. Mellita had felt that way about Nick. He glanced toward the road, it was empty.

"Konnen Sie mir hilfen, bitte?" the German said weakly.

"Nicht verstehe Deutsch." Nick explained he didn't speak German.

"Can you get help? My leg hurts," the German pleaded in broken English.

"I'll get some tape. Be right back. Do you understand?"

"Ja! Danke." He grimaced and rolled his head from side to side.

Nick noticed a wallet on the ground. He picked it up, and while walking to his bike, looked through it. He inspected three I.D. cards and slipped one in his own wallet. There was a picture of a man and woman and two children. He assumed they were his family. They could have been pictures of Americans.

He stuffed the picture back in the wallet and put it in his pocket. He grabbed the adhesive tape from his pack and rushed back. The soldier was too weak to talk, but he watched Nick's every move, eyes filled with trust.

He loosened the tourniquet. He pushed the wound together and taped it. He tightened the tourniquet again and shoved the wallet into the young boy's pocket.

Nick straightened the leg as best he could while the German let out a yelp. He leapt up and ran to his bike, and returned with a blanket. He covered the injured boy. He wrestled the motorcycle onto the road, and positioned it so that an automobile passing by would have to stop.

Nick decided it was time to leave. He knelt next to the German. "I have to go now, but I've put your cycle in the middle of the road. The next car will stop and take you to the hospital. You will be fine." Nick started to move away, but remembered the tourniquet and loosened it. The blood seeped from the wound, but at a less dangerous rate.

"Warten Sie eine Minute! Don't leave me."

"Your leg's not bleeding. You'll make it until someone comes," Nick said.

"I don't want to die. Don't leave me."

He continued to tremble, so Nick pulled off his coat and laid it over him.

"I'm afraid," the boy whispered.

"All right! All right, I'll hang around until I see someone coming. Then I'm going." Nick hoped he wasn't making a fatal mistake.

"Danke, danke," his thankful words could barely be heard.

"What's your name?" Nick asked.

"Helmut von Schott. I'm Field Marshal Hans von Schott's son. You will be rewarded for saving me."

Nick wondered how he could be rewarded -- leniency if captured, maybe? He doubted that. A German Field Marshal saving him. Forget it! The name sounded familiar. Was that the name of the Field Marshal that came to Mellita's house?

As they waited, Helmut shivered. Nick crawled beside him and wrapped his arms around him. He still shivered. They lay together close for what seemed like an hour. Nick knew Helmut was fighting for his life, and he couldn't help think of the picture of the boy's family. Those people were waiting for him to come home, just like his own mother and father were, back in the U.S..

Half an hour later, the moon still shined down on them, and Nick heard the distant buzz of a motor. He leaped up, and saw car lights. He grabbed his coat, and took a quick look at Helmut's

85

leg. There was no blood. Nick looked into the dull, colorless eyes and said, "Someone is coming. I'll watch to make sure they take you with them. Good luck. I'll be thinking of you. You'll be all right." He clasped Helmut's hand.

Helmut shook Nick's hand and whispered, "Danke."

"Don't tell them about me, please." Nick hunched over and ran toward his bike. He grabbed it and wheeled it along the ditch, watching as they screeched to a halt. When two men got out of the automobile and looked around, Nick felt relieved. They walked off the road toward Helmut. While they were occupied, Nick pushed his bicycle onto the road and sped off as fast as his legs would pump.

After a few miles, he saw a town up ahead. At the same instant, a car roared from behind. Nick shot off the road across the drainage ditch and up the opposite slope, toward the cover of a clump of trees. He turned to see the car head into town. It must be Hofen, he thought, as he slid his bike into some brush. He dug out the flashlight from his pack and began to scout around. He worked his way further into the woods.

The moonlight streaked through the bare tree branches, bouncing off the snow. It seemed almost like daylight. Nick realized how exhausted he was from the long journey from Mellita's house. He pulled out his two blankets from his pack and scrounged up branches and leaves to complete his bed. He lay there thinking of Helmut von Schott. Nick hoped he'd be all right.

He gazed toward the lights of Hofen and remembered Mellita telling him what her mother had said. Because of the railroad system, it was a military center. She had mentioned new improved tanks were being loaded on trains for shipment to the front.

He tried to relax but his mind wouldn't let him. He looked back, the way he'd come, toward the Schwartz's in Dambach. Nick wished he was back there. He missed Mellita. But now he wanted to find the U.S. front lines and his unit. He took a deep breath of fresh cool air, and wondered how his brother Wylie was doing in the Pacific War. Nick was proud that Wylie was a fighter pilot. Only special and qualified men were chosen for that job. His brother was special.

Chapter 24

Wylie Jordan revved the motor and primed it as he watched Jim Mckay's P-47 shoot into the sky. The letter's 'D.C.' painted on Jim's cowling, just above a volumptuous girl, changed to a dot as it disappeared from view. Wylie's friend was from Washington D.C.. Wylie from Washington State, named his P-47 the Rain Queen, because he came from Hoquiam, one of the wettest towns in the country. The young pilots felt these names and pictures brought good luck.

Wylie was tense knowing they were headed to the Japanese mainland, and their most dangerous mission yet. He scanned the instrument panel. It looked normal.

He shoved the accelerator. The Rain Queen moved slowly at first and then shot forward and up into the sky. He flew into position beside another plane and they circled the area waiting for the rest to get airborne.

When the last aircraft lifted off the ground, the group headed for their target. Wylie kept close to the LEAD Colonel, following precisely forty five degrees behind and to his right. He felt some comfort being only one in a group of eighty aircraft.

He remembered the last flight when his fuel wouldn't transfer. He hoped his guardian angel who told him about switching the five circuit breakers was still around. He needed all the help he could get.

He glanced at his fuel gauge. No problem. His plane had done good for him, and he prayed it'd keep on.

Wylie peeked out of the canopy and looked at his world of sky above and ocean below with aircraft scattered everywhere. He couldn't spot Jim's D.C. on the other side of the formation. He scanned the sky for the smallest speck that might be an enemy plane. It reminded him of the many times he searched for golf balls.

They were nearing their target. Wylie wanted to get it over with fast. Make his dive, empty his guns and run like hell.

There it was! Japan! Smoke exploded around him. Guardian angel stay with me, he thought as he followed his leader downward. He banked the Rain Queen from side to side to make him a harder target. He spotted two Japanese Zero's closing in on him. The orange sun-like insignia's stood out on the fuselage. They swooped for the Rain Queen but Wylie banked sharply. He slammed the control stick full over, jammed the throttle forward and pulled into a gut-wrenching climb. The P-47 shuddered into a steep bank and stalled. He rolled out to the right, completing his climbing U-turn in front of and four hundred feet above the zero's.

Stay calm, Wylie. Stay calm. The enemy planes swung toward him. He pinpointed one of them in his sights and pulled the trigger. His machine guns burst into action. At the same time he heard the zing of bullets and the whump of heavy weapons fire.

He jerked his whole body around and looked for the enemy. His heart caught. Make sure, Wylie. Make sure. He tugged the trigger back. Then, banked the Rain Queen, he saw smoke bellowing out of a Zero. It was going down. He felt another whump and prayed he hadn't been hit. His mouth felt full of cotton as he searched for the other enemy plane. That's when he spotted a speck disappearing to the east. The pilot had seen his partner go down so he took off. Wylie was thankful. He'd won the dogfight.

Wylie heard a monstrous explosion and knew the advance planes had hit their target. His stomach tightened. Please don't let me be hit.

The Rain Queen bucked! What the hell? More bumps! Wylie saw his target. He activated his guns, and the bullets sprayed the Japanese trucks on the road. He saw a direct hit as he pulled up into the sky. He felt another thump, but his P-47, Thunderbolt, kept on flying.

Wylie reached for his shoulder when a jab of pain hit it. It reminded him of the time he and Nick had stirred up a bee hive and both were stung several times.

The Rain Queen gave a heave and slowed. He fought to get more speed but nothing worked. The altitude gauge was gradually moving downward.

His shoulder ached. He slipped his hand to his shoulder, and swung it away from his jacket. He saw the blood. "For God's sake, I've been hit." He glanced at the fuel gauge. It was Ok. He switched on the radio.

"Wylie Jordan in Rain Queen, I've been hit. Power's down. Can't keep speed or altitude up. Will limp back as long as I can."

"The Colonel here. We'll stay with you and keep you covered. Don't get wet, keep her going. Roger and out."

Wylie looked the gauges over and punched the accelerator. Nothing. His radio crackled and another voice came on:

"This is Captain Stoddard. Jordan do you know there's a hole in your right wing big enough for a elephant to walk through. See you back at the base, Wylie."

He looked out of the canopy to his right wing and prayed again that his guardian angel was near by.

The gauges had stabilized. The fuel was transferring.

His main thought was could the Rain Queen keep going just a little longer. It was slow going, but all the planes nearby encouraged him onward. He spotted McKay's D.C., cruising past and Jim gave him a wave. Wylie gave him the thumbs up signal.

There was no more blood but Wylie's shoulder had stiffened. He peered down and saw the water. Oh, so close, the waves looked like they wanted to grab him. He tried again to get the altitude up with no luck. Wylie, sensed that their little island home base was close now. His heart started to beat again.

The Colonel had called ahead to let the ground crews prepare for a possible emergency. The crews were prepared for the worst as the crippled Thunderbolt approached.

While the other planes flew over watching and waiting their turn, Wylie shoved his landing gear down. But the wheels only came partway down, and the plane hit hard with a thud and a hop. Then it went into a skid that went on and on, until the P-47 spun around and came to a sudden stop against a light pole.

Ground crews sprinted from all directions, but Wylie was already climbing out when they arrived. The Rain Queen had delivered him safely. As Wylie climbed down, he wondered if his guardian angel had helped along the way.

Paul Jordan arrived home from the golf course. He and Blanche played to help keep their minds off of Nick.

Paul picked up the letter from Wylie that they'd just gotten: He started to reread it:

3/29/'45

Dear Mom and Dad,

Just got back from a scary mission. Two Zero's
dived on me. But thanks to our faster and more
manuverable planes, I won the dogfight. I got one
for Nick. The Rain Queen got hit so many times it
looked like a sieve. It lost power on the way back
but we made it.
I got nicked on the shoulder by a bullet or shrapnel.
I'm told that I'll be receiving a Purple Heart.
Jim Mckay was on the mission. He flew by me and
waved when I was coasting back.
I had a letter waiting from you and Sally. She seems nice.
She sent her picture. Pretty cute.

Hope you're both fine.

Your loving son,

Wylie

While reading the Sunday paper, Paul scanned the war articles. The progress against the Germans was improving day by day. The big German surprise attack had failed and again the Allies were driving the Nazis back toward Berlin.

Over and over he had read of the suffering the GI's endured due to the bad winter in Europe. He wondered if Nick had suffered a lot before he died.

He and Blanche talked about Nick every day. They reminisced about the things that happened during his life. It was comforting to be able to laugh about all the special things over the years.

Paul still remembered one Fourth of July when Wylie put a lit firecracker in Nick's pocket. To both their surprise, it set off a chain reaction with the package Nick had in the same pocket.

The many times when he was rough on Nick came to mind. He wished he could have let him know that he loved him.

Paul switched on the radio. The news was on, and the announcer was detailing the war progress. He switched it off and sat in silence, visualizing the nightmarish picture of his son being shot by a Nazi, slumping lifeless to the frozen ground. He jerked out of his reverie when the doorbell rang.

Paul moved swiftly to the door and opened it.

"Telegram for Mr and Mrs. Paul Jordan."

"I'll take it."

He signed for it, then closed the door and stared at it. It was from the U.S. Government. More details on Nick's death, he thought. He hesitated, but then carefully opened it and began reading:

Dear Mr. and Mrs. Jordan,

New information about your son has been uncovered.
Based on our most recent reports, we have established
That Nicholas P. Jordan is alive behind the German lines.

Therefore, your son's status has been changed to
Missing-in-Action.
Any further news of him will be relayed to you
without delay.

Sincerely,

Captain Joseph Sinclair
U.S. Government

Paul's heart leaped with unbelievable joy. He smiled at the news as he read the telegram again, savoring each word. "What a guy!" he shouted. "I should have known." Tears flooded his eyes as he dropped into the big overstuffed chair, in the sitting room.

His adrenaline pumped so much, he jumped to his feet and ran out the door. Outside, he screamed to the world, "He's alive! He's alive!" he looked up and down the street. There was no one. Blanche wasn't home, he had to tell someone. He rushed next door to the Wick's house and pounded on the door.

When it opened, Mrs Wick looked startled. "What's wrong?"

"Nick is alive! I got a telegram saying he's hiding behind the German lines. Isn't that the greatest news?"

Mrs. Wick's eyes watered as she said, "That's wonderful. What great news! I'll bet Blanche is thrilled."

"She doesn't know yet. She'll be home any minute. I can hardly wait to tell her. She'll go crazy. She'll be delirious."

"I'm happy for you. You've been through so much. You deserve some good news," she said warmly, sharing the joy.

"Bye now! Talk to you later," Paul said as he leaped off the porch and squinted down the street where Blanche would be coming. His grin widened across his happy face. He glanced down the driveway and saw the basketball hoop. Nick and Wylie will be playing one-on-one again after all, he thought.

As he entered the house, he turned for one more anxious look. Mrs. Wick stood on her porch smiling in his direction.

He went to the phone and called Cora across the street. As he told her the story, Blanche's car pulled into the driveway.

"She's here, Cora. Talk to you later." He hung up and headed for the back door.

Blanche was still in the garage when he jumped out in front of her, laughing ecstatically. "What's so funny?"

"Nick is alive! He's behind German lines. Can you believe it? They talked to him by radio. Paul threw his arms high in the air and danced around Blanche. They've changed his status from Killed-in-Action, back to Missing-in-Action."

Blanche exploded with happiness. They embraced and clung together smiling and laughing. The tears flowed. Their faces beamed as they separated and entered the house.

"I'll call Marilyn. She'll be so happy.. She never did believe he was dead. Let me see the telegram."

"'This is the best news ever. Let's pray this damned war ends soon." Paul wiped a tear away as he handed it to her.

Blanche called Marilyn, but there was no answer. "This is Sunday. They always go to their cranberry bog. I'll call her later."

The Jordans sat that afternoon, reading and rereading the telegram. They talked of Nick's danger, but prayed he would be safe until the war ended. It was a great relief to know he was no longer considered Killed-in-Action.

The Jordans called their close friends and told them the news.

"I'll call the newspaper," Blanche said. She did and relayed the story from the telegram.

Later, she made contact with Marilyn, who rushed to the house. She read the telegram in total awe. Her lovely face lit up and she screamed, "Hallelujah! He's coming back to us." She broke out laughing and they all joined her. The whole group found themselves simultaneously laughing and crying tears of joy.

After awhile they stopped and Blanche said, "Nick is such a good kid. He gave us no problem growing up. If we wanted him to do something, he'd get it done without a complaint. I couldn't ask for a better son. Wylie two years older was more independent. He could always take care of himself. Being the youngest, we were easier on Nick. Thank goodness, he's all right. I know he's going to be coming home safely."

"This calls for a celebration. Let's all go out for dinner and come back to the house for ice cream." Paul said.

Chapter 25

The sun woke Nick at mid-morning. After a stretch, he searched for a better hiding place. In the woods further away from Hofen, he heard the soft rustling flow of water and came upon a rambling creek. He scooped up a little water in his hands and drank. Refreshed, he moved along the water's edge.

Nick pulled a sandwich from his pack. Mellita had made it for him before he left her. While he ate, he realized how much he missed her. After he'd finished, he scooped up more water and felt stronger and ready to move forward. The day was full of hard sunlight. Meager clouds looking like white foam began to evaporate. It was dead quiet.

In the distance, he spotted evergreens, clusters of eucalyptus and sycamores. But in the far back ground, a tall stump caught his attention. Wanting a closer look, he forded the creek and crashed through the brush. Vines and thorny bushes tore at his arms and legs as he moved through the dense thicket. The leafy branches whipped across his face. Finally, at the stump, he wondered what kind of tree it was. It reminded him of the old growth cedars, firs and hemlocks back home. It was near six feet high and four feet in diameter. He hoped it was hollow inside. As a youngster back home, hollowed out stumps made great hiding places.

Nick dropped his pack and pulled himself up a nearby tree to look down. Sure enough, it was partially hollow. He climbed out on a branch and lowered himself into the stump. Using the shovel from his belt, he scooped the rotten wood out. It was a perfect spot to hide and would give him protection from the weather. He kept working until he could kneel and not be seen from the outside. He enlarged three small knotholes with his pocket knife to give him peep holes.

Then, swinging himself onto the branch, he climbed down. He removed the binoculars from his gear, and tossed the pack into the stump.

Stepping on the larger rocks, he crossed the shallow creek, and headed for his bicycle. He moved it into thicker brush and being careful to keep out of sight, started to hike toward Hofen.

The sky was grayer. More snow coming, he thought. He was amazed how close he could get to the town and still be under cover of the forest. He followed the road with his binoculars as it entered the town from the south, curved left to the west and then out the other side of the city.

Nick worked his way to the railroad station, easily identifiable with all its activity. He saw four engines, one with passenger cars hooked to it, and others linked to boxcars and flatcars. The cars spread out over several blocks and were closely guarded.

The snow floated lazily down. He glanced at the flat cars. There could be tanks under the camouflaged tarps. He spotted an area away from the railroad yard with allied vehicles of all types. He wondered what else they were storing there. The area wasn't being guarded very well.

Later, when darkness set in and the snow was falling more heavily, he slipped cautiously into the storage facility. He saw several stacks of boxes in the back of a truck, and jumped in to check the inventory. He found boxes of M1 rifles, carbines, browning automatics, pistols, and shells. What especially caught his eye, however, was a half-full crate of hand grenades. Nick pulled the box toward the tailgate and froze. Was that a noise? There it was again. Footsteps crunched in the snow. He slid back deep into the truck and hugged the floor. Sweat broke out under his shirt as he waited and worried that he might be spotted.

After a moment, he sensed the guard stood beside the truck. Nick held his breath when a light flashed in and drifted slowly out. The footsteps moved away and Nick gave a sigh of relief.

After a moment of silence, he looked out then climbed down. With the box of grenades in his arms, he fled to the woods, In a dense clump of trees, he sat the box behind a huge root. Then ran back to the truck to pick up an M1, a pistol, and ammunition, and dashed away. He went back one more time to retrieve a broken barrel and a pail laying beside another truck.

Once he'd gathered his supplies, Nick sat against a tree to rest. What was he doing sitting in the snow, alone in this foreign country? He pictured his home, family, and Marilyn, as clearly as if they were beside him. It tempted him to give up his plans and get the hell out, and find the U.S. lines.

But he knew he couldn't do that. Kane wouldn't have passed up this chance to help the Allied cause. Nor would Branch even consider turning his back on an opportunity to cream the enemy. He visualized Nelson's face, encouraging him to fulfill his duty.

With fresh resolve, Nick loaded the pistol, placed some shells in his pocket, carefully attached a hand grenade to his belt. With darkness coming, he checked for his flashlight, and headed toward the railroad station. The heavy snow made for poor visibility.

Nick crept close to the trains, and crouched behind a dense bush. He watched the guards as they patrolled their routes. There were three soldiers guarding the train. They looked like trouble, and Nick hoped he could handle it.

After observing for awhile, he saw a pattern to their pacing. There was one guard posted at each end of the train, and one in the middle. The ones on the ends each covered a third of the train, circled the end, and covered a third on the other side. The soldier in the middle followed a similar pattern, crossing between two boxcars over a coupling to cover the other side of his third of the train. Nick kept an eye on the soldiers moving about the station, thankful that they were too far away to notice him.

At the right moment, he darted toward the nearest open boxcar, and climbed into it. With his flashlight, he checked the contents, it contained ammunition and fuel. The others had the same.

Then, he crept toward one of the camouflaged flat cars. It was covered by a huge tarpaulin. Sliding up under it he found himself next to a new steel tank. A large menacing gun protruded from the turret. A chill ran through him when he thought of the chaos it could create. He directed his flashlight into the tank and saw the wide array of controls and gauges.

Nick slid from under the tarp and ran back to a boxcar. He pulled himself in and grabbed a burlap sack he found lying on the floor. He folded it and tucked it in his belt. He peeked out and jerked his head back. A guard approached. He held his breath and dove into a far corner behind some gas cans. Feeling weak. His heart pounded. God, don't let me be found out. As the footsteps drew closer, Nick froze.

Chapter 26

As Nick kept low in the back of the boxcar, he gripped his pistol tight. It trembled in his hand. Would he be able to hit his target? He tried to steady the gun, to no avail. Relax, Nick. Relax. He hoped the element of surprise was on his side. There was the chance the German might hesitate to shoot into the fuel. His concern was if the soldier shot, the explosion would blow him to bits.

He heard the slow, measured footsteps outside his car. He stared at the door. As he watched, the German stopped and flashed his light inside. He hesitated, then climbed into the car, scanning the interior again with the light as Nick readied his gun. Nick was barely able to suppress a sigh of relief when the guard sat down in the doorway. The soldier looked out in both directions. He put his rifle down, pulled a pack of cigarettes from his pocket and lit one up, peering out into the night. He puffed and relaxed, and slipped his helmet off and put it on the floor beside him.

Good instincts tell you what to do long before your head figures it out. So when Nick found himself silently creeping up behind the unsuspecting German, he didn't need to think twice. He swung hard sideways against the man's temple, hitting him with the butt of his pistol. The guard slumped over without a sound. His limp body started to fall out the open door when Nick caught his collar and dragged him back into the car.

Nick grabbed him under the arms and pulled him into the corner where he had been hiding. He picked up another burlap sack, cut it up and proceeded to tie the German's wrists behind him as he lay face down. Then, he tied the ankles and placed a gag in his mouth.

The guard still lay unconscious as Nick left the boxcar, and returned to the copse of trees where he had stashed the grenades. He took the burlap sack from his belt, and placed about fifteen grenades in it. With the sack over his left shoulder and his M1 rifle in his right hand, he turned and headed toward the train.

He felt the sweat on his body, and the tension inside him. It reminded him of when he was getting ready for the mile race in the state track meet.

When he got back to the train yard, he placed the sack of grenades behind a set of wheels and checked the boxcar where he'd tied the German. It was quiet, so he climbed in and turned the light on the guard. His eyes were open and showed fear. He'd turned over but had been unable to free himself.

Nick called on his high school German experience, and said, "Stehst du hier bis Morgen! Verstehe? Ja! Gut." The soldier nodded, understanding that he had to stay put until the next day.

He picked up another sack and shredded it into strips, leaving some and taking the rest with him.

Instead of following the side of the train, he went some distance from the tracks and moved toward the south end. He spotted a guard walking around the caboose. Nick froze and watched him until he went to the other side. Nick moved closer to the train and crouched low to see under it. After a few moments, he saw the German's legs on the other side of the boxcar. Soon the guard headed back toward the caboose.

When the coast was clear, Nick climbed a ladder between two boxcars that led to the roof. He waited, and noticed sweat under his shirt. He heard the crunch of boots as the guard approached. Nick held his breath, his heart pounded hard against his chest.

The soldier stopped below him and tossed his cigarette butt out into the snow. It sizzled as it hit the snow just as he brought the butt of his rifle downhard, it slammed into the German's neck. The thud sounded like a baseball smashing into a catcher's mitt.

He leapt to the ground as the guard screamed out and struggled to his feet. Nick swung the rifle into the man's jaw. This time the man was knocked out, and Nick quickly tied his hands and gagged him.

In a moment, the German had regained consciousness, obviously in pain. Nick forced him to his feet and pointed the barrel of his rifle toward the boxcar where the first guard was tied.

He prodded the guard with his M1 until they reached the car. He tapped the man's shoulder and pointed inside. Nick boosted him up, and pushed him into the car. Then climbed in, and sat the man down next to the first guard. Then, tied the second German's feet As Nick raised up, he froze when he heard a noise and a beam of light streaked into the car.

The words, "Was ist los?" came from a voice outside. Nick ducked and scrambled away from the light. He fired a quick shot in the direction of the beam. In return, a shot whizzed past Nick, barely missing him. He fired again, and there was a scream and the flashlight fell crazily to the ground. He rushed to the door, and both men fired at each other at the same time. Nick felt a twinge of pain in his shoulder. He crawled to the door, and aimed at the soldier. But when he saw the man lay helpless, Nick shoved his gun into his belt.

He slid down, and glanced in all directions. Then he forced the third guard to join the others. He checked out the German's wounds and decided they weren't bad.

Nick gathered the strips of burlap he'd cut and jumped out, closing the door behind him. He found his sack of grenades, threw it over his shoulder, and hurried toward the farthest flat car.

He hoped there wouldn't be a change of guard now. No matter! He had a job, and he intended to accomplish it. He owed it to his country, his family. Also, he thought, in memory of Nelson.

Seeing no one, he rushed to the nearest boxcar and climbed in. He flashed the light briefly to locate one of the fuel cans, and forced it open and poured it around the car. He placed a strip of burlap so one end was in the gasoline and the other near the door. He ran to the next boxcar and did the same. Eventually, Nick had set up all the cars in the same way except the ones next to where the guards were tied.

Next, he rushed to his sack of grenades. He took one out, climbed onto the flat car and on top of the tank. He lifted the hatch, and pulled the pin, and dropped it inside. He took off on the double. He grabbed the sack as he heard the muffled explosion that destroyed the inside of the tank.

He grabbed another grenade, climbed onto the next flat car, and repeated the process. Exhausted, Nick kept on with this pattern until all of the tanks were immobilized.

When done, he lit the burlap fuses, starting with the car closest to the railway station. Hurrying along the row of boxcars, he lighted one after another. After the last one, Nick sprinted toward his hiding place in the stump. He looked back. Despite the commotion, no one was pursuing him. He prayed luck would hold as he continued deeper into the trees. Rushing through the deeper snow, he swung past the spot where he had left the bucket and small barrel and picked them up.

Suddenly, an ear-splitting blast cut through the air. Nick took cover, then found a spot where he could glimpse the area. He saw the boxcars burning and exploding and both soldiers and civilians running in all directions

He noticed that the boxcars where the German guards were tied were not aflame. He smiled to himself and said, "You can change the guards now."

He got up and headed to where he'd placed the empty box with the grenades. He put the bucket in it and rolled the barrel stays to fit inside. Lifting it, he hurried away from the stump. He back tracked and circled to mislead anyone that might follow. The snow came down harder and would cover his tracks.

Exhausted, Nick was tempted to sit down, but couldn't chance it. He'd go the extra mile to prevent anyone from tracing him to the stump. He walked in the creek, and jumped from rock to rock, first in one direction, then another.

When he reached his hideaway, he dropped each item one at a time, into the hollowed out stump. Finally, he climbed the tree he'd used before, moved out on the branch and dropped into his new shelter for the night.

Nick's strength expended, he had to push himself to shovel out the accumulated snow, scattering it so as not to be noticeable. He tossed some of it over the spot where he'd climbed the tree to cover his footprints. The snow floating down reassured him that his tracks would be covered.

After that, he straightened out the barrel stays and lifted them up above the opening. Then spread them out like an umbrella and sat the whole assembly back down on the top of the stump for a roof. Even with the gaps, it helped to keep the wind and snow out.

The little grenade box became his chair, and he stored the bucket in the open end of the box. Though worn out, his adrenalin kept him wide awake.

The damage inflicted on the tanks and supplies might bring about an earlier end of the war. The thought pleased him; he'd get home that much sooner.

Memories of recent events flashed through his mind. He thought of the injured son of the Field Marshal von Schott, and hoped he was all right. The three guards he'd tied up in the boxcar should be safe from the flames and explosions.

As he relaxed, he began to dream of being with Mellita again. The more he thought of her, the greater his desire to see her again. He'd go to her house once more before finding the U.S. lines.

His mind wandered on to thoughts of his family. His loved ones back home had no idea what he'd been through, let alone that he was hiding in the woods in a hollow stump in the cold, snowy winter somewhere in Germany. They'd be proud of what he'd done...if he survived to tell them about it.

Chapter 27

A sound nearby woke Nick, his eyes popped wide open. Maybe, a German soldier looking for him, he thought. He listened, it sounded like an animal digging at something close to his hideout. Then, there was a shuffling noise, as whatever it was scrambled off. After a sigh of relief, he shifted to find some comfort. There was none. His legs tingled and claustrophobia swept through him. The urge to push the snow-covered roof off and climb out gripped him.

If soldiers were searching for him he hoped they weren't familiar with the virtues of hollow stumps. Nick remembered the happy days he'd spent at Lake Quinault back home in the Pacific Northwest. He'd enjoyed the green beauty of the coastal forest and hiding from his friends inside the many hollow trees. Here he was hiding in one an ocean from home. Now, it was life or death rather than the fun of hide and seek.

He peeked through a knothole. Snow flakes still drifted down. The scene was picturesque, with snow covering everything.

He found his flashlight and shined it on his pack, then picked out a sausage and sandwich that Mellita had packed. He savored each bite and washed it down with water from his canteen. Water would be no problem with all the snow, but food would have to be rationed.

He focused his light on three blankets, the lantern, and a small can of kerosene. Mellita had also supplied him with a box of matches, extra batteries, tools, a roll of twine, and wire.

Nick clipped a piece of wire, bent one end into a loop and threaded it through the slats in his makeshift roof. After turning the wire and retracting it, he grasped the end between the next opening with his pliers and worked it down. Twisting the ends around the handle of the lantern, and poured some kerosene into it. When the wick was soaked, he ignited the end with one of his precious matches. The place lit up and revealed details of his cramped quarters. There was no room to move about, or stand. He had to endure the discomfort.

A chill shot up Nick's spine as he heard distant sounds of barking dogs. They were tracking him now. He turned his lamp off and waited. He knew how hard it was to fool dogs. His family used to try to trick their dog by hiding in the woods, but it seldom worked. He hoped his effort to cover his tracks would pay off.

Nick felt around for the pocket on the side of his pack and lifted his pistol and stuffed it in his belt. He pulled his blankets around him and listened to the faint barking.

He stiffened, realizing the sound was getting louder. Closer, yes, dammit, they were coming directly for him. There was nothing he could do, but wait and pray. Barks roared in his ears, and he envisioned the hounds leaping at the stump, revealing his whereabouts.

At that moment, between the barks, he heard the German voices. Soldiers were closing in, he'd had it. They'd discovered him, and there would be no Kane to rescue him. They might shoot him, rather than take him prisoner.

The dogs got more excited, and his heart pumped faster. He tried to calm his breathing, but it sounded like the roar of ocean waves crashing against towering beach cliffs.

The voices were beside him now, outside the thin layer of rotted wood and bark. He froze, waiting for the inevitable. Despite the cold weather, sweat coated his body. He strained to keep calm, knowing any movement or noise such as a sneeze could be fatal.

Time crept forward slowly, and it seemed like a lifetime before the barks became less frantic.

He listened to the soldiers scream at the dogs, and he picked out several "Neins".

Since they probably don't know he's there, maybe they'd pass on by him. He hoped they weren't familiar with hollow stumps. He prayed they weren't, The dogs were still nearby sniffing, but not barking.

Then, there was a change, he heard panting and clawing right next to him. A dog whined, barked and jumped at the stump.

A German shouted at the dog. Boots crunched in the snow as someone walked by. Nick prayed as hard as he could. He shook from cold -- or fear. He held his breath, expecting the worst. But instead he heard a scuffing noise and snap, followed by a yelp from the reprimanded dog and the sound of the animal running off. Relieved, his nerves settled somewhat. There were still movements outside, and breathing. Someone was still there. Maybe he was suspicious that a person could be hiding close by. At that moment, a splattering noise against his tree, created an image of a soldier pissing. Nick listened as he heard a zipper being worked. Then came footsteps crunching in the snow as the German left.

Nick rose and peered through the knothole. His eyes hurt from the brightness, and he looked away. He let them adjust and tried again. At first there was a white blur, but soon focused on movements in the distance. The soldiers and dogs were grouped under a clump of trees. While some sat resting, others stood talking.

How long are they going to hang around, he wondered.

A pain shot into his right calf. A cramp like a vise gripped his leg. He rubbed and pounded on the muscle, but the agony continued until he could barely stifle a scream. Nick gripped his calf tightly and clenched his teeth. Finally, the pain eased and he sat back on the box. Thank God it hadn't happened when the Germans were near.

He peeked out the knothole, nothing had changed. The Germans were goofing off. The U.S. soldiers called it gold bricking. He wondered what the Germans called it.

Nick needed to leave his hideout and stretch his muscles. The stump had concealed him well. He reached for some food tried to relax, but he had to keep alert. So much had happened in such a short time, it was hard to believe he had been in Europe for only a few months.

Chapter 28

Nick looked through his peephole and watched the soldiers prepare to move out. With twilight coming on, it was time for them to head back to town for the night.

When they left, Nick turned on his lantern. The little flame made him feel warmer just looking at it. He inched about in his tight quarters, and stuffed a piece of sausage into his mouth. He ate hungrily.

He settled in for some sleep, but couldn't keep the thoughts of home from surfacing. It had been a long time since he'd seen his family. It was as though they lived in another time. But in his thoughts, they came to life. They were right there, encouraging him to survive and come back to them. He drifted into a restless sleep that carried him until just before dawn.

He spent the day watching for the soldiers. They never came. The next one dragged even more slow.

The lamp didn't take the chill off anymore. When another cramp made him squirm in agony, he felt he needed to get out of his hiding place. Every muscle in his body ached; he couldn't take it any longer.

Nick looked out and saw billows of white. The snow was coming down heavily. The wind picked up, and it howled through the knotholes. The layer of snow made the lid of his house difficult to budge. After a struggle, he was able to slide it off. He stood and looked around.

Wind whipped swirls of snow limited visibility. Had he taken the roof off too soon? Snow drifted in around him. He peered over the rim of the stump and saw the roof on the ground, already covered by falling snow. Should he climb out and hoist it back on? He decided not to, and stomped in place to keep warm. Chilled to the bone, he ducked back down. He huddled in his blankets.

The wind picked up until it developed into a blizzard. He looked up and saw a kaleidoscope of white flakes as the snow twirled above him and the wind howled. It blew all that day and into the night. With the constant roar in his ears, Nick finally dozed off.

Early the next morning, a loud bang and a crushing pain shocked him awake. He clutched his left side, and felt a jab, like a knife, in his rib cage. The pain wouldn't let him move, and he shivered as he realized the snow covered him like a blanket. He felt a solid round object pressed against him. In a haze of panic, Nick understood what had happened. The weight of the snow had caused a branch to give way. The sides of the rotten stump had crumbled, and the branch pinned him down, cracking against his ribs. He tried to work himself free from the searing pain.

Panic engulfed him. He was trapped. The stark reality of his predicament blasted through his mind. His hopes of returning home were shattered. Helpless and alone, he'd freeze to death or starve right here, pinned under this branch.

This is it, he thought. How could his hiding place become his grave! Dazed, Nick stared up into the whirling snow as the storm continued its ferocious course. Despair spread through him as he felt the cold and pain penetrate his body.

With his free right hand, he tried to move the branch off his torso, but it had fallen on the decaying stump with such force that it wedged into the rotten wood. In desperation, he looked upward again, and prayed to God for mercy.

Nick felt sick and light headed as his mind grappled for a way to get this damn branch off

99

him.

He tried again to work his way out from under the branch, but to no avail. His mother's face flashed before him. She would want him to survive more than anything. He had to get out of this trap for her. God wasn't going to lift it off, but maybe He had given Nick the ability to figure a way out. His right hand slid to his rib cage, fingers probing to see if there was any way to relieve the pain. Nothing helped. He moved his hand to his pocket. His fingers wrapped around his pocket knife and a feeling of hope washed over him. He pulled the knife from his pocket.

Working with his teeth and his free hand, Nick struggled for several minutes before the blade finally snapped open. He picked a spot on the branch and began cutting. Each movement caused a jab of pain in his ribs, as he sawed back and forth but he kept going.

Time passed. His hand ached and he had to stop. He was shocked at how small the wedge was that he'd cut. It wasn't going to be easy. He resumed his work, until his hand shook from the strain and he was forced to stop again.

The pain in his ribs grew worse. His hands felt numb. He had to get free before he froze to death. At times, thoughts of Mellita filtered through his mind. It gave him hope. He went back to sawing.

When he stopped to rest, he reached for his last remaining food and ate it. He needed more strength to continue. He took a drink of the cold water from his canteen. The wind and snow had tapered off.

Glancing at his hand, he saw the blisters. It throbbed, but the pain from his ribs had eased slightly.

He went back to work, trying to apply more pressure against the branch. Shortly, he stopped again and saw blood on his hand. The skin had worn off and all that remained was raw flesh. He continued on.

Hours went by and he became exhausted and discouraged. He lay back and rested. He looked at his mangled hand and shivered. But then felt heartened when he saw that he'd gone more than three fourths through the branch.

It wouldn't be long before he'd crawl out of his prison, and soon after join his Company. He pulled his blanket tighter about him, but still shivered. His exhaustion became too much, and he dozed off.

When he woke, his hand throbbed and he was hungry and thirsty. He took another drink and stared at the deep furrow on the branch. Maybe, if he stared hard enough the cut would get deeper, but he knew it wouldn't. If he worked hard, maybe he could cut through in another hour. He dived back into the job with determination. His food gone, and maybe his life. With his hand numb and getting more tender with each swipe of the knife, he worked on and on. His strength ebbed each passing minute.

His heart leapt with excitement as the final slash of the blade severed the branch. He dropped the knife, and lifted the branch. As he groaned, it moved and one end slid out of his stump. He was free.

Chapter 29

Nick forced himself up-right and leaned against the rim of the stump. He stood alone, the only sound a distant trickling of water rambling down the creek. The beauty of the white coated surroundings wasn't missed by Nick as he tossed his belongings out onto the ground. He climbed down, feeling great to be out of his confinement and free to move on.

The storm had passed and welcome patches of blue brightened the scene. In spite of his raw hand and aching ribs, he felt good. God gave him yet another chance.

Nick realized the snow was too deep to use the bicycle. Dambach and Mellita were too far for hiking. He'd explore the area and find another hiding place near, or in, Hofen. He had to be cautious and remain undetected.

Nick scooped water from the creek into his canteen and took a swig. He refilled the canteen and plowed through the snow toward town. Food was his main concern, but he must stay alert. As darkness settled in, Nick heard airplanes. They came closer and the roar of the motors became louder and louder. They must be American - the Germans would be pounded with bombs. The planes kept coming. Even with the air noise, he could pick out distant artillery fire. It reminded him of July fourth celebrations back home. The end of the war must be near. He wouldn't have to look for the American lines because GI's will soon find him. It was bound to happen and he'd be free to head home. He visualized his platoon led by Lieutenant Kane coming down the street.

He crept close to a few houses near the outskirts of Hofen. One place looked dark and empty. It reminded him of Mellita's home. He climbed over a fence, being careful with his ribs and sore hand. Nothing stirred as he pulled a low window open and scrambled into the cellar. There was enough light to see around the dingy room. In one corner, was a huge pile of coal. He worked his way over it and slid down against the wall. A safe place for the night. Tomorrow he'd look further for a cleaner, but still a good spot.

The airplane motors kept buzzing overhead. There was no let up all night, and the steady small arms fire and artillery continued.

Just as he was about to doze off, he heard footsteps and sprung awake. A minute later, the light in the cellar beamed around. Nick froze and didn't move a muscle. On the opposite side of the pile, the sound of a shovel scooping up coal and dumping it into a bucket vibrated in his ears. Someone was so close, Nick could hear him breathing. Shortly, there was a clunk as the shovel hit the wall, and the person lugged away the coal and snapped off the light. Nick felt a lot safer in the dark.

The next day when no one was home, he sneaked up stairs and foraged around sampling each bit of food without taking enough to be noticed. He kept the same routine for a few days. Carefully entering cellars and sometimes kitchens, sneaking bits of food into a sack to eat later. Then one night he ventured out and spotted a beat-up American ambulance in a junk yard full of old vehicles.

That night he entered a barn with packed dirt as hard as concrete covering the floor, and a giant haystack on one side. He tunneled into the backside of the stack and made himself comfortable. The first thing that entered his thoughts was Wylie's hay fever. No way his brother could survive in this barn. How lucky not to have that problem.

Nick and Wylie used to play in their Grandpa's barn.

Nick remembered the distinctive scent of hay, cows and horses, mingled with tractor oil and maybe a little sweat. They swung on a straw-stuffed burlap bag Suspended by a long rope from the rafters, then leaped to a cushioned landing in the soft hay. The pleasant memories left him looking forward to someday revisiting the old place. In the meantime, this barn didn't look too impressive, but Nick hoped it would be a good hiding place.

Bombers continued on their mission to blast another German target. If he could hang on awhile longer, he'd be liberated by his own troops. Each night, Nick would sneak out from his hay stack and explore the area. He managed to find enough food and water to keep him going. One night he checked out the bullet riddled ambulance, and was surprised to see the key in the ignition. He turned the key, and the vehicle burped slightly and died. He went over to a smashed jeep and unhooked it's battery and exchanged it with the one in the ambulance. He switched it on and the motor kicked in struggling to run. Then it roared faster, he let it idle awhile before stopping. It could come in handy if he had to make a run for it.

During his nights scrounging the vicinity, he came up with more blankets and every imaginable type of food. It seemed as though he could exist indefinitely, but he was getting anxious to move on.

Each day, there were less people in town, The Germans were gradually leaving as the artillery shells came closer and more often. Nick visualized himself soon having the place to himself. The next morning the intensity picked up with more sounds of war closing in. The German military had taken off, and only a few brave civilians remained. White flags sprung from up stair windows. The time finally arrived, the Allies were near.

Nick went to his ambulance and drove it to his barn. It felt eerie moving about without the danger of being captured. Hofen appeared like a ghost town. The sound of war bellowed everywhere and shells exploded closer. It was louder than the worst thunder he'd ever heard.

The idea that maybe he'd be better off to get out of town struck him. He'd drive the ambulance with red crosses on each side toward the Allied Forces. It seemed safer than being a sitting duck in Hofen. He found a pump in a garage and inflated the tires. Surprisingly, the gas gauge showed half full.

In a cloud of dust he took off wondering which direction was best. He glanced in his rear view mirror and saw pockets of smoke and fire.

He started to turn left when what he saw curdled his blood. In front of him was a platoon of German Storm troopers, with clubs, goose-stepping toward him.

Nick stopped and slowly backed up trying not to be noticed. He watched as they took a left into an alcove. His right hand shook on the steering wheel as he tried to figure which way to go. It was time to make his move and find some GI's. If he could track down his old platoon, and explain to Kane why he disappeared it would be great.

Chapter 30

Blanche and Paul had read the telegram so many times it was nearly in shreds. As the days passed, anxiety heightened and they feared for Nick's life. Could he hide out until the war ended!

The thought of Wylie flying his P-47 against the Japanese was a worry. Having both sons in danger left them emotionally exhausted.

"That letter from Wylie scared the hell out of me," Paul said. "He could have been the one to follow his Commander in the second pass on the target. Please, God, hope luck holds out and both come home safely."

Blanche glanced at the letter, "Wylie is having mixed emotions. He's thrilled at hearing Nick's alive but so sad, his friend Jim McKay was killed."

"After telling the men so often not to take a second pass on a target, strange the Commander himself did it. A fatal mistake. Jim is dead because of it. The Commander luckily survived, bailed out and was seen captured by the Japanese." Paul said.

"Remember when Jim and Wylie first met at the Officer's Club. Wylie hated his guts. Jim wouldn't leave the ping pong table when Wylie beat him time after time. There was nothing Wylie liked about the guy. Jim kept hanging around Wylie until they became good friends and roommates. Wylie always credited Jim for bringing Sally and him together as pen pals. I'm surprised, he's so interested in her. He never dated a girl before." Blanche said.

"Let's pray we hear from both the boys again soon. The war is winding down and will soon be over. Thank God!" Paul said, as he put his arm around Blanche and pulled her close.

Chapter 31

Nick jerked the steering wheel to the right. The ambulance spun around on two wheels. He pushed the accelerator to the floor and the vehicle lurched forward. In the rear view mirror he saw German soldiers still goose stepping down the street. To his left he saw a truck, parked on the side of the road, the Germans were probably heading for. He thought they might chase him and hoped they had more pressing duties. He sped on and took a right at a fork in the road, and hoped he was headed for the Allied lines.

The road narrowed and curved one way then another, definitely not a main highway.

It occurred to him that the soldiers were going into the houses where white flags hung to beat the civilians. He wouldn't put it past the Nazi's.

After driving a few miles, he spotted the outskirts of another small town. A narrow cobblestone street angled toward the center square. Everything appeared calm along the way. He passed houses more frequently.

Up ahead an old man with a cane walked on the side of the road. Nick pulled over, opened his window and leaned out. "Do Americans occupy this town?"

"Nein. Nein. The Ruskies move in. You American?"

"Yes." Nick, surprised the old man spoke English.

"Trouble if no papers. Better get out."

"The Russians wouldn't arrest me! We're on the same side."

"Go!"

"Danke." Nick thought he'd made a big mistake leaving his haystack.

Continuing down the rough street, Nick was astonished at the ruins from the war. The little town did have an eerie feeling about it. Did the old man know what he was talking about?

At the next corner, several jeeps moved toward him on the side street. He made a U-turn, and started back.

He drove slowly. He sure didn't want their attention. In the rear view mirror he saw two small trucks speed up. He tromped on the gas pedal and hoped they weren't after him. Nick saw the old German he'd talked to before. The man stared with his mouth hanging open, no doubt thinking . I told you so.

Nick pressed onward. He had to get out of the Russian zone. In the mirror, he saw the trucks closing on him fast.

Out of the city now, the ambulance bounced along on the narrow gravel road. He slowed to avoid losing control. Then he saw a convoy of Russian trucks up ahead. He swerved and headed across the field. The ambulance shook like a log truck but kept up a good speed. Nick clenched his teeth. He'd get away if it was the last thing he did.

A quick glance in the mirror showed he had pulled farther ahead of his pursuers. "Keep on going, you old clunker, and we'll get out of this mess." The sound of his own voice calmed him.

Suddenly, the front wheels caught a ditch, the ambulance careened into a culvert and came to an abrupt halt. He threw the door open, leaped out and sprinted toward a nearby cluster of trees.

A burst of gunfire swept the ground in front of him. He looked back and saw a huge Russian soldier with a gun aimed at him. His heart sank. Nick stopped and raised his hands.

Chapter 32

The tall Russian scowled as he frisked Nick and shoved him toward the soldiers who stood with guns aimed at him.

Nick's hands shaking betrayed his fear, he stumbled along as if in a trance. He'd lost his chance to get away.

As he studied the hostile faces, his breath caught in his chest. He forced himself to stand tall and act brave, even though he felt weak enough to faint.

The big Russian in charge looked like an officer to Nick. He rattled off some words to his comrades. Nick felt his face flush when he picked out the word -- German.

"I'm not German! I'm American. I want to talk to a U.S. Officer."

The Russian smacked him across the face, and blood gushed from Nick's lip.

The Officer shouted at him, it sounded like, "Heine slob." He motioned and a soldier grabbed Nick, twisted his arm and pushed him into the back of a car. Pain shot through his shoulder. His free hand went to his lip. Blood coated his fingers.

A soldier climbed in on both sides of him while the one in charge got in the front seat with the driver. The car jerked forward and took off. Since Russians believed he was an enemy soldier, they'd probably kill him.

He felt humiliated sitting helpless between the soldiers. Could he prove he was an American? He should have hung on to his dog tags. Nick tried again to communicate with the soldiers, only to be cut off by harsh Russian words. He'd keep silent until they got to a destination where there might be someone who spoke English.

He peered out the window to keep his bearings. Why did he bother? He didn't think he could get away. The Russians had him cold.

They entered a large city, demolished beyond recognition. Very few structures still stood. An unbroken window amid all the destruction was a rare sight. Rubble had been pushed from the streets and piled against the side walls. This must be Berlin, Nick realized. The car pulled in front of one of the few buildings still standing. He felt himself jerked out of the car and pushed toward the entrance. He looked at the squat concrete building, and recognized all too well the hammer and sickle insignia that decorated the building's main doorway.

Inside he was handcuffed and shoved into a small room. He sat on a hard little bench, and wondered what was to come.

After what seemed like hours, a burly Russian with deep set eyes entered, and read questions off his clipboard, then grilled Nick in German.

"Ich verstehe nicht! I'm American. Can you speak English?"

"Don't try to fool me," the Russian said in English.

"I'm a medic for the United States Army. The Germans captured me. I escaped behind their lines."

"Don't lie. We know you are a German. It's obvious you're trying to act like an American to avoid punishment. We've been through this with others. There is no use in continuing your deception; you're going to prison," he said. "Now, the truth or your punishment will be greater."

"No! I'm telling the truth. Go ahead; contact the Americans and check me out. I'll give you my name, rank and serial number. They're no doubt looking for me already.

105

I'm not German."

The man only shook his head. "We Russians are not so easily fooled. Many of you Germans speak English. Those who tried this tactic first got away but they were the last to escape us. None of the others have been set free, and neither will you." He checked the last item on the clipboard.

Chapter 33

Alone, Nick felt a wave of fear wash over his body like a stream of ice water in his veins. He'd never anticipated a problem with the Russians. With the war ending, changes no doubt occur between Allies. How stupid to fall into this dilemma! The U.S. Government would surely come to his rescue. There had to be a way to convince his captors who he was. Discouraged, he still knew he couldn't and wouldn't give up.

Shortly, two armed soldiers came into the room and hustled Nick out into a waiting car. They drove off, and when Nick asked where they were going he got only silence. He gazed out the window looking for landmarks. He saw the blur of an unfamiliar landscape, but his thoughts still grasped for some hope.

After perhaps an hour of driving, they pulled up in front of a drab looking ivy covered building, surrounded by a high fence with heavy-duty barbed wire at the top. It could be nothing else but a prison. The thought struck a chill through him. How had this happened? He'd been so close to freedom!

Nick glanced at the guard towers with machine guns mounted. He was a prisoner, and had no idea for how long. He'd heard the horror stories of Russian slave camps. He prayed they were untrue. Nick struggled to keep his faith.

Stark reality, dashed his hopes as Nick pondered his situation. No one knew he was alive but his captors. There would be no inquires, no government feelers. He was alone.

"Out! Out!." The guard jerked him from the car and shoved him through the front doors. They directed him into a barren room. A tall, thin scruffy man in a wrinkled uniform frowned at him. Russian conversation flew in all directions but he could make no sense of them. An instant later, a guard pushed him sharply from behind down a dim corridor until he stumbled into a cell, tripped over a bucket and fell on his hands and knees.

The door slammed and Nick heard the bolts thud home. A brilliant light in the ceiling came on, bringing the room into sharp relief. He crawled across the stone floor and pulled himself onto the single rickety chair in the cell. He leaned back exhausted. Stark white walls stared at him. In the door of the cell, a small open window offered him the only view from his isolation. His world now consisted of a narrow cot, a small table, the chair he sat in, and a bucket for his toilet.

Nick leaned forward with his face in his hands. A harsh sob burst forth from somewhere in his heart, and he felt sick. He looked up at the ceiling and thought of his far away home in Washington State, a place he might never see again. No one knew where he was; they probably all thought he was dead by now. Nick glanced around the room. Perhaps he was.

Chapter 34

When school was out, Marilyn headed home. As usual, she thought of Nick. Her walk was a special time for her to daydream and feel close to him.

When she arrived, the same loneliness she felt every day gripped her heart. Would this be the day the Jordans would get news of Nick? Letters always took forever to arrive during war time.

To keep her mind occupied, she started reading for a book report. As she read, she reached over and switched on the radio. The music made it easier, and she enjoyed the love songs that made her dream of Nick.

The music was interrupted by an announcement. The urgency of the words grabbed her attention. Something important had happened. She heard the words "President Roosevelt" in ominous tones. Leaning over, she turned up the volume.

"Our President, Franklin Delano Roosevelt, is dead.

He died today, April 12, 1945. He was at his vacation home in Georgia when he was struck down by a stroke."

Marilyn, shocked, wondered if this would have an effect on the war. She caught the end of another announcement:

"...to administer the oath of office to Vice President Harry S. Truman."

Truman! Marilyn had heard little of the Vice President and now he was the new President. She became frightened as she listened to reporters analyze the situation the rest of the afternoon.

When her parents arrived home, she was still upset. Her father comforted her, and told her nothing would change. The war wouldn't last one day longer because Roosevelt had died. "That's why our country is so great, honey. The people run it, not one man like Hitler or Mussolini. America is a democracy, controlled by the people."

Over the next few days, Marilyn listened to the news. Russia was racing toward Berlin from the east, and the Allied forces had crossed the Rhine from the west.

The Germans were fleeing for their lives. Hitler had said, "We may be destroyed, but if we are, we will drag a world with us -- a world in flames." Now it looked like only Germany would go down in flames.

One day Marilyn had the radio on, and she heard the announcer cut in with another bulletin.

"Word from Europe is that on April 30th, with Russian troops only blocks away, Adolph Hitler committed suicide. It is believed, Hitler and Eva Braun hiding in a bunker below a street in Berlin died together in a suicide pact. We will report further information as it arrives."

Marilyn leaped out of bed and ran downstairs to her parents room. "It was just announced that Hitler is dead. Nick will be on his way home soon. Thank God!"

"How did Hitler die?" her father asked.

"He committed suicide. The Russians were closing in, so he and Eva Braun killed themselves. I hope it's true."

"I wish they'd captured him alive," her Father said, "He got off too easy."

A few days later, Marilyn sat in her history class listening to Mr. Allison ramble on about a boring incident of the past.. He was interrupted, to Marilyn's relief, by the crackle of the intercom.

"This is your Principal, we received word the war in Europe is over. The Germans have agreed to unconditional surrender. The papers are to be drawn up and signed in Rheims, France within 48 hours. General Jodle will represent Germany and General Eisenhower will sign on behalf of the Allied Forces. This is the happy day we've been waiting for. We'll have an assembly tomorrow afternoon to celebrate the occasion. Thank you."

After school, Marilyn ran home. As usual, she went directly to the mailbox. There was nothing from Nick.

Once inside she called Blanche. "Did you hear the good news ?"

"Yes, isn't it fantastic!"

"Let's hope we hear from Nick soon."

"I suppose it'll take awhile."

"I get so anxious. I keep searching through the mail, expecting a letter but knowing better. Even if he mailed one now, we wouldn't get it for a couple of weeks at least."

"We might hear from the government before we get a letter from him," Blanche said.

"Yes, that's true. Let me know the minute you hear. Is Wylie doing all right?"

"The last we heard Wylie is fine. We do worry though, he's got a dangerous job."

"I'll call you again, Blanche. Bye!"

The Jordans were thrilled about the war ending in Europe. It meant Nick could come out of hiding and the war against Japan would end sooner. But in Blanche's subconscious, there was a nagging distress signal she couldn't get rid of, a throbbing pain somewhere in her, like an emotional sore tooth. She wouldn't be truly happy until both boys returned home.

Chapter 35

The sour stench of food drifted through the cell. Nick stared at the ugly mess. It reminded him of the skunk smell in the woods back home. Closing his eyes, he sneaked the spoon into his mouth. Then gagged and spit the food out. He tried again, but couldn't swallow. He took a deep breath and forced it down. He felt sick but didn't throw up.

He moved to the door and looked out the tiny window. He saw only a blank wall. He looked around the desolate room. It was a dismal cell with no way out. Sitting in the lone chair, he grew sadder by the moment. He looked at the opening in his tiny cage. How stupid to get trapped in this predicament. He must force himself to keep active in mind, if nothing else. To pass the time, he'd think and dream of happy days, past and those yet to come. Writing poems for his Mom and Marilyn would help keep him occupied. Also, golf would be a good game to think about.

He probed his thigh, it wasn't as painful. His hand went to his lip, still tender and swollen. He wondered if the scar on his cheek would ever go away? His main concern was getting out of this hell-hole alive.

Part of a poem came to him out of the blue:

> Outside my window, a new day I see
> and only I can determine
> what kind of day it will be.
> It can be busy and sunny, laughing and gay,
> or boring and cold, unhappy and grey.
> My state of mind is the determining key,
> for I am the person I let myself be.

Nick thought about home and his Mom and Dad. They must be worried to death. Was Marilyn still waiting for him? Lots of questions drifted through his mind. His thoughts settled on Marilyn and their first date. It was April 17,'43. The same day he had his first trackmeet. A day he'd never forget. The exciting day began to reel through his mind like a movie.

Nick's last two months in high school became the most memorable of his school years. Two important events changed his world.

It started when the high school cancelled the golf season because of war restrictions. Without golf, his high school athletic career would be over, and the thought left him dejected.

Nick's neighbor, Jim Parker, insisted he try out for track. Jim ran track the previous year and thoroughly enjoyed the experience. Jim persisted in encouraging him to give it a try.

Nick ran a hundred-yard dash and came in last, so, he tried the mile with Jim and a fellow basketball player, Joe Martin. In his first attempt, he dragged behind five teammates. But in a matter of days, he moved closer to the front runners. Then, a few days before their first meet, he found himself pressing Joe Martin, the number one miler.

During the same period of time, he met Marilyn in his typing class. She captivated him instantly with her shiny dark hair flowing to her shoulders, and slate blue eyes that seemed to penetrate his being. One day in class the teacher rearranged the seating, and Marilyn ended up next to Nick. He couldn't keep his eyes off her. They began a friendship of gentle conversation.

One day, Marilyn asked Nick to a tolo dance. It hit him like a sledge hammer, he was so surprised and thrilled. It seemed from then on he thought about her constantly during the day and dreamed of her at night.

In his first track meet ever, Nick made mistakes during the race. He'd sprint, then slow up at the wrong time. He'd pass on curves instead of on straight-a-ways. When he saw Jim pass by, it surprised him and he shifted into high gear. At the home stretch, he found himself wedged behind the Aberdeen miler and Joe Martin. Nick pushed forward but there wasn't room. Joe glanced over his shoulder and took a step to the side. Nick squeezed through and went past them to win the race. Thrilled by the victory, Nick felt on top of the world.

Nick's mind shifted to the night he went to the tolo with Marilyn. The whole evening was so pleasant, Nick could still picture every bit of it like it had just happened. They hit it off great, and Nick looked forward to seeing her again. It was the beginning of a lasting romance. Nick talked to her every day in school and called her every evening. Her magnetism drew Nick closer and closer each day.

Nearby sounds brought Nick out of his dream world. The cell door flew open and a guard motioned him out. In the corridor, the Russian nudged him to follow the other prisoners as they moved down the hall. The group wearing German, French, and Danish uniforms, walked in a narrow dark stairway and out into a courtyard. The yard was a little larger than a basketball court, and the ground was packed dirt.

The sun felt good as he followed the flow of about forty other prisoners. He gazed around the compound. It was a place with no way out. Armed guards stood in each corner, and above were towers with mounted machine guns. But there was still hope, if he could convince someone he was an American.

As he walked faster, he turned his attention to the other men. There must be someone who spoke English. The guards kept the men moving, not allowing conversation between them. But Nick noticed some of the men whispered back and forth when not noticed by the guards. from then on he tried to make contact with someone by throwing out English, but without luck.

He felt discouraged as they were herded back to their cells. He hated the tiny room. Being alone, and not knowing what the future held, did peculiar tricks on the mind, Nick wasn't sure he could handle it. Each night became an endless bad dream, with memories from past and present all scrambled together. Like a person with a terminal disease, he longed for sleep but his mind refused the plea. In prison, a man lived his life in an iron cell, alive and dead at the same time, swinging between the two like a pendulum.

Chapter 36

Nick looked forward each day to heading out to the exercise yard. While waiting he imagined the words he'd write to Marilyn, if he were allowed to do so:

"My Darling Sweetheart,
I have been here only two days, yet it seems like an eternity. I'm convinced that the first thing that happens when one sets foot in a prison is a total rupture of one's sense of time. A second becomes a minute and a minute becomes an hour. So, when I say that I miss you and think of you constantly, it is because in a part of my mind, it has been a very long time since I held you in my arms. I think of you always and those thoughts help me survive this nightmare. I try to think that someday we'll be together again, and then it will be for the rest of our lives..."

His mind shut off, and later that day he came up empty in the yard.

The next day, two new prisoners showed up. One, short and stocky with a limp who seemed in his thirties. The second in his twenties with an athletic body. The younger one held back his stride to stay with the shorter man. Nick timed his walk until he came up behind them. He said, "Hello!", and to his surprise, the younger one replied, "Bonjour!"

They were both French, and one spoke English. As they walked side by side, Nick explained his dilemma to them. After telling his story, the whistle blew. The guards yelled and they headed back to their cells.

Nick found out their story the next day. The two men celebrating the end of the war with a group of French and American soldiers became drunk. On the way back to camp, they wandered into Russian territory. Since friends witnessed their arrest, they expected to be freed soon.

Nick's heart pumped faster, "When you get out, do you think you could do me a great favor?"

"If I can!" the Frenchman said.

"Could you let Pierre St. Croix in Nancy or the American Headquarters in Rheims know that I'm in this prison?"

The Frenchman vowed that he'd be glad to do it.

A few days later the same men passed him in the yard and whispered, "A guard asked us if we were all right. He dropped a hint to the effect that we'd be leaving soon."

"Great!" Nick said, his hopes soaring. "Don't forget me in here."

"No chance! We want to help. Good luck in the meantime."

"I appreciate whatever you can do."

"Au revoir, My friend."

The next day, Nick's hopes leaped when the two Frenchman were gone.

Time dragged and disappointment grew with each passing day. Would he ever be free again?

One bleak cloudy day while exercising, there came a flash of lightening and a blast of thunder. Drops of rain came down and he moved to the door where others gathered. Nick heard a quick shuffling behind him. A combination of instinct and reflex caused him to duck. It was too late, everything went black.

The next thing Nick remembered was waking up on the ground with a gigantic headache. A guard lifted him to his feet and helped him into the building. He entered a small sterile room where he sat down. A bushy-hair man with dark rimmed glasses examined his head. The man painted on antiseptic and bandaged the wound. Then directed him to another office where he waited.

Finally, two Russian Officers arrived to question him. One Nordic looking, with blonde hair, pale skin and blue eyes. The other with dark hair, and a wiry build with bulging eyes. The last one spoke English to Nick's surprise.

"Why were you attacked out there?" The man gestured in the direction of the courtyard.

"Probably because I'm the only American, and they know it. Someone wanted to get rid of me. They're still fighting the war. If I hadn't ducked when I did, I'd been killed!"

"If you're American, what are you in here for?"

"I was a German prisoner but escaped. I crossed into the Russian zone by mistake. I'd come from German territory. They didn't believe me when I told them I was an American."

"I'll talk to my commanding officer about you. Your head is all right. A slight concussion, nothing more."

Nick was escorted back to his cell, all the while fostering hope of being released.

As he lay there, he wondered who was the person that jumped him. He had no idea but he would be more aware from now on.

The next day Nick stuck close to a guard the whole time. There was no problem. He scanned all the faces but there was no clues to who had done it.

As the days went by there was no word on being released. He figured the Doctor's inquiry about him had been ignored.

It had been two weeks since the Frenchmen had left. Was he destined to live out the rest of his life like a caged animal? Would he ever see his family again? Marilyn would find another man. He'd miss out on all those dreams they had made together. It was difficult to breathe as the pressure in his chest built up.

Alone in the darkness, a tear traced its way down his dirt smeared cheek.

Chapter 37

The war ended, and still no word from Nick, the Jordans grew more concerned with each passing day. Nick's situation weighted on their hearts. He was listed as Missing-in-Action, and no new word left them fearful.

One afternoon Blanche made her regular stop at the post office. No mail from either son. Dejected, she made her way down the gray stone steps. A voice interrupted her day-dreaming.

"Have you heard anything from Nick yet, Blanche?'

She looked up to see Joel Pierce, their minister, standing in front of her. "Hello, Reverend. I didn't notice you. No, we haven't heard, and we're nervous. It's been so long."

"Sorry to hear that. I'd be glad to come to your house and say a prayer with the family."

"I'd like that, Reverend." Her voice broke and tears formed in the corners of her eyes.

"I'll call tonight and talk to Paul. We've had our differences, and I want to be sure it's all right."

"He'll want you to come. He's upset about Nick and we've been praying every night." Blanche smiled and called out, "See you tonight." She moved toward her car.

When Blanche got home, she called Marilyn and invited her to join them.

She told Paul about it when he arrived home. "We need all the help we can get." He said with a grin.

"He wasn't sure whether he'd be welcome or not."

"I don't hold it against him for kicking Mike and me out of church. We deserved it. After all, brothers can be a little on the wild side when they're kids."

"You could have made amends sooner, you know," Blanche chided him. "I'm sure he would have forgiven you."

"Reverend Pierce's temper isn't as mellow as it could be for a man of the cloth. He threw us out bodily and told us not to come back. We tended to take him for his word.

We were young and thought we knew it all, but things change. We eventually grow up. I guess, It takes some longer than others." Paul admitted.

A short time later, Reverend Pierce called and set the time for eight o'clock.

Marilyn arrived at seven forty-five. Paul, and Blanche chatted with her as they waited for the Reverend.

"How's it feel to be out of high school?" Blanche asked. "Oh, I'm glad, but sometimes I have mixed emotions about it. College sounds scary."

"You'll do fine," Blanche reassured her.

The doorbell rang, and Paul hurried to answer it. He greeted the Reverend enthusiastically. "We appreciate this, please come in."

They shook hands and the Reverend said, "My pleasure. I've known Nick a long time. If I can be of help, I want to. He's a fine boy. Hello, Blanche."

"This is Marilyn, Nick's girlfriend. Marilyn, this is Reverend Pierce," Blanche said as her eyes moistened. "She wanted to join us tonight. I hope you don't mind."

"Not at all! I'm glad you came, Marilyn."

They moved into the living room. Reverend Pierce took the overstuffed chair and faced the group. "By the way, how is Wylie doing?"

"He's doing fine. You know he is a fighter pilot in the Pacific!" Paul said.

"Yes. I knew he'd be a good one."

"He flies a P-47. A superb airplane, according to Wylie. It's the fastest plane in the skies now, and gets up to 49,000 feet. So reliable handles like a dream and its range is fantastic!"

"That's interesting, Paul. You don't hear much about flying."

"He wrote us a compelling letter on formation combat flying. He said it was tough, maybe the most difficult part of flying. You're constantly trying to hold your wing position. You're always moving the throttle as well as the flight controls. The idea is to hold your position, and it's not easy. That position may be three feet from the wing of the next plane. He said, one does what one must to hold that spot. Your very life is in the balance! You must stay in position. Get eight feet away in heavy clouds and poof your leader can be gone, and you're on your own to get yourself down. More than likely you are not prepared to do that, especially if your navigation or radio is out of commission. Nothing in flying is more dangerous and unforgiving as losing LEAD PLANE during thick clouds."

"Wow! If anyone could stick with the formation, it would be Wylie. He's got the courage to do what he has to do. I've seen that trait in him on our mountain climbing. I had him in my hiking group several times, Paul. He showed strong leadership when quite young.

"I didn't know Nick as well. He was always one of the best competitors at 'Y' camp. I'll never forget the times we took the group to the baseball field a few miles away. When the game was over, we'd make the kids walk or run along the road back to camp. Nick was always the first to make it back. He's a winner, and that characteristic has helped him survive. You can be proud of your boy.

"Shall we pray: Heavenly Father, Your word says that if we abide in You then Your Word abides in us. We can ask anything in prayer - believing - and it will become a reality.

"Delight thou in the Lord, and He shall give thee thy heart's desire. Commit thy way unto the Lord, and put thy trust in Him, and He shall bring it to pass.

"Today we pray that Nicholas Jordan be brought back to us safely. He has done his duty for his country, O Lord, and his family and friends pray for his protection. He is a special human being, created by You. Nick, whom we all love, is an inspiration for us all, and we pray he is returned to us unharmed."

Paul glanced over at Blanche and Marilyn and saw the deep faith radiating from their faces. He closed his eyes and felt strengthened.

The Reverend continued: "If this is not possible, we know You have called him for a special reason. In Heaven he will be at peace forever.

I now lift up my eyes and gaze into the face of our Lord.

He who has made the heavens and the earth and all the people in it has the power to help us, and I know that He Will. Praise the Lord!

"Thank you!

"In the name of Jesus. Amen."

There was a peaceful silence, broken first by Paul. "Thank you, Reverend. We appreciate your words. We'll keep praying for him everyday. It's been a long wait."

"I'll do the same, Paul. Amazing things can happen from the power of prayer. We'll count on it.

"I've enjoyed seeing you all. I'll keep in touch. If I can help in any way, be sure to let me know. Good night, everyone."

Later that night, Marilyn thought of the nice prayers the Reverend had spoken. She prayed for Nick, but her nagging thought persisted:

Where was he?

Chapter 38

Six months later, the dreary life in a Russian prison had taken its toll. Nobody had come to get him out. The French men who had been released earlier evidently had not been successful in contacting anyone for help. He'd been so sure they would. Frustrated, Nick let his emotions get to him. Drained of strength, he hadn't been out to the exercise yard in weeks. Fatigue left him curled up in bed most of the day. There seemed to be no hope. He had lost his will to live. Depression seized him and wouldn't let go. His dream of going home had died, and life had no meaning.

A noise drifted in from far off, it brought him out of his hazy babble of thoughts. His head whipped up. Fear shot through him like a jolt of electricity. His heart pounded so hard he could feel the pulse in his neck. He tried to think of what he could do with a brain that felt slow and cold, as though plunged in an icy surf. He heard a key in his door, followed by a grating squeak of it opening. Now what? There were the constant rumors of Russian brutality. He dreaded the thought.

A guard lifted his shivering body up by his arm and directed him out. Nick shuffled along the corridor wondering what lay ahead.

His mother's face flashed before him and he wished he could tell her he loved her. Had he ever told her? He couldn't remember! Probably not! "I love you, Ma!"

Nick stumbled as he entered a bright room. The guard caught him before he slumped to the floor. He glanced around and saw only dim silhouettes. Were these his executioners?

There was only silence in the room. What were they waiting for? Why didn't they kill him?

Nick jumped when a voice boomed, "Jesus H! That's him! It's Doc! Christ Almighty, Doc, you look like shit!"

The voice seemed familiar, but Nick was too weary to recognize it. The English words, however, brought him into focus as he peered at the blurred figures. The haze cleared and there sat a grinning Lieutenant Kane.

"Are you saving my life again or am I dreaming?"

"We're here to take you home, Doc. What the hell have they done to you?"

"They didn't believe I was an American." From a combination of enthusiasm and delirium, his mind was spinning. "I thought they were going to execute me or send me to Siberia. Nobody liked me, especially the other prisoners. They knew I wasn't German. Did the French tell you I was here?"

"Yah! It took a while to get anyone to believe their story. Colonel Walker called me to identify you. I was shocked when you disappeared, I didn't know what the hell happened to you. One day you were gone, and no one knew why."

"It's a long story."

The Colonel interrupted, "Tell us later. We need to get out of here before these jerks change their minds. It wasn't easy to convince them to release you. It took the support of General Eisenhower and President Truman to persuade them."

The Colonel spoke with the Russian Officer. Meanwhile, Kane took Nick's arm and pulled it over his shoulder and they headed out. After Kane helped Nick into the car, he climbed in beside him. When the Colonel came, they pulled away following the Russian escort car. Nick glanced back at the drab prison. What a relief to see it disappear behind him. He never believed he'd leave the place alive. Nick's old platoon leader sat next to him, and the Colonel sat in the front seat. Riding toward freedom gave Nick the greatest feeling of happiness that he'd ever had. Now he could tell his mother he loved her, in person. He smiled with a delightful inward surge of pleasure. Nick looked over at Kane's familiar handsome face. The nightmare was over, thank God.

He'd like to see his old platoon buddies again, but if there was a chance to go home, he'd grab it in an instant. His main thoughts were on his folks and Marilyn.

As they moved along, he looked at the bombed out buildings and wondered about Mellita. He'd still like to find her. But it didn't look like he'd ever see her or be able to pay her back.

Chapter 39

"How come it took so long to get me out?" Nick asked.

The Colonel turned toward him and said, "those Russians are stubborn, Jordan. It took time to convince them. They're wary of Americans and are reluctant to believe anything. We had to get tough; Eisenhower insisted we check this information out. They continued to maintain they had no American prisoner."

"When I escaped from behind the German lines, I had German identification on me. Like a fool, I hung on to it when I crossed into the Russian Zone. I had no idea there was a problem with them. They found the I.D. on me and nothing I said could change their minds. My only hope was that the French men would carry my message out to someone who knew me. Thank God they succeeded!"

The car bounced along in the rutted road that had been torn up by the shells during the blasting of Berlin.

"The two French soldiers you spoke with kept insisting you were in that prison," the Colonel said. "A guy in the French Army named Pierre St. Croix caught wind of it and wouldn't let it rest. He ended up going to DeGaul, the French military leader, who talked to Eisenhower, who in turn relayed the story to Truman. All that happened before we saw results. Finally, permission was granted for Kane and me to go in and find out what was going on. Even at that point, we weren't sure if you were there, or even if you were alive."

Listening in silence Kane said, "When you came into that room, I almost fainted. Doc, you looked a mess, so much older. But I knew it was you."

"Do you know if my parents know I'm alive?" Nick asked. "I don't. Do you, Colonel?" Kane said.

"We had no positive proof you were alive. Now we know, they'll be notified. We're getting you checked out at the West Berlin Hospital. Then, you'll be transferred to Rheims."

"Are you sure they'll let us out of here?" Nick asked. "Oh, yeah! They'd better, it's been cleared by the top brass," the Colonel reassured him.

"I don't trust these Russians." Nick said.

"Don't worry! You're a free man once we pass Check Point Charlie, and that's right up ahead," the Colonel said. "We've got all the proper papers we need."

"There it is, Doc! Right up the road!" Kane said.

The archway with its wrought iron gates was guarded by heavily armed Russian soldiers concentrated near the entrance. Rows of barbed wire fencing extended north and south as far as the eye could see. Nick tensed as they neared the mass of guards. He feared they might not make it safely through to freedom.

The car Nick was in pulled to a stop behind the escort car. A Russian officer in the sleek Mercedes got out and talked with a border guard, then Colonel Walker joined the group, handing them papers.

After listening to them and scrutinizing the papers, to Nick's relief, the guards stood aside and motioned them through. The gates swung open and they drove from the communist territory into West Berlin.

The United States flag flew from one of the buildings, and a chill surged through Nick. He was free and homeward bound.

"You can relax now, Doc, we're out of that hell-hole." "Thanks Lieutenant. You bring me nothing but luck." Nick relaxed as the tension melted away. He looked around and everything seemed cleaner and brighter.

The car swung to the curb in the side of Checkpoint Charlie behind a polished automobile bearing United States flags. Two Officers got out of the car and came to greet Nick. They grinned in pleasure as they welcomed him and shook hands. They referred to him as Sergeant Jordan. "I'm a Corporal, sir," Nick said.

"You've been promoted, Jordan. Right now, we're taking you for a medical evaluation." The Officer gave Nick a pat on the back and returned to his car.

When they got back in their car, Nick asked, "How's Branch doing?"

"He's home recovering. Thanks to you, he's all right." Kane said.

"If it wasn't for you, Lieutenant, neither of us would have survived. I couldn't believe it when you showed up today. I'm doubly indebted,"

"Bullshit! I just followed orders. You're the real hero, Doc,"

The two cars drove into the emergency entrance of the hospital. Huge round white pillars supported a roof that protected anyone from poor weather. Beyond the car, a sloped concrete ramp for wheelchair access led into the entry way. As they climbed out of the vehicle, Kane said, "I'm headed back to the outfit now. I'll tell the boys how you're doing. Come and look us up, when you can. Good luck, Doc."

They shook hands and Nick said, "I owe you. Thanks again." He got into a wheelchair, and a short-haired nurse pushed him toward the entrance.

Nick turned and watched his platoon leader as his car drove off. He'd always remember Kane for his nerves of steel in combat. Also, his kindness would never be forgotten. Kane's advice, don't underestimate the enemy and life is not always fair, would remain with Nick forever. There should be more people like him in this world.

Chapter 40

Paul Jordan, about to step out the door for his usual bridge game at the Elks Club, heard the Phone ring. One of the guys can't make it, he thought, as he hurried to answer it.

"Is this Mr. Paul Jordan?"

"Yes!"

"This is Colonel Joseph Sinclair, United States Government calling. Are you the father of Nicholas P. Jordan, 118 '0' St., Hoquiam, Washington?"

"Yes!" Anticipation lifted his voice.

"Good news, Mr. Jordan. We found him in a Russian prison camp, and as we speak, he's resting in a West Berlin Hospital. Sergeant Jordan is recovering from malnutrition but otherwise doing fine."

Paul's mouth opened, but no words came. Tears welled in his eyes, and he choked before words came out. "That's great news! We almost gave up, it's been so long, He's O.K., huh?"

"Yes, he's fine. We'll keep you posted on anything new. He'll be contacting you soon, I'm sure. Congratulations on getting your son back. I'm happy to be the one to pass on the good news."

"Thank you. You've made us the happiest parents on earth. Call anytime." Paul hung up.

"Blanche! Blanche! Nick is all right. He'll be coming home."

Blanche hurried down the stairs and slipped, covering the last few steps on her rear end. "What did you say? Nick's coming home?" Her face flushed.

"He's been found and is O.K.. He's been in a Russian prison. He's recovering from malnutrition in a West Berlin Hospital. Thank God!"

"How wonderful. We've waited so long. Wylie and Marilyn will be thrilled." Blanche's grin would last the rest of the day.

"I feel like we've been on a roller coaster. Emotions going up, down, up, down and up again. Maybe life will calm down. How great it is. Now, let's get Wylie home." Paul chuckled in delight.

*   *   *

Meanwhile in Okinawa, Wylie was preparing to make his last flight to accumulate the points necessary to be sent home. With the war over he was anxious to get home, but had to wait his turn. There were still flights every few days to ensure the safety of the postwar peace. So, here he was taking off to get in his final flying hours.

The weather was questionable, but after discussing it he was given permission for take off. When he got into the air, he wondered if he'd made the right decision. The tug of the wind bounced his P-47. Heading south he spotted a U.S. Battleship below going in the same direction. He looked to his right and saw the dark clouds moving toward him. The plane bumped and heaved. The weather was getting worse. He swung the plane around and headed back, visibility was getting worse by the minute.

Wylie got on his radio and called Okinawa. The operator yelled, "Get back now. The airport is about socked-in. The latest report says there's a typhoon building. Hurry."

121

Dark clouds made it seem like the middle of the night instead of one o'clock in the afternoon. No sign of the island. Where in hell was he? The storm turned ferocious as it smashed into Wylie's beloved Rain Queen, sending it whirling in all directions. He fought bravely to keep it under control.

The compass pointed north, but north could be anywhere. It didn't tell him where his home base was. He was lost. The thought of running out of gas and ditching in the ocean petrified him. There was no hope of surviving in that water.

The fuel dropped fast. Time was running out. He had to make a decision. He glanced out the canopy but there was nothing but darkness.

Wylie swung the plane west. His only hope now was

the Chinese mainland. Could he make it? If he did, then what? One more look at the gas gauge, it was low. He hoped there was more fuel than was indicated.

Where would he land? Please, guardian angel, I need help. Thought of Japanese soldiers waiting for him was scary. They could still be around in some areas, not realizing the war was over. He almost vomited as a surge of nausea gripped him.

For an instant, he spotted the ocean below. The plane wasn't bouncing as much. Maybe, he'd get lucky.

A flashing red light burst on above the word FUEL. The five minute warning signal. Did he have only five minutes to live?

Wylie's eyes strained, searching for a landing spot. A quick glance at the fuel gauge showed empty.

Below, he spotted ground but only rugged terrain. Wylie punched the button to retract the landing gear. A belly landing was his only hope. The Rain Queen slowed as the river and ground below came closer. A buzzer shrieked in his ears telling him there was no more gas. The sandbar by the mountain river was his only chance. Instead of his life flashing before him, his mom, dad and brother, were right there rooting for him.

He dropped onto the sandbar with a scraping roar that sent gravel and sparks in all directions. The P-47 slid and skidded for what seemed like forever. The plane spun around, and shuddered, to a halt with a loud thud. Wylie Jordan didn't hear the final crash or feel the sudden halt of the Rain Queen. There was only darkness and silence.

Chapter 41

Bullets sprayed around Nick as he ran for his life. He couldn't see the Germans but they were there on all sides. They were laughing at the poor Americans trapped and being picked off one by one by the sharp shooting SS. He sprinted on weaving, ducking, and hunched over. A burst of machine gun fire shook the ground near him. The vibration caused him to stumble and sprawl to the ground. He glanced sideways and saw the mines protruding from the ground on all sides of him. He was trapped, an easy target lying helpless. His heart pumping fast and body wet with sweat. A blow to the back of his head, jarred his whole being. He looked to see where it came from. He couldn't believe what he saw. The German prisoners from the Russian camp were standing there snarling at him then charged and began to pummel and kick him as he lay there helpless. They punched harder, and he felt a strong hand on his neck.

Panic surged through his whole body. He pushed the hand away and let out a blood curdleing scream, "Help, help, they're killing me." In self defense, he swung out.

"Sergeant! Sergeant! Wake up, wake up!" She pulled back and shook Nick. Then when he swung at her again, grabbed a glass of water and poured it on his head. His eyes slid open and stared at a pretty face he'd never seen before.

"I'm the night nurse. You were having a bad nightmare, and I wrestled with you to get you awake. You're better off awake than going through whatever you were going through. It's time to check your temperature and blood pressure anyway.

Nick found himself looking into the caring eyes of an older, beautiful woman. He liked her instantly.

"My name is Barbara. People call me Barb." Her smile was warm and sincere.

"If I were sick, I'd be cured just looking at you," he said, only half joking.

"You're nice. Are you feeling all right?" it was the most soothing voice Nick had ever heard.

"If I said I didn't feel good, would you stay longer?"

Her hand found his and held it gently. Nick felt the warmth of her kindness. He didn't want to let go, but after a long moment she drew her hand away.

She placed the thermometer under his tongue, bending close to look into his eyes. It was as though he meant more to her than anything in the world. He was enthralled by this angel out of the night. She treated him like a special person, though she'd never seen him before.

After taking his blood pressure, she said, "I'll let you go back to sleep. It was nice meeting you."

"Are you on the night shift tomorrow?"

"I have a furlough starting in the morning. I suppose you'll be gone when I get back. Good luck to you, and get well quick."

"Thank you." Nick responded, disappointed. He wanted to say more but was too discouraged to think of anything.

The nurse reached for his hand again in parting. After gripping it for a second, she gently pulled away and left the room.

Wide awake from the meeting, he could hardly believe the pleasant experience had really occurred. He'd probably never see her again. He'd never forget her, though. She was so nice, an angel named Barb.

When he woke in the morning, he glanced around the hospital room and wondered whether last night had been for real or if Barb was only a dream. But he knew she existed. Her kindness would never be forgotten.

"How are you feeling, Sergeant?"

"I'm fine!"

"My name is David. I'm your nurse today." He took Nick's blood pressure and temperature.

"That's the story of my life! I've seen these cute nurses in the movies, but what do I get? A male nurse."

"Sorry about that," David said with a slight grin. As he turned to leave, he said, "You're doing good."

Before he got out the door, Nick asked, "Do you have writing material? I need to write home. I'm not sure my family knows I'm alive."

"I'll find some," David said as he sped out the door.

*   *   *

He thought back to the surprise visit by Barb, the night nurse. He assumed she'd left on furlough, but then she burst in with a steaming cup of hot chocolate with a tall pile of whipped cream towering precariously on top. It was by far the best tasting cocoa he'd ever had. He wrote a little note, "Barb, the only thing better than your hot chocolate is your smile." He felt like he was back in grade school writing notes to the cute little girls.

*   *   *

When the writing material came, Nick stared at it, unable to begin. He finally pulled himself out of the trance and started a letter to his folks. He agonized over each sentence. Like extracting a wisdom tooth, slow and painful, he thought. Nick couldn't understand the reason, but assumed it had something to do with his ordeal in prison. He finally was able to tell them he was fine and would be soon heading home.

The letter to Wylie was similar, with many of the same words. It was hard to be creative, but he wished him good luck on the many dangerous missions in his P-47.

His creativity returned, as he spent twice as long with Marilyn's letter. He expressed his love, and about being together again. This time it would be for the rest of their lives. When he was content with what he'd written, he sealed all three envelopes and got them ready for the outgoing mail.

Nick savored the luxury of his time in the hospital. How different from the Russian prison. Here people waited on him and treated him special. The food was delicious. He ate every chance he could. What a switch from the prison slop. Colonel Walker checked on him regularly and reassured him he'd be leaving soon. However, Nick was enjoying himself so much that his original desire to leave had faded.

124

Chapter 42

With a healthy diet and good medical treatment, Nick's strength bounced back. One morning, Colonel Walker brought him a uniform with sergeant stripes. The time had arrived for him to leave the hospital. The contrast between his stay in the hospital compared to the Russian prison was dramatic. He had enjoyed the food, the rest, the doctors, and the nurses. He stepped out the door and a thrill went through him. This was the first leg of his journey home. Nevertheless, walking toward the car, his happy thoughts of home conflicted with the sadness of never seeing Mellita again.

Little dark round spots erupted on the sidewalk, as raindrops started to fall. His pace quickened until he ducked into the car with the Colonel. As they drove away, the rain blurred his last view of the old hospital. Nick fell into a relaxed, almost hypnotic state watching the windshield wipers sweep back and forth. It reminded him of home. He could hardly believe he was headed there now. He'd given up so many times. As he thought about it, he realized the strong bond with his family had given him the desire to survive that carried him through his long ordeal.

He focused his eyes on the drops pouring down. How often he and Marilyn had walked together in the rain. He longed to share those kinds of moments with her again. He prayed she was still waiting for him.

The rain eased as they drove through the city of Ulm.

"I can't believe the destruction. What a horrible nightmare for anyone to go through! I wonder if anyone survived," the Colonel wondered aloud.

"I doubt it, the way it looks." Nick replied.

Soon after that, they crossed into France and headed for Rheims. On the way, they passed field after field of gnarled grapevines clutching tiny green clusters of developing fruit and wineries that looked to be back in full production. Great bushes of broom grew wild, bordering the vineyards with brilliant yellow flowers on branching stems.

Entering the outskirts of the city, they passed houses bright with backyard gardens and occasional cypress trees jutting upward. Nick was in awe of the beauty of the French countryside. As they moved on, his attention focused on the facades were unlike anything he'd ever seen. He was surprised at the number of American soldiers touring the streets. "I feel proud to see our flag and all the GI's everywhere."

"Yes, there are probably as many Americans here as French right now." The Colonel said.

They pulled in front of their hotel and climbed out. Entering the lobby, Nick was struck by the brightness. Thick lush red carpets covered the floors, and overstuffed chairs and davenports were scattered in strategic locations.

Healthy plants and flowers decorated tables, and hanging baskets were in each corner. Beautiful chandeliers projected majestically from the ceiling. A unique staircase curved down from an upper floor.

With assistance from a bellboy, Nick found his room. He was impressed. It was a far cry from his former prison cell. The room was decorated in a sumptuous European style, with marble-topped furnishings. In the bathroom, he saw mirrors flashing back at him from all sides, as well as more of the dazzling marble. He glanced at himself in the mirror. His scar wasn't so noticeable but he looked older.

He stripped off everything but his shorts and sank into the softness of the four-poster bed. His thoughts settled on the memory of Marilyn's beauty. A picture of himself arriving home soon engulfed his mind. How great it will be!

Chapter 43

The next morning, Nick was whisked to an office where more briefing took place. Before he knew what hit him, he was on his way to the coast. The next day he boarded a victory ship, <u>The Gustavus Adolphus.</u> The small ship rolled and bobbed for nineteen seasick days across a stormy Atlantic to the United States.

Then came the unforgettable train ride from the East Coast to the West Coast. The scenery across the nation was breathtaking, but most of all, he loved the brief stops at small towns along the way. They were allowed to jump off the train for treats. Sometimes he'd get a candy bar - Baby Ruth and Butterfinger were his favorites, or cold pop, or a piece of pie. It was a freedom he hadn't enjoyed since before he entered the military. The trip was a relaxing few days, taking him closer to home with each station.

Finally he was back in Fort Lewis where he'd been inducted three years ago. The rows and rows of drab barracks were still populated with young soldiers, but the feeling now was so different from when he had arrived initially. At that time, he didn't know what lay ahead and now he knew exactly what to expect. He'd be mustered out with an honorable discharge within forty-eight hours. Then home and a new life with his family and Marilyn.

The next morning, after his last Army physical, he called home. He told his mother he'd be discharged the next day. She was thrilled. "Marilyn and I will come for you, so give us a call when you're free to leave. It'll take us about an hour or so to get there. We can't wait to see you."

When he hung up, his first reaction to Marilyn's coming with his mother was a surprise, but what at thrill! He tried to picture her lovely face, but couldn't. She must still love him or she wouldn't be coming.

The next day, he sorted his way through the red tape and finally got his discharge papers. Afterward, he rushed to the telephone and called Blanche. "I'm ready anytime, Ma!"

"All right, we'll be leaving in a few minutes. See you soon."

Everything happened so fast, Nick felt in a daze. It was hard to believe he was going to see Marilyn soon. How would she react after such a long time apart? She'd written those beautiful love letters for three years without fail. Now they were meeting face to face. The anticipation grew stronger as the time for them to arrive drew nearer. Finally, Nick gathered his duffel bag, swung it over his shoulder and headed out of the barracks.

It was a warm, sunny day as he walked down the sidewalk, feeling strong and indescribably happy. He spotted his mother coming toward him with a stunning young woman by her side. With a shock, he realized it was Marilyn. He felt conspicuously alone. As they spotted him and moved faster in his direction, Marilyn broke into a run. Nick dropped his bag and opened his arms just in time to catch her in midair. The force of her hurtling into him almost made him lose his balance, but he held his ground. He engulfed her in his arms as she wrapped hers around him, and they embraced tightly. She lifted her face to his and they kissed for a moment, until she pulled away to look at him and then kissed him again. After the second kiss, she said in a beautiful voice, "Welcome home, Nick. We've missed you so much."

Marilyn had matured into a gorgeous woman. Nick couldn't keep his eyes off her. His face flushed as he said, "You don't know how long I've looked forward to this moment." Marilyn stepped aside and Blanche, holding her handkerchief tightly in her hand, stepped forward.

Mother and son enjoyed a long-awaited hug. "You're out now for sure, Nick?"

Definitely, yes," Nick answered with a big smile. He picked up his duffel bag, and put an arm around Marilyn. They all walked slowly to the car.

When they reached it, Nick threw the bag into the trunk, and at his mother's request, got into the back seat with Marilyn. He looked at her and she smiled as her hand slipped into his. A surge of delight went through him.

Blanche pulled away from Fort Lewis and drove toward Hoquiam.

Chapter 44

Stunned, Wylie tried to lift his head off the instrument panel. His hand slid to his forehead where he felt a bump the size of a golf ball. The Rain Queen had collapsed around him, but not until he was on the ground and alive.

He heard voices but couldn't distinguish the foreign words. Strange looking faces bobbed about him. They'd be there for an instant then jerk away. Their heads were covered with peculiar hats and their faces were coated with wild hair. The eyes and skin coloring gave them away. He was in China as he'd hoped.

Wylie tried to raise up but couldn't seem to do it, until he felt the friendly hands tugging to help. He pushed harder with his legs and, with the help, pulled himself out of the canopy.

He took a step and stumbled almost hitting the ground. The Asian men helped him forward as his head throbbed. Wylie felt he was in friendly hands as they moved away from the crash site.

He glanced back at his reliable P-47 and felt a sadness. The old plane had carried him through many dangerous missions. Somehow, it got him down safely on an empty gas tank. It wasn't easy walking away and leaving it wrecked on this remote sandbar.

As he trudged along, his strength slowly revived. Surrounded by friendly faces, he tried to communicate without luck. The rugged terrain reminded Wylie of his high school days when he hiked into the Olympic Mountains to fish in Heart Lake. The serene beauty of the mountain water in the cool fresh air always remained with him. If he survived this ordeal and returned home, someday he'd make a marvelous return trip to the Olympics.

For now, he wondered where they were taking him. It wasn't long before one of the men pointed ahead. In the dusk, Wylie spotted a few shacks up ahead. Curious women and children came running toward them. They clustered around pointing and shouting at Wylie wondering where he came from and what a strange looking person. His air force uniform and caucasion skin kept them gawking and jabbering as they followed along.

He was escorted to a small one room building. Wylie immediately noticed the bars on the windows and the door. The weather beaten old shack must be their jail. Was he a prisoner, after all, he wondered! While he stood waiting, two men cleaned the one room place. The men chattered at him but he couldn't make out what they were saying. They continued to smile and nod which left him feeling all was all right. He entered the room which had a bunk bed on one side and a chair with a small table on the other side. By now it was getting dark and there was no light in the jail. They brought him some food and left him with the door open. He definitely wasn't a prisoner.

Wylie exhausted from his near fatal experience and elated from his good fortune slipped rapidly into a deep sleep.

Periodically through the night he'd wake to the soft tone of a flute.

The next morning, after a breakfast of rice, three of the Chinese motioned Wylie toward the river. They boarded a small boat and drifted down stream. Mid-day, the group pulled over to shore, jumped out and walked to another village slightly larger than the first.

The word spread rapidly of a United States Fighter Pilot being in town. Everyone wanted to see the first American ever to be in their area.

Wylie felt honored as the people swarmed to get a glimpse of him. They smiled and applauded as he walked past. It was as though he was very special.

The next day they continued down the river until they reached a larger town. There were more modern buildings, and the first English speaking Chinese greeted Wylie. Everybody seemed proud to have him in their town, and he was treated like a hero. The business leaders of the area hurriedly prepared a meeting to honor and meet the American. Wylie felt out of place but the cheerful smiles left him at ease. He enjoyed the center of attention that was poured on him. There was no longer a concern of getting back to base safely. These nice Asians would see to it for sure. Wylie thanked the Lord for these wonderful people. Was he lucky to find them or did his guardian angel guide him?

The leaders of the town formulated the plan for his journey out of the interior to Hong Kong and then to Shanghai. From there he could catch a plane to his home-base in Okinawa.

The trip to Hong Kong sped by like a blur and a flight to Shanghai placed him in position for the quick flight home.

While waiting his flight to leave to Okinawa, he walked the streets amazed at the size of the marvelous buildings and the huge number of people racing bicycles down the street. He had no idea China was so modernized. He glanced down and across the street and picked out a group of U.S. Navy Officers. He wondered what they were doing in China. He strained his eyes.

Chapter 45

On the ride home, Nick kept glancing at Marilyn reveling in her beauty. She didn't seem like the same girl he'd left three years before.

Marilyn noticed him staring and grinned back. She slipped her hand into his and gazed back. His heart skipped a beat each time their eyes met. He was thrilled by her enthusiastic response to him.

"I waited so long for you to come home. I can't believe you're really here. It's a dream come true!" Bravely, she leaned over and gave him a kiss on the cheek. When she pulled away and gave him a big smile, Nick blushed bright red.

"There were many times I'd wondered if I'd ever see you again. Especially when I was in prison. Thinking of you kept me going."

"Oh! You're a sweetheart.. I kept writing even after you were reported killed-in-action. I never gave up hope. When we didn't hear from you after the war. I wasn't so sure," Marilyn said, with a slight tremor in her voice.

On the way home, Blanche was content to listen to their talk. Her blissful expression and tears were testament to her happiness.

"I was afraid you might fall for someone else. I'm glad you didn't." Nick said.

"No chance, Nick Jordan! You're stuck with me. I dated two or three times, but realized right away you were the only one for me. The boys in my class gave me a hard time. They thought I should be going out with someone in my class instead of an older person. I ignored them, because I was in love with you. They finally got the message."

"The memory of what the soldier sitting next to me on the train to Oklahoma had told me, kept in the back of my mind the whole time I was in the war. He said, "If I had a girlfriend back home, she wouldn't wait for me. They never do." I felt upset about hearing those words, but I was sure you'd wait."

"Well," Marilyn responded without so much as blinking an eye, "that proves you can't believe everything you hear. There was never a doubt in my mind or heart about waiting. So, are you glad I did?" She asked coyly.

"Are you kidding? This is what I've been looking forward to, being back home with you and my family."

"Did you have a girlfriend while you were over there? I've heard about those German frauleins," Marilyn chided him with a smile.

Nick was caught off guard. He flushed and stammered, "No! I never had the opportunity." He wondered if his guilt showed. He'd never been a good liar.

Marilyn didn't seem to notice, nor did she seem concerned. He was relieved that his little lie had gone by unnoticed. There was no reason to bring up Mellita at this time.

Throughout the drive home, whenever there was a lull, Blanche would glance back from her driver's seat and ask a question. She filled in the silent gaps. Nick noticed what she was doing and appreciated it.

Nick looked out the front window and read the huge sign saying 'Entering Aberdeen'. He was nearing home now. Soon, Nick glimpsed the sign saying,'Hoquiam'. He felt thankful to be back home where he had grown up with so many good memories. What a great little town for kids to grow up in.

Crossing the Hoquiam Bridge, they followed the road down into the center of town. As they passed the Masonic Temple Building, he automatically glanced up to the third floor where his father's name was on a window. His dad was probably working up there right now.

They drove on through the familiar streets, getting closer to home by the minute. Nick would never forget the exhilarating feeling that surged through him when they turned onto 'O' Street and spotted his house. The home hadn't changed a bit, but to his eyes it looked like a jewel sparkling in a dull setting.

Nick's mind switched in a flash back to when he crouched low behind a tree hoping not to be seen by the German soldiers on all sides of him. With no apparent hope of survival, there was only one person he could count on for help. God always came to mind under the most dangerous situations. Nick prayed and somehow a miracle led him to safety, and now his dream is being played out.

He reflected on the poem by an unknown author: he'd read in a magazine on the homeward-bound train ride across America:

> God hath not promised skies always blue.
> Flower - strewn pathways all our lives through.
> God hath nor promised sun without rain.
> Joy without sorrow, peace without pain.

They pulled into the driveway and Nick smiled when he saw the basketball hoop on the front of the garage. How many hours had he spent with Wylie shooting at that basket? He glanced at his adorable Marilyn. Yes, how grateful to be home for good.

Chapter 46

In the garage, the first thing Nick noticed was the old familiar alder smell from the freshly cut fire wood. He loved the endless memories of the past.

The three walked through the back porch into the kitchen. Immediately, Nick noticed the bounty of pleasant aromas that filled his mother's house. They moved through the dining room to the living area, where the odor of his father's lingering stale cigarette smoke remained.

"How do you like being home?" Blanche asked.

"Fantastic! I'm going upstairs."

He took the stairs two steps at a time, turning right when he reached the top and traveled past the bathroom. Somehow, his room seemed smaller than he remembered. His eyes settled on the old radio that he'd spent hours listening to.

Marilyn followed him. "Are you glad to see me, too?" The look on her face was one of a child admiring a first Christmas tree.

"I'm happier to see you than anybody."

"Wonderful!" She said as she slid her arms around his neck. Nick leaned forward to embrace her and they kissed savoring their first moment alone in each other's arms. Nick's pulse raced. They were in no hurry to let the moment end, but Blanche was waiting. The two lovers walked arm in arm down the stairs.

When they got to the kitchen, his mother said, "Look what I've got!" She held up a lemon meringue pie.

Nick beamed and said; "Does that ever look good! Let's have a piece."

Blanche shook a finger at him in mock severity. "I'm getting dinner on now. We'll have it for dessert; Marilyn will be staying, and Dad will be here soon."

When they were gathered in the dining room over dinner, Nick felt strange, as though he'd never been away. The war seemed like a dream that never happened. Yet, he knew Branch, Kane, and Mellita were for real. If he doubted it, all he had to do was look in the mirror and see the scar on his cheek.

When the time came for Marilyn to leave, Nick offered to walk her home.

They walked hand in hand, just like they had in high school. The evening was beautiful, the stars and moon shining brightly, in the clear sky.

He remembered those summer nights before he went into the Army.

"Let's walk to Emerson School." Nick said.

"Yes, that would be fun."

They walked down '0' Street, toward the school. Nick was thrilled to have her beside him again. Shortly, they passed through the open gates of the school grounds. Without a word, they headed straight for the track. They strode along past the grandstand. "I remember the day when you and Ma were up there in the corner of the grandstand," he pointed. "It was the day of the County Track Meet. I was so inspired, having the two important women in my life cheering for me. I was surprised I broke those records. I remember feeling like I was on top of the world, and even happier I still had a date with you that evening." He squeezed her arm.

"Do you remember when we came here at the end of the dance and walked around the track?" Marilyn asked. "That was the first time you ever kissed me. I remember wondering if you were ever going to do it!" she smiled.

"I wanted to for a long time, but I couldn't get up the nerve." Nick said.

They slowed to a stop, and stood together staring into the empty stands. Turning to face each other, they embraced and kissed.

Marilyn rested her face on Nick's shoulder, and they snuggled together. After a few minutes, they continued around the track.

"I'm so glad you're going to school in Seattle. We can spend our free time together." She said.

Nick smiled, "Nothing can keep us apart. I'm the luckiest guy in the world."

After kissing Marilyn good-night, Nick walked home. On the way, he thought about how great his life was going to be with Marilyn. He could hardly wait to see her the next day. He started running.

He sprinted into the house, and found Blanche sitting at the kitchen table, smiling at him with a cup of steaming coffee cradled in her hands and a piece of lemon meringue pie next to her.

"I love you, Ma." He hugged her. "It's great to be home."

Chapter 47

Nick woke up and glanced at his precious old radio and time-worn chest of drawers. He was really home. It wasn't a dream. It was as if a new life stood before him. How grateful he was that he'd made it back alive.

Today, he'd visit his old haunts down town, and see Marilyn. Such contentment he'd never known. His years in the service were over, and in the fall he'd be in Seattle going to college with Marilyn. It was difficult to imagine but wonderful to look forward to. He thought of the many times during the war when he dreamed of coming home to Marilyn. They had to put their dreams on hold, but now they could begin again. First college, then marriage, kids, and a home of their own would be in view.

As he lay there drifting in and out of sleep, memories of the war stormed into his mind. For the combat soldier, the war was never over, it came back regularly especially at night as a vivid nightmare. Nick thought of his buddies who weren't so lucky. They didn't have this privilege of making it back home to live the happy life.

Mellita floated into his thoughts like an angel. He'd found her in the war and lost her so quick. She'd saved his life and he'd failed in his promise to help her when the war ended.

Marilyn was his first love and now he knew she was the only one for him. But he owed Mellita and didn't intend to forget her. She never let him down. Someday, he'd return to Europe and look for her. If she wants, he'd bring her back to the United States.

Nick hoped he could do the job. Sometimes the circumstances we face seem like Goliaths. They appear to be impossible. But when you confront them, you'll be given the strength to carry on, overcome, and maybe even help somebody else along the way.

Nick got up and began his first full day at home. He talked to his Dad and Mom in the morning. He listened with deep interest and worry about Wylle's dangerous missions against the Japanese.

Later, he walked to town. The memories of his younger days flooded his mind. First, he stopped at the YMCA where he'd spent so many hours competing in a variety of games and sports, especially basketball. He took a few shots with the basketball feeling more at ease with each one. It brought back a memory that was so vivid, it had played back to his mind like a record over and over. As a junior on the high school basketball team, we were having our first preseason game of the year against Everett, the number one ranked team in the State.

The Hoquiam gym was packed solid with local fans. The whole town followed the basketball team because they had done so well in recent years. Why such a small town had such a good record was a puzzle! But most had concluded it had something to do with the YMCA and Mr. Lovgren, the manager.

Nick had seen his parents arrive and sit in their floor level reserved seats. He watched his grade school coach, his doctor, and many other prominent Hoquiam people. He hoped he wouldn't make a fool of himself if he did get into the game.

It was a close game from the start. Half way through the second quarter, to Nick's surprise, Coach Huhta called his name. He was the first substitute to enter for Hoquiam. At that point, Hoquiam was two points behind and it was Hoquiam's ball out of bounds. Playing forward, Nick was down the court being checked closely by a Everett player. Walt Siden dribbled down across the center line. Nick ran toward him as Walt flipped the ball to him and screened. Nick dribbled twice and let fly a shot from far out near the center line. As he let go of the ball, the thought flashed through his mind that he could very well be in trouble for shooting the first time he got his hands on the ball and from so far out. He was wacked by the player guarding him, and lost his balance. Nick slid part way to the floor, but maintained his balance. The auditorium was so silent. Nick peered between players to glimpse the basket. The ball came down and twirled and spun around the hoop several times before dropping down through. The silence abruptly changed to the loudest roar Nick had ever heard. The fans had woke up and come alive.

The memory of those few seconds were so embedded in Nick's mind, it repeats itself over and over. Similar to the moments of near death episodes in the war. Those memories are always there, never to be lost.

Hoquiam won that game by two points and later went to State and won the Championship in 1942.

Nick walked upstairs in the old 'Y' and reminisced further in the pool room and game area. It had been so long since he'd enjoyed the place. He'd spent hours here while growing up and he loved it.

He left the building and walked a couple of blocks to the center of town. He went past the movie theater and remembered how he looked forward to going to the Cowboy matinee for a nickel every Saturday. Nick entered Nel's candy store next to the theater. He'd spent hours there playing the nickel pinball machine. You'd get three balls for a nickel and if you got so many points you would get five nickels back. A big deal in those days. He'd gotten clever at knowing how far back to pull the handle to get the ball to go in the right hole. Nick tried it and found he'd lost his touch.

He headed back home saundering along enjoying the view. What a wonderful little town to grow up in.

As he got closer to home, he passed Pete Ashenfelter's house. The memory of when he was twelve and he and Pete took their bicycle trip around the Olympic Peninsula came to mind. It was one of those once in a lifetime highlights that you could never forget. The two of them had started out pedaling from Hoqulam, and stopped the first night at a camp ground at Hoodsport on the Hoods Canal. We rode up the west side of the canal the next day and stopped at a State Park in Quilcene. It had this nice little creek running through it that intrigued us. We stayed there an extra day. Then, we went past Port Angeles to a camp near Crescent Lake. The next day we reached the Ocean, Ruby Beach. We played around the beaches for a day before we headed past Quinault Lake and got home that night for dinner. Thanks Ma for letting me have that great experience, he said to himself.

Nick ran into the house feeling terrific but immediately knew something was wrong when he saw Blanche's stricken face.

"Wylie's missing in a storm over Okinawa."

Chapter 48

With Wylie missing, Nick's homecoming took a drastic change. Paul and Blanche being devastated were in a sour mood. Marilyn was the one pleasant constant in Nick's life, and he spent more time with her each day. The instant they parted, a sadness swept him. Everyday, he wondered about Wylie. Where was he? Nick wanted to hop a plane and hunt for him. But that made little sense, where would he even start.

Time dragged waiting for news. There was nothing from the government. Three weeks after the notice about Wylie. The phone rang and Nick grabbed it.

"I'm Troy Meyer. I live in Centralia. My brother told me you haven't heard anything about Wylie. Is that true?"

"We haven't gotten a word. Do you know something?" Nick asked.

"Yes, I'm Tom Meyer's Uncle. Tom's a Hoquiam classmate of Wylie's. He called me from Shanghai; yesterday and told me he ran into Wylie on a street in the city. Tom was shocked to run into someone he knew. It seems Wylie had crashed in the interior somewhere and was working his way back to where he could fly to his base in Okinawa. My brother from Hoquiam told me, he thought you hadn't gotten the word -- so I gave you a call."

"What fantastic news! Thanks so much. What a way to hear about your missing brother. I'll take it anyway I can get it!"

When Paul and Blanche arrived home. Nick emphatically passed the word. Pandemonium erupted in the happy household and Nick called Marilyn to let her in on the marvelous news.

Two days later, Blanche, watched an official appearing automobile drive down the street and pull to a stop in front of the house. The car door swung open and a Military Officer, carrying a briefcase, stepped out and strolled up the walk. Blanche moved to the door and opened it as the doorbell rang.

They stared at each other a second, then the Officer said, "Are you Mrs. Paul Jordan, Captain Wylie Jordans Mother?"

"Yes! How can I help you?"

"I'm Colonel Rick Sanford of the United States Army Airforce. I'd like to talk with you about your son." He said, in a somber tone.

"Come in and have a chair."

"Thank you. Mrs. Jordan, you received a telegram a while back about your son being missing off Okinawa, right?"

"Yes."

"This is a follow up on that telegram, and I've been sent to inform you-- there hasn't been anything heard from him since the storm hit the area. It is presumed Wylie crashed in the Pacific, and is no longer alive. Sorry, I have to bring you the sad news. We want you to know we are willing to help you with whatever you need." He looked at Blanche surprised the usual cascading of tears hadn't occurred. He was amazed that her expression stayed calm and unchanged.

Neither had heard the car drive in but when the back door opened and closed. They both turned toward the footsteps as Nick strode into the room.

"What's going on?"

"This Officer just told me Wylie's dead, and I hadn't gotten around to saying, it's not true."

"Yes, a couple of days ago we received word that Wylie is alive and well. Probably back in Okinawa by now." Nick said.

The Colonel snapped open his briefcase and shuffled through the papers. He pulled out a file and scanned the pages.

"Someone has played a sick joke on you. Wylie Jordan is still missing and presumed dead."

"No, we found out a couple of days ago, he's safe. A high school classmate ran into him in Asia. He called his Uncle in Centralia and told him about seeing Wylie. The Uncle called us.

He explained how Wylie landed on a sandbar near a mountain river as he ran out of gas. Chinese people helped him out of the interior." Blanche said.

"If you're right, this is a first. Whenever I visit people, it's always a downer. I feel sick in my stomach when I leave their house. This time, I'll be whistling a happy tune all the way back to base. God, I hope you're right." The Colonel left with a wide grin that was still on his face as he drove off.

The next day, the Jordans received the long awaited call from Wylie. It was true, he was very much alive. He verified the near death experience and said he'd be home in a month. He added that he'd also talked to Sally.

Three months later Wylie arrived home, and the Jordan family was complete for the first time in years. Paul and Blanche were delighted to have the boys back and the worries lifted from their shoulders. It was a happy time. Nick and Wylie enjoyed golf together. Their competitive juices flowed strong as they battled each other in close nip and tuck games.

Nick saw Marilyn every evening and she often came to dinner at the Jordans. Their romance became stronger with each passing day. Nick felt Marilyn was the most incredible woman that ever drew breath and the most beautiful. They talked of getting married and having five sons for a basketball team.

But there were many nights, when the war came to his thoughts and the strong memory of Mellita persisted.

Wylie kept in touch with Sally everyday by phone. One day they couldn't stand it any longer and set a time to meet in Chicago. When they met, it was love at first sight. Wylie never one to procrastinate proposed on the spot. They made plans for a wedding in Hoquiam the next year.

Chapter 49

Nick worked the summer of 1946 at Hoquiams Blagens Lumber Mill. A tough job that left every muscle in his body sore. After the first month, he enjoyed the feeling of being in good physical shape. After work he'd enjoy a shower and dinner with the family. Later, he'd call Marilyn to make plans for the evening. It was a fun summer that eased Nick from the memories of war.

Wylie remained in the United States Air Force Reserve and the National Air Guard. He and Sally moved to Great Falls, Montana where Wylie was stationed. He continued his fearless, dare devil flying. While building up flying time to his credit, Wylie, secret from the world, buzzed U.S. Airfield's around the country. His object was to keep them on guard for an enemy attack. The Commanders of these basis scrambled his men and planes thinking an attack was in progress. When they discovered it was a false alarm, there attempt to trace down the person responsible failed. Wylie, time after time, outsmarted them and be long gone,

Also, Wylie loved to dive over Hoquiam tipping his wings and then speed back upside down. The whole town knew it was Wylie Jordan giving them a show. They loved it and seemed to enjoy the fact that they knew the pilot and he was a Hoquiam graduate.

Wylie mastered every type of Jet built, and rapidly was promoted to Colonel. Always active he developed an interest in ultralight aircraft. He assembled a kit and soon was learning the technique for flying one. His interest grew with each flight. Ultralights didn't need licenses because they were not officially regarded as aircraft. They were nothing more than a few aluminum tubes, cables, and some nylon sail cloth. They were driven by 20-30 horse power two cycle motors. The two seaters needed 6 foot more wing length, a 38 foot wing span. It had a lawn mower pull start or electric. Helmets and seat belts were a requirement. The pilot had to shift weight to turn, and use a foot pedal for left or right. There was a stick shift to power up or down. After receiving the plane from the factory, Wylie could assemble it in 30-40 minutes. His plane sounded like a flying sewing machine as he circled the field and prepared for the hazardous landing that was never easy.

His mind always working, it wasn't long before he was trying to manufacture his own. The hobby became a challenge that kept Wylie busy most of his spare time.

Meanwhile, Nick went on to college under the G.I. Bill, and two years later married Marilyn. Their family grew every couple of years until they had four daughters. After Wylie and Sally had six daughters, Paul and Blanche had ten granddaughters. Nick remembered the times he'd wondered if he'd survive to return home. Now, here he was enjoying each day with Marilyn and the daughters.

In the girls younger days, they would visit the Washington coast often. The girls loved the beach and digging in the sand. They spent hours working on sand castles and wading in a nearby creek. The whole family loved the fun vacations. Marilyn always dressed the girls real pretty and neat. The girls were perfectly behaved wherever they went. People glanced in their direction with approval. Mom and Dad were proud of the cute daughters.

Chapter 50

When Nick started at the University of Washington, he had no idea what he wanted to take. His high school buddy, Jim, thought because of his athletic skills, he should be a coach. His dad said there was no future in that line of work, and urged him to go into a profession. Blanche recommended dentistry because her brother Bill was a dentist and doing well.

Nick set up an appointment with a counselor. The man suggested Nick enroll as a pre-dent student for now and see how he liked it. He could always change if something else appealed to him down the line.

So, Nick started in pre-dent and then went into the dental school until he graduated as a dentist with a D.D.S. degree. Along the way, he hadn't been able to think of anything else he wanted to get into.

In Kirkland, they found a small house and thanks to a government loan were able to buy it for $11,500 at 4% interest.

Nick hired a young girl out of high school, Roberta, for his assistant. She turned out to be the best thing that ever happened to him. She was smart, willing and able to help the beginning practice. Later, Nick encouraged her to go on to the University of Washington, which she did.

Years later, they met again when she came to Nick and Marilyn's anniversary party put on by the kids.

Roberta was thrilled to be there and thanked them over and over for their generosity toward her. She presented them with a anniversary letter:

> Today marks a very special celebration!
>
> How fortunate are your family, friends, and business associates to be with you today and share your joy!
>
> I think of your lifetime of giving to others and enhancing their lives, contributing to your community and professionally caring for a host of patients while raising your four lovely daughters.
>
> You certainly made a difference in my life. You had the courage to hire me, a recent high school graduate, entrust me with your fledgling practice; and send me to the University of Washington. It was your investment in that training; the confidence you had in me, and the wonderful work environment in your office that

provided the initial springboard for me to be
successful in business and ultimately finish
college. I thank you.

Your generous caring way with friends,
patients, and family are an inspiration to each
of us. You are cherished and deeply loved.

Congratulations on your wonderful years together!!

Roberta

Roberta's letter topped off a tremendous and successful anniversary party. Her words were appreciated deeply by Nick and Marilyn. After the party was over, the happy couple read the poem Laurie had given them earlier:

ANNIVERSARY

On June 12th a happy day
    You can recall as yesterday
When as a groom and bride to be
    Some nervous joy your friends did see
Till down the isle Mom you danced
    And Dad so shy he didn't glance
Then wedding vows were sung to all
    Joy and love you do recall
Today we hope for both of you
    Just as your friends who loved you true
A happy life of love and peace
    Of passion that could never cease
And may your life together grow
    As God's own love that he does sow
So happy anniversary mom and dad
    We all love you and are glad
That on that day some years ago
    You chose each other with whom to grow
Your children love you. Yes they do
    And wish the very best for you.

Happy June 12th

Love -- Laurie

There is nothing more special than a poem from your own daughter. Nick and Marilyn thoroughly loved every word of it.

While Nick and Marilyn were discussing the fun party that evening, the phone rang. It was Wylie and Sally wishing them a happy anniversary. Also, Wylie was going to make one of his quick trips to visit in three days. He was still in the National Guard, so he would be coming in his jet. He would be calling them before he took off. They always enjoyed his wild visits, he was a man on the move. He couldn't even sit in a chair and visit. He had to be walking. They both looked forward to seeing him.

Chapter 51

Marilyn and Nick scanned the sky looking for a speck that might be Wylie's jet. "There it is." Marilyn said, as she pointed to the northeast. It took Nick a second before he spotted the dark spot moving toward them. "Amazing how fast he gets here." He called us a half hour ago. We barely beat him here." Nick said in an excited voice.

They watched as the black dot in the sky got larger, circled the field and came in for a landing. "He sure knows how to handle that jet." Marilyn said.

"He keeps wanting me to squeeze in beside him and go up for a spin. But I have no desire, I'm perfectly satisfied to watch my brother do the flying."

Wylie always checked the plane over and then signed in at the headquarters building. He'd schedule his departure time and date, which was usually the next day or on a long stay the day after.

Wylie didn't talk much but when he did you listened. He didn't waste words, no idol conversation.

Marilyn took care of the dinner, while the brothers talked about flying. "I'd have claustrophobia in that Jet, and the instrument panel is mind boggeling. I couldn't do it. Did some of the pilots in the war have a problem with fear."

"Your first aim is to not get shot down. Fear's a big factor, especially as the action drags on and on. The main thing is learning to live with it. Some can't. We call it LMF, lack of moral fiber. The fact is that as range decreases, accuracy increases. You've got to close the range. Some blaze away from afar, and he runs out of bullets and heads for home. And there's the one who somehow always loses the bird he's after in the clouds, or who finds the foe and aborts the mission. The time I was wounded and my plane was shot to hell, none of the others in my squadron had a scratch. It turned out I was the only one that dived down close enough to hit the target. I hit it on the nose but got shot up in the process. I was lucky to make it back. The others didn't get close enough to make a hit. The fear factor played a part. They wanted to get back in one piece. I was proud to have hit the target but came close to being killed. So, who is the smartest?"

"You were definitely the most courageous, Wylie. Fear was rampant with the combat soldier, also. Every so often, a GI would fall apart, begin to sob. Someone would console him, but it never helped. They would take him back to the rear, not to be seen again. The emotions left them useless for fighting a battle. I'm not sure if they sent 'em home or put the guy in a rear position desk job."

Wylie would go to bed early and then leapt out of bed before sunrise and take off walking. He'd walk miles usually picking up some type of treat at the store. Marilyn and Nick would still be sleeping when he returned.

Wylie loved to have breakfast at a Redmond pancake house. When Nick and Marilyn got up, they headed for Redmond.

Nick always ordered a hot chocolate. At this restaurant, they gave free refills on cocoa. They were generous with whip cream on the top which always reminded Nick of when he was in the Berlin hospital. When Barb, the night nurse, surprised him with the hot chocolate and towering whip cream. She had left a pleasant impression that he'd never forget. The memory of her triggered his mind to unwrap other war episodes. That night he tossed and turned, trying to fight off the tide of memories. The many sleepless nights he'd had was one of the reasons why for years he didn't talk about the war. Now, in later years it was like he had to get it out. He found himself telling war stories, and often noticed the bored expression of the son-in-laws. He figured he was talking too much about his experience and had better try not to.

During those wakeful nights, Mellita would come to life. He prayed she survived the war and was happy now. He'd told his family how she'd saved his life. How she'd hid him and nursed him back to health. Then smuggled food to him for months. But he never elaborated on his fondness for her nor anything about their romantic episodes. No need to stir up a possible problem.

He knew all along he was destined to marry Marilyn. She was meant for him and she was a fabulous mother.

However, he definitely was and always would be attracted to the sweet Fraulein who he owed his life. He could not forget her and she consistently showed up in his dreams to remind him of their moments together. The one nagging regret, his failed promise, still bugged him.

One cloudy Sunday, the phone rang at the Jordan's resident and Nick answered.

"Is this Nick Jordan former member of the 42nd Rainbow Division?"

"Yes."

"I'm Mellita Schwartz's cousin calling from New York." Nick stunned, couldn't find the words.

Chapter 53

"Do you remember, Mellita?"

"No way I could forget her. I wouldn't be here today if it wasn't for her. Is she all right?"

"She is fine, except for being trapped behind the iron curtain. She'd love to escape to freedom in the West. Her husband died two years ago going over the wall."

"Oh! I'm sorry. I~ promised to help her but never did. Didn't find her after the war."

"Mellita, doesn't expect help. She wanted to find out if you were all right. I've been trying to locate you for years. What a surprise when your name finally popped up on my computer when I was scanning through the 42nd Division Veterans Association records. She'll be so happy to find out about you. I'll send you her address."

"Thank you. I can't believe this. I'd given up, after all these years."

After hanging up, Nick dropped into a chair, exhausted from the news about Mellita. He pictured the beautiful young Fraulein that had befriended him in time of need. Now, she needed help and there was nothing he could do.

A few days later, he explained the complete situation to Wylie on the phone. A man of few words Wylie listened with his usual silent interest.

But a week later, Wylie called with his astonishing conclusion. "Lets do something. I've got a plan."

He explained his idea of getting to East Berlin by using the premise of selling an ultralight franchise to a communist business man. "Nick, I can fly her out."

"No way! You'd both be killed. Too dangerous." Nick realized the thought sounded like something Wylie would come up with. His brother was fearless and had the confidence he could do it without a hitch.

Nick tried to talk him out of the idea to no avail. He wouldn't take 'No' for an answer and hung up.

In three weeks Wylie called back with the whole plan arranged. Nick had doubts, but knew his brother usually accomplished whatever he set his mind on.

In spite of strong objections from Blanche and the kids, the plans went ahead on schedule. Sally and Marilyn, also fought the idea to no avail.

The process of obtaining required passports and the other necessary papers was started. Nick and Wylie put their heads together for hours studying maps of Germany and especially the Berlin Wall.

The dividing line between West and East in Europe runs through Germany. It was a curious thing that on both sides of the line, the people are Germans. They speak the same language, and those who were born in the earlier decades of this century share a common experience. Many of them can remember when Germany was a single nation whose might and power threatened the whole world. Free patriotic men like Nick and Wylie and thousands of others stopped the Nazi's for good.

The line is real: an 858 mile border strip of wasteland, barricades, and barbed wire. On one side lies the Federal Republic of Germany, usually called West Germany. On the other side is the German Democratic Republic, known as East Germany.

Nick hardly had time to think about the whole scenario, before he and Wylie were landing at the Frankfurt/Main Airport. They hiked through the terminal and caught a flight to the West Berlin Airport Tempelhof. Wylie hailed a cab and they sped directly to the Kempinski on Kurfursten-Damn, a very old but beautiful West-Berlin Hotel.

They were told that just the year before it had been O.K'd for phone connections between West and East Berlin. Nick couldn't wait to call Mellita. She answered and they both could hardly believe they'd made contact after all the years. They reminisced all the good memories of the past, and each could hardly wait for the soon to be reunion.

Wylie watched Nick while he and Mellita were talking, a grin covered his face the whole time. What a thrill for his brother! Wylie called Rudolph Haupt and made plans to meet in East Berlin to discuss the ultralight business.

The next day the brothers boarded a train for East Berlin, they left the Bahnhof (train station) and a short time later came to a clanking stop. It was checkpoint charlie and on the far right was the West Berlin police building on Friedrich Strasse. Nick had enjoyed the characteristic odor and atmosphere of the train even though there was an underlying fear of what was up ahead. Could Wylie pull it off, he wondered?

They pulled out their pass port and visa papers as uniformed guards came down the aisle.

"What's the purpose of your visit?" With a scowl on his face, the guard waited.

"We have a business meeting with Rudolph Haupt to discuss a sale of a franchise." Wylie said, knowing the East Germans were lenient with Westerners with business interest in the East.

"Very well." He moved on to the next person.

The train soon chugged forward slowly for a few blocks until they were further into the Eastern sector. The Americans for the first time had a good look at the 18th century triumphal gateway, the Brandenburg Gate and the wide vista of Uter den Linden.

The next stop was the Friedrichstrasse "glasshouse" the East Berlin Checkpoint. They were 'Behind the Iron Curtain' as they exchanged their passports for numbered slips. Watching as the slim blue books with their oblong patches of white slid through the slot into somewhere to be processed.

Numbers were called and people went to the counter, moving on after to the customs.

At last their passports slid out of the slot again. They went to the counter and handed over their numbered slip and the officer compared it with the part he had retained.

He opened the passport and looked at the photo, back to Nick and back again to the photo. "Thank you. That is all."

At the next counter they handed over their customs declaration, filled in and signed.

They moved on finally through all the procedures. Nick and Wylie couldn't help noticing the metal barriers and guards and the steel doors to thwart would be escapees. From the confluence of Leipszigerstrasse and Friedrichstrasse, they looked back at Checkpoint Charlie illuminated by bright lights. It was the opening in the Berlin Wall between the Communist East and the Capitalist West halves of the city. It looked like a tollbooth plaza: 10 lanes where I.D. papers were checked and rechecked by East Berlin guards to make sure that those leaving were not East Germans.

Wylie winked at Nick, they had no intention of crashing through the numerous obstacles. Wylie and Mellita were flying over the top for a touchdown and freedom.

Chapter 54

Nick and Wylie walked to a nearby cab stop and hopped in the first one that arrived. Nick noticed as they drove along that East Berlin, even though they had the colorful sidewalk cafe's, was drab compared to the West. The people looked similar but not as happy.

They got off in front of the "Adlon" Hotel on the famous street unter den Linden. This is where they had a room reserved for their stay in East Berlin. After sauntering through the Hotel observing in awe the elegant decor, retired to their room. They were exhausted and decided on a short nap for rest.

An hour and a half later, the phone rang and Rudolph Haupt was on the line. Wylie made plans with him to meet later downstairs and talk about the idea. When they got together Wylie explained all the details concerning ultralights and the information necessary for business knowledge in the field. Haupt got excited about the whole project and could hardly wait to move forward. "There should be no problem with the government. They were at a time when they encouraged outside business because they desperately needed foreign money to up the lagging economy."

Wylie went back up to their room and told Nick, "Haupt is hooked! We're set to go. I'll order the ultralight. It'll be a week or two before it arrives."

Nick contacted Mellita and set out with Wylie to find her place. As they left the "Adlon" with a city map, Nick thought of Wylie's ingenuity It reminded him of how the inexperienced G.I.'s out of high school outsmarted and out fought the precisely trained, war oriented, Nazi soldiers in World War II. Patriotism and freedom were greater incentives than whatever means the evil Hitler could contrive. He remembered how the G.I.'s attacked then retreated when overwhelmed by shear numbers and firepower zigzaging out of range only to return and eventually beat the so-called best soldiers on earth. Wylie was a perfect example of the American know-how and bravery that won the war.

His mind flipped directly to Mellita and all she'd done for him. How nice to finally see her again. He wondered if they'd recognize each other. Nick hurried his walk with longer strides with Wylie sticking beside him. They hopped a bus and headed to one area of town and got off and found another bus, being careful no one followed them. When they were sure; they walked toward Mellita's.

"There's the number." Wylie said.

Nick looked over the pleasant looking small grey with white trim house. "She's kept it up good." His voice trembled slightly. He grew more nervous as he got closer. Nick gently knocked on the door as Wylie stood behind him eager to meet the woman who had saved his brothers life. There was a shuffle of feet on the other side of the door and it slowly swung open. A long moment of silence prevailed, as they stared at each other.

"Mellita its been a long time. I'd almost given up ever seeing you again. How are you?"

"Not bad considering I've been stuck in the East all this time. Come in Nick."

Nick stepped forward and the two hugged for a long moment. When they seperated, he noticed her blue eyes and smooth soft skin seemed the same. Her hair wasn't as blond and she was slightly heavier but otherwise the same Mellita he'd known.

"This is my brother, Wylie."

"Nice to meet you."

"My pleasure. Nick told us, how you nursed and saved him during the war. Now, we want to help you."

"My brother and I have a plan to get you out. Are you willing to try?" Nick said.

"Yes, although it scares me. My husband was killed trying to slip over the wall."

"There's no doubt about making it. We'll do fine. Don't worry." Wylie said.

"If my brother says he can do something, I believe him."

"I want to get out so bad. I'll try anything."

"OK! We'll go for it." Nick said. He went on and explained the whole plan.

The thought of flying out in a fragile ultralight frightened Mellita, but she still was ready to try the escape anyway she could. Nick thought she was very brave not to falter in her desire for freedom.

They decided it would be safer not to see each other until time to make their attempt out. So, they embraced good-bye and Nick and Wylie left.

The following week the crate with the ultralight arrived. Wylie began to assemble the plane at Haupts field, and Rudolph watched with growing interest and excitement. Soon, Wylie tested the plane by flying around and landing with a bounce, to the cheers of Haupt. With each trial flight, Wylie was observing each landmark to be familiar with the area. He'd casually drift closer to the border mapping their escape route. All the while Haupt was so excited about his new pet project, he had no suspision of Wylie's plan.

In preparation, Mellita had shipped her valuables out of the country. The plans were ready and the time had come to make their escape.

In the middle of the night on June 12, 1971, Nick left the side door of his Hotel and headed for Mellita's house. Wylie had left an hour earlier for the airfield. Nick hadn't slept a wink, his mind kept flashing to the details of the plan ahead. If anything went wrong, it would be his fault. Wylie was doing it for him, there was no other reason. A loyal brother with nerves of steel, had only thoughts of success. Mellita; a brave lady with a strong desire for freedom. It had to work. The thought of failure was to dreadful for words.

He glanced up at the cloudy sky as drops of rain started to trickle from the sky. Perfect weather for the dark ultralight to sprint for the border. He peered around to be sure no one followed him. The streets were empty.

Mellitas place was dark, but she was waiting for him. They climbed into her car while whispering to one another about their apprehension. This was the most important night of their lives and previous confidence had become shaky. It reminded Nick of those moments in the war when they'd hike all night not knowing what lay ahead but fearing the worst. Mellita drove without incident to the airfield where Wylie waited. The two seater ultralight sat ready to take off.

Nick shook hands with Wylie, "Good luck. I'll meet you on the other side of the wall. Take care."

"You bet! I'll be there."

Nick gave Mellita a hug, "I'll be praying for you."

"I hope we make it," Mellita said with a slight uncertainty in her voice. Wylie and Mellita climbed into the plane and waved.

Nick watched the shaky take off and then got in the car and headed for the "Adlon". He grabbed his suitcase and stepped on a bus to the border. The tension and fear of going through the grueling steps again ahead of him. The process seemed slower than ever as suspicious eyes followed him every inch of the way. He gave a big sigh of relief when he finally stepped through Check-Point Charlie onto West Berlin soil. He didn't realize it 'til then that his shirt was saturated with sweat.

He sprinted to his rental car. As he opened the door, there was gunfire in the distance. Nick froze and shuddered at the thought that those shots were probably aimed at Wylie and Mellita. He prayed they weren't hit, but fear mounted.

He turned the ignition on and sped forward toward the baseball field, south of West Berlin. He hoped all would go well and the ultralight would show up as planned. All of a sudden, Nick realized in his eagerness he'd missed his turnoff. He found himself on the slippery Autobahn, desperate to find an off ramp. It was rainy and dark with little traffic that time of morning. Nick drove on for what seemed like forever before he found an off ramp. As the rental drove along, Nick hoped he was going in the right direction. But inside, he knew he was lost. He headed back toward Berlin hoping to spot the right area. The field lights were set to come on, so he watched for them. Wylie and Mellita were on his mind every inch of the way. He often glanced up in hopes of seeing them but never did. Where was he? Where were they?

Chapter 55

Wylie and Mellita were living a nightmare, both hanging on for dear life. The plane bumped and rolled with each gust of wind. Wylie secured his helmet and took a deep breath and let it out. He wanted the clouds but not the high winds and heavy rains. It was obvious this wasn't going to be a joy ride. He pulled back on the throttle and the plane lunged forward. Flying low to avoid radar but high enough to stay above power lines. At times he dropped too low before he realized his altitude. In spite of the difficult flight, Wylie felt confident and in control. Hoping not to draw attention, he flew away from the border. After a few miles, he angled back toward the Wall. The wind and rain swarmed around like angry bees. The plane was getting harder to handle, it leaped up, down, sideways, like a roller coaster. Wylie was having a difficult time trying to pick out the landmarks, he was so familiar with. He spotted lights in the distance, it had to be the Berlin Wall. He leaned back and went higher. A flash of lightning lit the sky, and probably their plane. During the flash, he glanced back at Mellita. There was fright written across her face. Her life was in his hands. He clenched his jaw determined to make it for Mellita and Nick. He thought about how Nick for years had worried about not fulfilling his promise to Mellita. Now that it was so close, he needed to succeed.

The plane, not that strong, was being hammered hard, he hoped it would hang together. Somehow, it kept on going, like his old P-47 did. If they survive, he'll name the ultralight "Rain Queen". The rain kept pouring harder. He kept pushing ahead toward the border. Time to shut the motor and coast over the Wall. He didn't want the motor to be heard.

Another flash of lightning exposed them to whoever might be watching. Two powerful search lights came on moving in their direction. For an instant a beam drifted past. Then to his horror, it came back and focused on them. Machine gun fire swept past on all sides. The first barrage luckily missed the plane. Wylie frantically pushed the starter. The motor sputtered and then caught. The plane lurched forward as bullets ripped at the dacron wings. Memories of the war when he flew his thunderbolt over Japan and had his plane riddled with bullets flashed through his mind. He made it back then, and he can do it now. He kept the ultralight zig zagging in different directions. He glanced back at Mellita again, and she hadn't been hit. She was hanging on for dear life as though riding a bucking bronco in a rodeo.

Another blast from the ground caused a loud popping noise. Wylie felt a jab of pain in his right shoulder but the sound of the motor stopping bothered him more. They glided forward not sure where they were headed. Again, a volley of bullets sprayed near bye. This burst didn't cause any damage, so Wylie wondered if they might be out of range. The plane kept moving forward slowly losing altitude. Wylie was alerted to the fact he'd have to set it down soon. His eyes strained in every direction, hoping to see a good spot. There was no sign of the designated field where he and Nick had planned to land. His intuition and experience told him he was too low. He had to make his move quick before he hit something. Wylie spotted a group of lights to his right. He leaned in that direction, it was his only chance.

****

Nick pulled into a gas station and small grocery store. He rushed inside and inquired about the school, and charged back out and sped off. Hoping there was sufficient gas to make it to the field. The territory started to look familiar. There was no sign of the ultralight in the sky. If anything happened to them, he'd never forgive himself. Ever since he heard those first shots, he'd been fearful for his brother and Mellita.

At that moment, Nick caught a glimpse of a dim light in the sky to the south. Could it be! The rain had let up, improving the visibility. Driving with his eyes darting around in the sky, Nick spotted the lights again. He kept going, praying it was them. Suddenly, he realized he was coming up on the autobahn.

The weight of two people took the plane down faster than Wylie wanted. Before he could think, he spotted a car below on a freeway. A memory flash took him back to China when his 'Rain Queen' settled down on the sand bar as his gas tank screamed empty.

Luckily at 3 A.M., there was practically no traffic. The car below sped forward and Wylie's experience helped him to gently angle the plane above it. If the driver looked in his rear view mirror at that moment, he'd be shocked and probably react wildly. He might swerve off the road and crash. But like most drivers, his eyes were fixed straight ahead not aware of anything behind him.

Wylie stiffened ready for the impact. He hoped Mellita would be all right. His legs were already running as they hit the ground. The ultralight hit with a thud and bounced three feet in the air, wobbled one way then another. It slid sideways and skidded off the highway and banged hard against an embankment.

151

Chapter 56

Nick found the on-ramp going southeast. The lights on each side of the Autobahn improved visibility. There was no sign of stars in the cloudy sky. The rain had changed to a mild drizzle. Up ahead he spotted flashing lights. He slowed as his heart pounded. If it was Wylie and Mellita, he hoped they were all right. He drove up to the scene. Nick saw the ultralight smashed against the side embankment. He slammed on the brakes and leapt out and ran to the tangled wreck.

Two men were helping the stunned Mellita from the crushed plane. Wylie with blood flowing down his face already sat shaken beside the road.

Nick rushed to him, "You made it, Wylie! Good for you. Are you all-right?"

"Yep! A little shoulder wound and a bump on the head, nothing serious. How did you find us so quick?"

"Just luck. I was lost driving around in a fog. I headed this way when I saw a light in the sky. It was you thank goodness." He left Wylie and hurried to Mellita.

"Are you injured Mellita?"

"No, Shaky and scared to death. Thank God we made it."

"I'm glad. I was really worried, especially after hearing those shots." He reached out to her and took her into his arms. She put her head on his shoulder and hung on to him.

Evidently one of the Germans had called for help, because an ambulance with its siren screaming and lights flashing arrived just ahead of a police car.

The Medic worked on Wylie and then headed toward Mellita. Nick grabbed Wylie's hand and as they shook, the Medic talked to Mellita. The two that escaped from the East were escorted into the ambulance and driven off to the hospital for an examination.

The policeman questioned Nick, and he clued the officer in on the escape from East Germany. The policeman's interest increased as he listened to the complete story. He took notes in total amazement at what he heard. Nick finished the interview and sped off to the Hospital.

"Why did your brother bring the woman out of East Germany? Is she a relative?" The reporter asked Nick at the hospital.

"Wylie did it for me. Mellita saved my life in World War II. I'd promised to return the favor after the war. I never found her, instead I landed in a Russian prison camp. She was caught up after the war in the communist sector. My brother was a World War II fighter pilot. With his training and experience, he never had a doubt about trying to fly her out. He's a brave and loyal brother to do it for me."

The reporter quized Nick for an hour, then flew out the door to get the exclusive into his paper. It proved to be the first printing of a story that spread around the world. In no time, 'News Breaks' on TV in most countrys told about the thrilling escape out of East Germany and the story behind it.

Marilyn Jordan and the four daughters heard the news first on TV. They were back and forth on the phone with each member of the family, laughing and yelling in their total enthusiasm. The girls knew their Dad and Uncle were brave, but now the whole world knew. They all looked forward to meeting the mystery woman, Mellita.

The Jordan's believed the publicity would fade, but instead it skyrocketed. The people wanted to know more about the whole exciting story.

Mellita became an instant heroine in West Germany. Her picture was in every paper and magazine available, and the world learned of the World II episode plus the recent escape out of the Iron Curtain. Wherever she went, she was mobbed and treated like royalty.

Wylie recovered rapidly, so he and Nick began their journey towards home. Throngs of people hovered wherever they showed up. It hadn't occurred to them that the world would react so enthusiastically to what they accomplished.

Chapter 57

Nick and Wylie bid farewell to Mellita, knowing they would be together again soon. The three had bonded into such strong friends nothing could keep them apart for long. It was a mutual admiration that would last forever. Mellita appreciated their bravery and her freedom. They in turn owed her for World War II. Nick was exuberant that his promise to her had been fulfilled.

Mellita promised to visit them in America soon. Nick and Wylie both hugged her good bye before they departed.

"Looking forward to your visit. Make it soon." Nick said.

"I want to meet Marilyn and your daughters. See you next month, probably."

Wylie and Nick arrived back to the United States, and were shocked by the amount of money being offered for movie, book, tabloid, and TV Rights. When the brothers executed the escape plan for Mellita, there was no thought of monetary reward. So, what a surprise to be returning home millionaires.

A month and a half later, Nick, Marilyn and daughter Jane drove to Sea-Tac Airport for Mellita's arrival from Europe. They spotted her coming out the ramp with a handsome young man beside her. The Jordans greeted her with hugs and happily welcomed her to the State of Washington.

Mellita smiling acknowledged everyone, then said, "This is my eldest son, Rudolph Nicholas Schott." After a moment of hesitation, she went on, "He is your son, Nick."

Marilyn looked at Nick as the color drained from his face. Nick caught her glance and flushed. "You're not kidding!" Nick said.

"No, really."

Nick stared at Rudolph. "I've always wanted a son."

He moved toward Schott and they embraced. "This is so neat, what a surprise. I can't believe it."

"Hello, dad. I'm proud to be your son."

"I'm happy to be your father. How great it is! This is my wife Marilyn and daughter Jane. You have four sisters, Nancy, Lisa, Laurie and Jane."

"Your mother saved our daddy. If she hadn't, we wouldn't be here today and neither would you. Welcome to the family -- brother Rudi." Jane said.

Nick beamed with pride, his ultimate dream come true. He thought about the many times he came close to being killed. How lucky to have lived to enjoy this life.

Paul Jordan passed away from multiple myeloma at a young age, leaving Blanche a widow. After two more years in Hoquiam, she moved to Napa, California where she was raised. A beautiful sunny area with fields of grapes surrounding the pleasant city.

Blanche remarried two years later, and continued her active life. She won the Napa Valley Country Club's, Women's Championship several times, and built friendships that made for a happy long life. She played bridge regularly, and did volunteer work once a week at the Community Project thrift shop. Every Christmas she traveled to Nick's house for a three week visit. When she's home in Napa, Nick and Wylie each call her on the phone at least twice a week.

Wylie and Sally settled in Tucson, Arizona, where the warm sun seemed to always shine. Wylie played golf in the morning, shooting his age or better regularly. Some of their daughters settled near them, and others were spread around the country. Wylie and Nick kept in regular contact by phone.

Nick and Marilyn moved to Kirkland, across Lake Washington from Seattle. Their four daughters settled in the area, Nancy in Redmond, Lisa in Kirkland, Laurie in Bellevue and Janie in Bothell. The girls and grandchildren have fun visits with Nick and Marilyn frequently. The four sisters plan weekend trips several times a year to get off by themselves. They each look forward to the enjoyment spent bonding with their siblings.

Nick's son, Rudolph Schott, met a charming girl in a computer class at Bellevue Community College. After dating regularly for a year, he asked her to marry him and she accepted. Rudolph found a job in Olympia working with computers. Mellita found work as a designer in a florist shop not far from where Rudi worked. After being employed there for six months, the owner, Adam, presented her with an engagement ring. Adam was a pleasant gentleman that kept Mellita happy.

Mellita and Rudi, a big part of the Jordan family, attended every function possible. There was a strong bond between Nick and Mellita that brought a closeness between all of them. Nick loved his new found son, and they frequently met to attend and enjoy special sporting events.

Meanwhile, Nick made plans for a family reunion.

Wylie and Sally set up a trip from Tucson to Kirkland. Wylie had yet to meet Rudolph, and Sally wanted to meet both Mellita and Rudi.

One afternoon Nick and Marilyn picked them up at Sea-Tac Airport. In the car, Marilyn and Sally sat in the back seat talking and laughing all the way. They always enjoyed their time together.

Nick and Marilyn were always amazed at how pen pals between strangers could turn out to be such a perfect match. They, also, had produced the sweetest and prettiest daughters imaginable. Somehow, it was a match made in Heaven.

An hour later, Rudi and Mellita arrived from their hour and a half drive from Olympia.

"Rudi, this is your Uncle Wylie, and Mellita this is Sally." Marilyn said, as they entered the front door. After the introductions and small talk about their trips, Mellita said, "Rudi has always been interested in flying. He was thrilled to find out his Uncle was a fighter pilot. I'm sure he'd like to hear about it, Wylie.

"Anything special you'd like to hear, Rudi?"

"How about the procedure you follow when you take off and fly the jet."

"Oh! First I'd talk to the crew chief. Then I'd investigate the plane to make certain everything is satisfactory. Once I get in the cockpit and strap myself in, and the engine is whining, I look over the instrument reading. Then signal for the shocks to be removed and begin talking with ground control and the tower. I close the canopy. Once cleared to take off, we light up the afterburner, speed build up at a high rate. We lift the nose up and the bird goes into the air. I bring up the landing gear and turn out of traffic, cut the burner and head into the stratosphere.

I was super trained not to run into other planes, I head for where I intended. I can practice some maneuver, skim above a layer of clouds or go under clouds or go in and out of whatever clouds you want to have fun with. I have options to look over lakes and mountains, the choice is limitless. I often flew straight up or dived straight down for enjoyment. I could fly supersonic speeds but usually don't.

Most will never know the danger and pressure of hanging on someone else's wing during heavy weather and at night. It is another world, very dangerous indeed.

A fighter plane has only so much fuel - not like an airliner. Not much in the world is as troublesome as when you have made an instrument approach only to hear a guy on the radio say, "Our field is closed." I would rather eject out of a burning jet fighter than have to go to an alternate field at night with your fuel low.

It is a thrill to get the fighter into position to land and maneuver it on to a touchdown with speeds far above anything in automobile traffic. It is great fun."

"Thanks, Uncle Wylie that was interesting."

"My pleasure. Call me, Wylie. I'll bet it's time to eat now."

"We've got reservations down on the Kirkland waterfront at Anthony's Homeport. We can head out in a half hour." Nick said.

During their dinner they all commented on the beautiful view. Birds dived here and there and all sizes and types of boats drew their attention. Across the lake you could see Seattle's skyline. They all enjoyed the tasty meal.

Marilyn and Sally giggled often and Mellita seemed to enjoy their laughter with a perpetual smile on her face. Rudi kept glancing proudly at his new found relatives.

"When we get back to the house, why don't you tell Rudi about how an enemy became your best friend?" Nick said glancing at Wylie.

"If he wants to hear it, I would be glad to."

"Yes,it sounds interesting," Rudi said.

Content with full stomachs, the group arrived at Nick's and Marilyn's house. Shortly thereafter, Wylie started his story for Rudi.

"I was a 20 year old pilot graduate and second Lieutenant in the Army Air Corp. It was almost a blur. They teach you to do a lot of maneuvers, then night flying and some instrument flying. My greatest skill finally showed, when they graded us on how well and how short we could land after going over a fence. At last we could use initiative and talent if we had any. I made it with no problem.

Then some P-40 training at Matagorda Island off of Texas. Then they shipped me to P-47 flying in Bruning, Nebraska. The air base was "FIRST CLASS" with lots of P-47s and many many personnel. The very first night there; being an officer I wandered over to the Officer's Club.

I looked in at the huge dining room. The entire club was totally full of people. I walked around a bit~I found a game room. Men playing ping-pong. A game which I was very familiar. I watched the games, and realized that the way it worked was when someone lost a game, the person who was next in line played the winner. I got in line to play. When my turn finally came up, I won the game. Then played the man who was next, and beat him. I had a good back hand and forehand. What I had over most anyone was 'Defense' My brother Nick taught me that before the war. Anyway another player faced off with me. This guy was obviously extremely cocky, egotistical, ultra flamboyant, good looking, husky, a fine athlete - dark wavy hair. He had a friend with him. I won the game. But instead of him going to the end of the line like every loser does, he stayed at the table, insisting on playing me again. Obviously he figured he could beat me. The next game was on. Another great game but even with his flamboyant confidence and talent my defense killed him again. I won. This guy refused to leave the table. The whole room was packed. Everyone knew what was going on. I should have insisted he leave the table. But on my first day on the base. We played again, I won. My opponent was not a happy man. In fact, he was down right mad. He and his buddy did leave the table. I played another game, lost and went back to the barracks in a somber mood. Apparently having made an enemy on my very first night there. Time went on. I soon found out my enemy and his friend were in the same class as I. Along with many others, learning to fly the P-47. In flying fighters you soon learn a lot. You find out who is an excellent pilot, who is average, who is poor. It is a fact. Both Jim, my enemy, and his friend were from Washington D.C.. They had funny accents especially his friend Bill. I don't hold a grudge and apparently neither did Jim. In time Jim and I had built respect for each other.

We were sent to Dalhart, Texas for more flying. The squadron commander had been in combat in Italy. He called us all together in the hanger for a meeting. "Boys we are all going to combat together. There is one axiom we will go by and never ever vary off of that; never make two passes at the same ground target. It is that simple. Don't you ever do it." A few weeks later the C.O., again calls us together and gives us the exact same speech. It makes sense, if we go back a second time, the ground gunners will be ready and waiting.

My old enemy Jim, requested at Dalhart that he and I be roommates - and we were. Later on our squadron arrived on Ie Shima. We had our planes and we flew them there.

A month earlier Jim had asked me if I would write to his girl friends, girl friend? I had said "Yes" if she would write first. So, anyway the next day on Ie Shima, the schedule would be posted on a telephone pole just who would be on the very first mission; up to an Island north of us, "Amamio Shima". Probably like a practice mission. Certainly nothing like going to Yokohama, Tokyo or Osaka. Then it was posted. Jim would be on it. The Commanding Officer would lead the mission. The Operation Officer and more pilots were scheduled but not me. The rest of us did not attend the briefing, but we heard them take off real early. We waited hours so as to find out how it went. We got the report in total. The Squadron Commander had made one pass at the building, circled around and made pass number two with the other 15 planes. As such, the C.O. and the Ops. Officer and another were shot down. Jim, also, went down and was killed. A PBY rescue plane fished Jim's body out of the water.

That afternoon when we had mail call. My first letter from Washington D.C. (Sally) arrived. I sat down and wrote to her that Jim had been killed. Sally had known Jim before, too. I didn't expect the letter and information to go through, as most mail is censured. But the letter went through without a hitch. Sally felt obliged to tell Jim's girlfriend, as they worked at the same place. I don't know who informed Jim's Mom. When the war ended, the Commanding Officer and Ops. Officer were rescued as they had been captured and were P.O.W.s.

After the war, Sally and I met in Chicago. A few months later we got married in Hoquiam. What a wonderful wife I got. Six daughters and grandchildren on the way.

Did you know an enemy can later become your very best friend. It happened to me, and of course never make two passes on a ground target.

Chapter 58

The four daughters joined the group to get better acquainted with Melitta and Rudi. It was exciting for them to talk with the woman who saved their Dad's life, and to meet their handsome half brother. The pretty girls mingled around the room talking to each person.

Nick mixed a variety of drinks for all, and then gave a toast in honor of Melitta for saving his life during the war. "Without her diligent effort to help me, I wouldn't have made it home. She scrounged up food that tasted awfully good to me. She put up with me when I hallucinated with fever. You name it, she did it. But the greatest thing that came from my stay in her house was Rudi.

We're all so fortunate to have him. God bless Mellita and Rudi." Nick held his glass high, then drank his champagne in one gulp. He put his glass down and walked over to Mellita and hugged her tightly and kissed her cheek. Everyone in the room followed Nick's lead and did the same. Mellita was thrilled by the honor. Rudi observing it all grinned the whole time.

They all participated in friendly conversation for a couple of hours enjoying the time together. When most had left for home, there was a moment where Mellita and Nick found themselves alone for the first time. Nick stared across the room at her, she stood motionless unable to speak as her eyes met his. He moved toward her and took her in his arms. They hung together and Nick gently kissed her cheek. "Mellita, you are my very best friend and you always will be."

The next morning, to keep Wylie happy, they headed for the Redmond Pancake House. Half way through the breakfast, Sally asked Mellita about her first husband, "How did you meet him?"

"He was the son of a German Field Marshal that my mother worked for. I had met him several times. Helmut and I were both caught in the Russian sector when the war ended. Later on, we ran into each other in East Berlin. He asked me to dinner and our romance began. I was pregnant with Rudi but it didn't matter to him. I had given up on ever seeing Nick. We eventually married and had our own children." Mellita stopped as she put a bite of bacon waffle in her mouth.

Rudi took over the story while Mellita worked on her breakfast. "Helmut was a good step father. He'd been a soldier in the German army. His dad was a Field Marshal and a good friend of my grandmother. Dad was upset about the life in East Germany. One day he made a break over the Wall. He'd planned on getting Mom out later but it didn't happen. Fortunately, us kid's were allowed to visit grandmother in the West, and Mother had us stay there. We didn't like leaving her but there was nothing we could do."

"You said, Helmut, a son of a Field Marshal!" Nick said.

"Yes. Helmut von Schott my step father."

"I met a man by that name the first night I left Mellita's house in Dambach. In fact, I saved his life. He was a German soldier riding a motorcycle. He was headed for Hofen when he spun out on the ice. I was hiding in the brush watching when it happened right in front of me. The cycle landed right on top of him. He was badly hurt with a gash in his thigh that severed an artery. Lucky for him I was a Medic and knew how to treat him or he would have died right there."

"That was my Dad, he told us about the incident. He said an American saved his life. I guess, we never connected it up as being you. I can't believe it."

"Talk about a small world, to think I saved his life and later he married Mellita and raised my son. He paid me back and much more. I remember worrying about whether he survived or not.

He seemed like a nice guy. I liked him immediately. He reminded me of myself. Little did I know he'd survive and become involved in my world. No wonder, I liked him so much. I'm sorry he's not alive so I could thank him. What a world of coincident's!

God works in mysterious and often wonderful ways."

"Unbelievable story." Wylie said.

"Isn't that like Wylie; condenses the whole story down to two words." Sally said, bursting into laughter. Marilyn giggled and the two woman joined in wild laughter. Mellita smiled broadly and seemed close to joining them. Rudi looked puzzled and slightly embarrassed.

"Rudi, don't pay any attention to those two. They go through this giggling business all the time. It doesn't make much sense." Nick shrugged, and slid his jacket on. They all got up and moved out. Nick stopped at the counter and paid the bill.

Chapter 59

They all thoroughly enjoyed their visit, but as the time came to depart for home a sadness swept them. So, plans were made to meet again in the near future. A friendship had developed that they wanted to keep alive.

Rudi was proud of his uncle and dad. They had served their country honorably. Both decorated veterans in different branches of the service. One a daredevil fighter pilot with a Purple Heart; the other a combat medic with a Bronze Star for putting his life on the line to save others. Medics had an enormous responsibility treating the wounded while under fire from the enemy. They both came close to death many times but managed to survive. Both admitted, surviving was out of their hands. It could have been fate, luck, or the Lord looking after them. They were not sure, but so thankful to be alive to enjoy their present life with family and friends.

Nick felt empty when they all left for home. It had been fun being able to reminisce happy moments, although, at times, it brought out buried memories of the war. Flashbacks popped up so real, so strong, so fresh. It's like I was right there in the snow covered foxhole peering out in fear a German is creeping up on me. I'm running, ducking, zig-zagging and praying a bullet doesn't rip through my body. I'm madly racing toward Drusenheim with German soldiers in pursuit, and 88's whistling overhead and exploding nearby. If I could have, I would have climbed into my helmet.

With heavy artillery in the distance and bullets zipping all around, I stepped cautiously but quickly into the mine field while scanning the ground, until I got to Goodwin. His foot was blown off, and I remember he was bleeding profusely. I treated him and helped him until we made it out where a litter bearer took him to the rear.

On a patrol, in the middle of the night, I'm spotted by the Germans. All hell breaks loose as bullets spray and ricochet everywhere, it was like the whole enemy army was shooting at me. I jumped into an alcove where I came face to face with a German soldier. I breathed a huge sigh of relief when he turned and ran the other way as fast as he could.

Heading to relieve a machine gun nest, there's another German ambush. A medic has to be the last to retreat in case someone is hit. Up ahead a GI screams for help. His knee is thrown out of joint. Nick extends the leg and twists. It worked, but the soldier still has to lean on Nick as they move out--but it's too late. The Germans surround them.

Hiding in a hollowed out stump, a snow covered branch breaks, and traps him. The struggle to free himself goes on and on.

Flashbacks never faded. They always lurked ready to erupt at any moment. Nick's heart is still full of the sounds and the words and the fears of those days. Sometimes in the middle of the night it all comes back so clear. He almost becomes the kid he was--back then. Nick remembered the feeling of great joy when he saved a buddy, and the horrible sadness when he tried to save a dying friend and failed. He'd tried to do his best but sometimes that wasn't enough.

The words of Stephen Grellet were so accurate to Nick: "I shall pass through this world but once. Any good, therefore that I can do or any kindness that I can show to any human being, let me do it now. Let me not neglect it nor defer it, for I shall not pass this way again."

During the war, Nick fought to get back home and he made it. Now, he felt blessed to be with his family and friends. How grateful to have the love and respect that he had around him. Mellita kept in constant contact with the Jordan's. The past had brought them together and the future would bring them closer.

As time went on, the group of Nick, Marilyn, Wylie, Sally, and Mellita and her new husband Adam set up a schedule once a year for a vacation together. Each year they picked a different location to visit. On occasion, Rudi and his family would join them. Sometimes one of Nick and Marilyn's daughter's would arrive for the fun.

When they got together, they always began with a big laugh about the media reaction to their arrival in West Berlin. The reporters were desperately looking for a story, and they found it at the Berlin Hospital.

Discovering the escape occurred because of something that happened during World War II, they quickly made it 'Breaking News' around the world. It was the 'Top Story' on every broadcast. The Jordan's and Mellita couldn't believe the commotion, they had caused.

Year after year, their conversation settled on the fabulous memories of World War II and the escape from East Berlin.

THE END

About the Author

Rollin Hurd received his dental degree D.D.S. from the University of Washington in Seattle. He practiced dentistry for forty years in Kirkland, Washington before retiring. He is now a life member of the American Dental Association, Washington State Dental Society, and the King County Dental Society. He achieved recognition in high school sports especially his final year when he turned out for track for the first time. Rollin broke the school and county mile record without losing a race. At 18 years of age he went into the army and fought in Europe during World War II. He became a combat medic in the 42nd Rainbow Division. He was awarded the Bronze Star for treating and saving many lives while under enemy fire. His company also put him in for the Silver Star and another Bronze Star for heroism. At one time he was listed as missing—in—action, but a group of seven of his platoon managed to escape. Dr. Hurd and his wife have lived in Kirkland, Washington for 47 years. They have four daughters and nine grandchildren. His mother Blanche ninety-seven lives in Napa, California.

Brother Edgar a veteran of World War II, flew combat missions from Ie Shima to Japan and China in P-47's. During Ed's later years he flew jet fighters in the Air Defense Command, and became a successful Real Estate Broker.